J.O.B.

J.O.B.

THE LEGEND OF
Jonathon Oliver Biggs

KEVIN SHORKEY

Tate Publishing & Enterprises

Published by Tate Publishing & Enterprises, LLC
127 E. Trade Center Terrace | Mustang, Oklahoma 73064 USA
1.888.361.9473 | www.tatepublishing.com

Tate Publishing is committed to excellence in the publishing industry. The company reflects the philosophy established by the founders, based on Psalm 68:11,
"The Lord gave the word and great was the company of those who published it."

Published in the United States of America

ISBN: 978-1-61566-737-6
1. Fiction / Christian / Classic & Allegory
2. Fiction / Suspense
09.12.16

Dedication

To Sheila, whose love and encouragement is always invaluable.

To Becky and Kim, my English-teaching daughters for lovingly editing and correcting my writing.

To Colleen for motivating her dad when I needed to persevere.

To my brother, Frank, for good advice at the right time.

To my parents for believing in this project.

Prologue

The Tucson night was clear. The moon shed a soft glow over the desert. The sounds of the desert at night were interrupted only by the erratic growl of two all-terrain vehicles making their way across the landscape. The man on the lead vehicle was concerned about being seen, as he skillfully led his partner around the saguaro cactus and toward the herd. Rustlers were common in this part of the country. These ranches covered thousands of acres, making it difficult for the ranchers to keep track of their cattle. Rustlers used this to their advantage, working under the cover of darkness—a cover that was not available tonight. If they weren't pressed by a deadline, the leader would not have proceeded with his plan. He did not want to get caught on Jonathon Oliver Biggs' range. But time was of the essence. Waiting was not an option.

The men dismounted a short distance from the herd. The second man carried a small black backpack from which he took a smaller black case.

"Let's take our time and do this right," instructed the leader in an anxious whisper.

"Stay low so no one can see our silhouettes from a distance." The second man was concerned as well. "These are not the best conditions."

"Open the case," the leader commanded hoarsely as they crept into the herd. The cattle were calm and didn't react to their presence. Most of them were asleep standing up. The leader selected a cow toward the middle of the herd and placed his hand on her neck just above her shoulders.

"I'm almost ready," the man with the case responded, furtively glancing around, knowing that they could be easily seen. He extracted a large syringe and a bottle of serum from the case. He poked the needle through the top of the bottle and drew the serum into the syringe. "Ready now."

"I'll pinch the hide. Go in fast but steady. She'll move her head when she feels the needle, so stay with it until all the serum is in."

The lead man was at the head pressing his chest firmly against the side of the cow's head as he grasped her hide at the predetermined spot on her neck. "Do it now!" He wasn't sure how long the cow would let him hold his position.

The second man inserted the needle steadily into the pinched area of the neck. He moved it gently, side-to-side, trying to feel between the vertebrate. When the needle found the right spot, he pushed it hard into the spinal column and quickly plunged the serum home.

The cow threw her head, easily pushing the leader away. She mooed with irritation and discomfort. She dropped her head and shook it vigorously while striking out at the men with her back leg.

"Are you clear?"

"Yes, we're good to go!" The second man carefully capped the needle and placed the syringe back in the case with the empty serum bottle.

"Good, let's go." The leader looked around and saw no one. The cow was walking around the herd, angrily shaking her head and bellowing occasionally. The leader was glad that they had found this group of cattle so far away from the ranch house.

The two men carefully wove their way back through the desert. An hour later, they loaded the ATVs into a covered truck and drove away.

"This has been a long time coming," the second man exclaimed with a slight grin.

"Yes it has," responded the leader with firm confidence. "Soon Jonathon Oliver Biggs' life will come tumbling down!"

Both men laughed as if they had already won.

J.O.B.

PART
ONE

Chapter One

"Mad cow disease?"

"Yes, sir."

"How many?"

"One for sure, and six others are being tested right now."

"This is really bad!"

"I know."

"We still have plenty of assets to help us ride this out."

Jonathon Oliver Biggs' last statement fell on the dumb-founded ears of his executive vice president, Eli Moore. Moore was a bright young star at Biggs International. He amazed his colleagues with his ability to see problems coming and solve them, before they turned into crises.

He didn't like surprises. "We've never been hit with any-thing like this. Biggs International will be all over the news. Our stock will drop. We may have to close the Tucson ranch or destroy the entire herd. I need to start working on damage control."

Jonathon Oliver Biggs, President and CEO of Biggs International, had inherited the cattle empire from his father, who had inherited it from his father after whom Jonathon was named. He had lived up to his father's expectations and had expanded their holdings from two-to-six ranches in the U.S. The company had diversified under Jonathon's leadership and had made a kill-ing in its four-year-old industrial division. Eli had discovered a very lucrative market for farm-equipment-replacement parts.

Original equipment manufacturers were gouging farmers on the price of replacement parts. Eli had set up an engineering firm and purchased the rights to manufacture various commonly replaced parts. He also set up a network of factories overseas and even put together a group to sell rebuilt parts. Farm co-ops went for it like starving people who had been invited to an endless BBQ.

The intercom buzzed. "Mr. Biggs, it's Mr. Holt for you."

"Thank you," Jonathon said as he punched the speaker-phone button.

"Don, I'm here with Eli. How bad is it down there?"

"It's bad." The pained reply came of the usually jovial Don Holt, Executive Director of the Tucson Ranch. "We have one for sure, and we've randomly selected six others to be tested immediately. Mad cow is usually a result of bad feed. I think we may lose the entire herd. The USDA has been notified and will be here within the hour. They said that they won't hesitate to force us to destroy every head, if necessary. I'm sorry, Jonathon. I didn't see this coming. We haven't cut corners, and our standards are still the highest in the business. The feed we use is the best in the industry. I have no clue how this hit us."

"Don, let's make sure we cooperate completely with the USDA on this. I want our integrity to be intact when this is over. Give them anything they ask for."

"Will do, Jonathon. I'll take full responsibility for this, even though I don't know how it happened. You'll have my resignation before close of business today."

"*No!* Absolutely not!" Jonathon was adamant. "Don, I hired you because you're trustworthy. That hasn't changed. I won't leave you hanging out to dry all alone. We don't operate that way. Our values haven't changed."

"Thanks, Jonathon. I'll keep you posted." Holt hung up.

"Eli, let's set up a video conference with the other five ranches within the next two hours. We need to keep everyone informed as this unfolds. I'll clear my schedule for the rest of the morning."

"Yes, sir!" Eli responded with anticipation in his voice. "We'll manage the fall-out and come out of this on our feet."

Jonathon managed to get through some minor administrative tasks over the next ninety minutes. The minutes seemed to tick by very slowly. He had a sense of foreboding but didn't know why. He hadn't experienced this feeling before today. He caught himself playing out different scenarios in his mind—all negative. When he had called his wife, Rachel, he had come off as being very pessimistic. She had asked him where his usually optimistic attitude had gone and said, "Jonathon, you're a great leader! Great leaders always know what to do when the time comes. Go with your instincts. I have confidence in you! And by the way, I love you, Bigg Time!"

When he hung up, he took a moment to be thankful for marrying Rachel. She had been trusting, affirming, and encouraging him for twenty-eight years. Much of his confidence came from her. When she called him "Bigg Time," he always laughed. She gave him the nickname when he first went to work for his father. He started as a highly educated, interoffice communications liaison. Rachel called him "the mail boy with an MBA" and told him to get to know people on his way to the "Bigg Time." "Be a good guy first, and you will become a great leader!" She was right. He could handle this.

The video conference was Eli's show. Jonathon explained the situation, and Eli acted as the discussion facilitator. They were a great team. Eli was asking probing questions and providing quick, concise reviews as they went, while Jonathon was formulating possibilities and interjecting directive sound bites. None of the other ranches had noticed anything unusual, nor had they heard of any problems with neighboring herds. They decided to grant media interviews as a way of letting the public know that this was an isolated problem. Eli thought that Jonathon should fly to Arizona and hold a press conference at the ranch. All agreed, and Maggie, Jonathon's administrative assistant, ordered the company jet to prepare for the trip. Jonathon would leave immediately. He called Rachel and asked her to accompany him. She would make arrangements for the kids to stay with Joshua and Jane overnight. Jonathon and Rachel had five children. Joshua, the oldest, had been married for three years to Jane. Megan was a newlywed, and her husband, Daniel, was fitting into the family like he'd always been there. Jon was a sophomore in college. Kathy and Kelly were two years apart in high school.

Jonathon usually enjoyed traveling on the Biggs jet but not today. His mind was occupied with thoughts of how mad cow disease had come upon one of his ranches. This was not a good time to have this kind of trouble. He was working on expanding the holdings of Biggs International, and this was an immediate threat to the well-being of the company. Jonathon hoped that people would not lose their jobs as a result of this problem. He felt a strong sense of responsibility toward his employees and their families. He believed that success was a result of hiring the right people and taking care of them.

"I hate press conferences," he moaned as the Biggs jet soared from Kansas City to Tucson. "And this one might turn into a royal disaster."

"At least you'll be proactive with the press. Maybe they'll tone it down some." Rachel was trying to be positive as Jonathon's mood became more and more depressing. Their lives had not been filled with difficulty. After all, they were both born into wealthy families with well-established businesses. They had been to the best schools and had been blessed with great opportunities to succeed. Life had been good.

"You always like going to Tucson in April. The temperature is in the seventies with the sun always shining. It beats the chills back in Kansas City!" Rachel was intentionally trying to distract her husband. It didn't work.

Jonathon forced a tight smile. "That is true."

As he looked at his wife, Jonathon thought back to their beginnings. He and Rachel met in college. They both attended Kansas State University. When Jonathon first saw her, he was immediately enamored. Rachel possessed striking beauty complimented by an ever-present smile. Jonathon was tall at six feet four and gangly at one hundred and eighty pounds. He possessed a sense of confidence without the arrogance that was common to young men. Jonathon sat next to Rachel in Business 101 the first day of class. He immediately asked her out for coffee—a date that lasted six hours. They seemed to have everything in common. Jonathon wanted to become an influential business man with a reputation for caring about the people with whom he worked. He was concerned about his integrity and that of the people closest to him. Rachel appreciated that about him. She had always been pursued by men who were more interested in her beauty than anything else. Jonathon wanted to learn about her as a person.

"You know, Bigg Time, character is revealed through crisis. This will be good for us. We'll be tested. We'll learn about ourselves. We'll grow as people."

"I know, babe," replied Jonathon with a sigh. "Remember when we went to that core-values seminar in New York?"

"Yes, and we saw *Cats*."

"Right. I still believe in and talk about the core values of the business all the time. The first thing we value is truth and the next is people. Our values are the key to our success and happiness. I'm going to stick to them during this whole mad cow thing."

"You always say, 'At Biggs International, we infuse integrity into everything we do!'"

"Sir," interrupted the flight attendant, "you have a call from Mr. Moore." She handed him the phone.

"Eli, what's up?"

"Jonathon, we have a problem! And it's huge!" Eli blurted.

"Okay, take a deep breath and talk to me." Jonathon's heart was pounding, but he'd managed to sound calm and in control.

"Jack Harris called in from the Sierra Vista Ranch. They think they have a mad cow. He's quarantined the herd and called in the USDA."

"We just talked about this, and Harris said the herd was healthy!" Jonathon always became irritated when he thought his people were holding back information or showed up to a meeting unprepared. Jack Harris had been managing the Sierra Vista Ranch for six months. "I hope he can explain this!"

Eli related that one of Jack's foremen was out on the range and discovered the sick cow all by itself while they were meeting. He reported in an hour later."

"Have any of the neighboring ranches discovered anything?" Jonathon's voice was barely in control.

"No, but we're contacting them at least to keep them informed," Eli practically yelled into the mouthpiece.

"This is really strange. The ranches are a hundred miles apart. Ask Jack if we've transferred any of the herd between the ranches lately." Jonathon knew that sometimes individual cows or small groups were moved around to mate with a particular bull at a different ranch. Breeding quality beef cattle required good bloodlines. Large-cattle brokerage firms put a lot of value on a ranch's quality of breeding.

"Jonathon, do you want me to come down there?" Eli asked.

"No, we need you at headquarters to run things from there. I'm glad I have you around to work through this with me. Hang tough, and we'll be fine." Jonathon knew the importance of affirmation during a crisis.

"Anything you need, Jonathon. Anything you need!"

Chapter Two

"Kelly will be totally surprised!" said Jane Biggs, Jonathon and Rachel's daughter-in-law. Since she had married Joshua, Jane had become the family organizer. She made every birthday, anniversary, graduation, or any other event special. "We're the Biggs, and with us everything is a big deal!" was her favorite line when recruiting other family members to get involved.

Megan and Kathy got together to plot the surprise and make Kelly's sixteenth birthday party a landmark event in her life. The girls were very close and loved to get together to talk and plan.

Kathy was enthusiastic about the home her parents had just built. She really liked her new room, which she decorated herself. Rachel had wanted a home that was practical yet suitable for entertaining and to serve as a gathering place for the family. She anticipated having grandchildren and designed the home as a place for them. Rachel, Jonathon, Kathy, and Kelly had moved in last week. Rachel teased Joshua and Jane about waiting to have children and challenged them to give her some grandchildren that she could spoil.

"Let's throw the party at the new house!" Kathy said.

"Great idea," said Jane. "Will Mom and Dad be back from Tucson by six on Saturday?"

"I just talked to Dad, and he said that the plane would be on the ground at four; so they can be in the 'copter at 4:10 p.m., landing in the backyard at 4:30 p.m." Megan kept track of all the family details.

Jonathon and Rachel gave each of their children a car for their sixteenth birthday. It was always a Honda Accord, and Rachel chose the color and interior details. Jonathon felt that the Accord was a safe and reliable car that was sporty enough for a teenager without actually being a sports car. Although Kelly knew that she would be getting her Accord this year, she didn't know how it would be delivered. Jonathon had unique ways of delivering the gift. When Kathy turned sixteen, Jonathon gave her a series of clues to follow. It took her all afternoon, but she found her Accord in the mall parking lot wrapped in a bow.

<hr>

"I don't see how the two could be connected. The ranches are a hundred miles apart, and we haven't shared herd in over a year." Jack Harris had driven up from the Sierra Vista Ranch to Tucson to meet with Jonathon and Don Holt.

"This is bizarre!" interjected Holt.

"We have to stay calm and investigate both ranches." Jonathon knew that the USDA would do an investigation of their own. "The USDA investigation will take forever, and we don't have that kind of time. Let's do our own with an independent firm. I want to make sure that the results are accurate and timely."

"Who do we get?" Holt inquired.

"I'll have Eli call Bills and Masterson. They work in the international arena and do herd evaluations for import and export companies. They're very good at discovering problems and tracing them back to the source. Their credibility is excellent, and they tell it like it is."

"Weren't they involved in the mad cow situation in England?" asked Harris.

"Yes, and they were the key to keeping the problem from spreading." Jonathon and Miles Masterson had known each other through their fathers' friendship.

The three men continued to discuss their own investigation

and the USDA investigation. They speculated on the outcome of each; the conversation soon shifted to the upcoming news conference. They decided that the best approach was to include both ranches and focus on the upcoming investigations.

"I know it's not much information, but it's all we have right now." Jonathon was resigned to the fact that the fallout would be bad for business.

⟶✦⟵

"Eli." Jonathon was on a video conference with his executive vice president. "We need to talk about the financial repercussions."

"Right now, we can cover our margins. But if it's a slow news day and the media chooses to use us as their main story, it could get ugly."

"They do have a tendency to fill in the blanks with damaging speculations. And we have plenty of blanks right now." Jonathon was concerned about Biggs International's latest acquisition. He wanted to expand their holdings into South America and decided to buy a large ranch and a beef-processing plant in Argentina. He had borrowed the money to make the deal against his shares of Biggs International stock. He considered it a minimal risk, because Biggs was a stable company that had a sound financial base. As long as the price of their stock didn't plunge dramatically, he would be fine. Biggs stock had never fallen more than twelve cents in one day and had gone up consistently for the last fifteen years. The trip to Argentina had been successful and the deal made. Both Jonathon and Eli expected the stock to begin climbing as soon as news of the acquisition became public. The news conference had been planned for tomorrow.

"Rachel, you had better call Jane and let her know that we may be late for the party." Jonathon had moved the news conference back an hour, because he wanted the Bills and Masterson team there with him. He wanted to show the media that Biggs International was moving quickly to resolve the mad cow problem.

"What time should I tell her we'll be there?"

"Six thirty at the latest, probably sooner, and maybe as early as five thirty. The car won't be delivered until seven, so we should be there in plenty of time." Arrangements to deliver the Honda Accord to Kelly's party had been made with her Driver's Ed instructor, Todd Carpenter. When Kelly hadn't passed the test to get her driving permit, Carpenter had met with her a few times to tutor her. She passed the second time without missing a question. He had become Kelly's favorite teacher. He was to drive the Accord around to the back of the house and pull up on the patio between the pool and the house in front of the dining room windows.

"Are you sure that Kelly can back the car out of there without ending up in the pool?" Carpenter said. He'd always had a good sense of humor.

Chapter Three

Breslin Kline had been with the USDA for twenty years. He considered himself the best of the best and, as a result, had developed a condescending attitude toward just about everyone. He was slight in build for a man six feet tall. The tight wave of his short black hair combined with his narrow brown eyes, thin nose, and small straight mouth gave the initial impression that he was chronically picky. Both of his ex-wives said that he was a rude, insensitive bore, who drove them away with his demanding perfectionism. His first wife warned the second before the wedding that it was impossible to please Breslin Kline. Life never seemed to live up to his standards, making him constantly disgruntled.

Jonathon was amused at Breslin Kline's initial approach. No introductions were made; Kline simply walked up to Jonathon and made his announcement.

"Both of your ranches are shut down pending further notice. If you do not cooperate fully, this will be a more difficult experience than you can imagine."

"We will give you anything you need," Jonathon replied.

"I will be taking part in the press conference," Breslin Kline informed him.

"I expected you would," Jonathon responded.

"I will tell them what they need to know. The American public must be protected."

With that, the conversation ended, and Breslin Kline walked away.

—◦►◄◦—

"My name is Jonathon Biggs. I am the president of Biggs International, and I'm here to talk about the mad cow situation on two of our ranches. We first discovered the disease at our Tucson ranch this morning. One cow displayed strong symptoms. Upon testing, it was determined that the cow has mad cow disease. Later today, we discovered a diseased cow out on the range at our Sierra Vista Ranch. Mad cow has been identified in that situation also. The Sierra Vista Ranch has only one diseased cow that we know of at this time. We are rounding up both herds and conducting a thorough inspection of each head. We will not be selling or processing any beef from either ranch until we are satisfied that it is safe to do so. We are cooperating with the USDA. Biggs international has also retained Bills and Masterson to conduct the inspections and perform a complete investigation into this situation. Bills and Masterson is a highly reputable firm, which has an international reputation for being meticulous and honest. We anticipate getting to the source of this problem with their help. I will now turn the podium over to Breslin Kline, a senior inspector for the USDA. We will then take questions."

"Mad cow disease is a serious problem and a threat to the health of the American public. I will be leading the USDA investigative team. Both ranches are under quarantine, effective immediately. We will be looking into the cause of this situation and into the operating procedures of all six of the Biggs ranches. I will be communicating with the media as we go through the process." Breslin Kline took two steps back from the podium and crossed his arms.

Jonathon's cell phone vibrated gently in his pocket. Only a few privileged people had his number. He instantly retrieved the phone and noticed on the screen that Eli was calling.

"Eli, I'm in the press conference right now," he whispered hastily.

"Jonathon, find a way to close it, and get out of there!" Eli was in panic mode. "Our Montana ranch and one of our New Mexico ranches have possible mad cow situations. I'm talking to them now to find out what's going on. You need to bail out on the media immediately!"

"I'll call you back in three minutes." Jonathon was disconnecting from Eli as he walked to the podium. "It would be better if we held our questions until we have further information. Thank you for coming."

Jonathon walked away to the rustling of reporters with unanswered questions. They yelled after him, hoping he would turn and answer. He ignored their clamor and walked directly to the limo where Rachel was waiting.

"That was an interesting twist—what happened?" she said.

"We have two more affected ranches, Montana and New Mexico. Eli called me while the USDA guy was talking. Everything is at risk."

<hr>

Jonathon was troubled by the new developments at the Montana and New Mexico ranches. Mad cow disease was transmitted through bad feed and took time to show up in a cow. These incidents of the disease were showing up at different ranches in a short span of time. And it was only showing up at his ranches so far. This was unusual and suspicious. He wondered if the testing was fraudulent, or if his herds were being infected intentionally. He had some enemies but had been careful to be forthright and honest in all of his business dealings. "We infuse integrity into everything we do" was his motto. He began to think about the people who may want to hurt him. Jonathon didn't like feeling suspicious, but he was.

<hr>

The flight home was uneventful. Rachel refused to let anyone on the plane listen to the news. She wanted Jonathon to have time to shift emotional gears from the stress of his business problems to the joy of his daughter's birthday party. Rachel knew he would have a hard time not thinking about the ranches tonight. While he had worked his way up in the business, he had never really experienced harsh adversity. His success followed his father's, and the expansion of the company seemed to fall into place easily. People were amazed at Jonathon's ability to maximize his opportunities with minimal risk. He was careful to give credit to those who worked with him, but in his heart he had a sense that he was specially blessed.

Jonathon decided to have the Biggs jet land at a different airport than originally planned. He was concerned about the press besieging him. He didn't want to be detained and miss Kelly's birthday celebration. He was anxious to see her face when the bright yellow Accord was delivered. He would ask her to pull the curtains in the dining room, and the car would be sitting there with a big red bow. He loved to see his family laugh and enjoy each other's company. Tonight would be difficult for him, but he would still appreciate the family time.

The Biggs jet landed at the secluded airstrip, and a limo was waiting for them. The early evening was cool and cloudy. The air felt good on Jonathon's face as he disembarked from the plane. Jonathon had asked for the helicopter but was told that Eli didn't want it to be followed by media people.

"I'll get you to the party on time!" the limo driver insisted as they drove quickly in the direction of their new home.

"This will be the first big test for the new house," said Rachel. "Our first party with the whole family there and friends too!"

"I'm glad you designed it to be a party house. This will be great." Jonathon was working hard at sounding enthusiastic, even though he felt like he'd been run over by a truck. He was determined to make Kelly's sixteenth birthday a good memory for her. He leaned his head forward and closed his eyes for a long moment.

"Jonathon, are you okay?" Rachel's voice gave away her worry.

"I'm praying."

"I'll have to meet you at the party. We have had a disastrous day, and I still need to clean up some of the details." Eli was speaking to his wife, Debra.

"I'll wait for you," was her response. "You know how important it is to me for us to show up together." Her tone of voice told him that the discussion was over. Debra was a very socially correct person. She had been brought up in high society and knew the rules. Her parents had taught her to be concerned about how she appeared to others. "When things aren't quite right, the word gets around," her mother used to say.

"Okay, I'll be there at six thirty. We can make the party by 6:45 p.m., if we hurry."

"Good, we'll be fashionably late!"

Eli hung up shaking his head. Sometimes Debra was a pain in the neck. She was self-absorbed and expected his life to revolve around her and only her.

Eli had one more call to make to Bills and Masterson about their investigation. Mad cow disease was the rancher's biggest nightmare, but Eli wasn't a rancher. He was a business executive. He wanted to gather as much information about mad cow as possible, hoping to control the damage and minimize their losses.

Jonathon's quiet moment was interrupted by the vibration and then ring of his cell phone. It was Breslin Kline.

"Breslin Kline, USDA inspector here, may I speak to Jonathon Biggs, please?"

"Hello, Mr. Kline, this is Jonathon. I'm on the way to my daughter's birthday party. Can this wait?"

"No, Mr. Biggs, but I'll keep it short and simple. I received the report on your Montana and New Mexico ranches. We're already looking into those situations. This is shaping up to be a unique scenario. So far this outbreak seems only to have affected your ranches. The pattern is unusual, and the reports of infected cattle have come within hours of each other. I don't know what's going on, but I suspect that you are doing something on your ranches that has caused this to occur. I'm asking for your permission to extend my investigation to include all six of your ranches. If you decline, I'll get a court order within a few days anyway. The way this is unfolding, I expect that your other two ranches will report the disease within the next twenty-four hours. I'd like to try and get ahead of this now."

A sickening fear ran through him. "Mr. Kline, you have my permission and complete cooperation. Please let me know what you discover. Thank you and good evening." Jonathon turned the cell phone off completely. "I'm going to the party." He said to the phone as he put it back in his pocket.

Chapter Four

Rachel was excited about the party and worried about Jonathon at the same time. "Driver, please turn right at the next road. We'll go in the back way. The roads in our neighborhood aren't paved yet, so drive slowly."

"Yes, ma'am." The driver turned right.

"Okay, now take this quick left … right here. This is the construction road leading to the back of the house. I'm sorry, but it's not kept up. Be careful, it's narrow and winds through twenty acres of woods before you get to the back of the house."

The limo moved gingerly in the ruts caused by construction equipment.

Rachel was talking through the window now rather than the intercom. "See that row of evergreens on your right? The road makes a sharp right turn there, and then you'll see the house."

The limo slowed as they approached the row of trees. Suddenly, a ball of red and yellow flame erupted from the house.

"What the …" exclaimed Jonathon.

Rachel screamed.

The limo stopped dead.

The ball of flame was replaced by a pillar of acrid, black smoke.

The house was gone.

The driver threw himself across the front seat. Jonathon instinctively pushed Rachel to the floor and covered her with his body. He wrapped his hands around his head. Unable to absorb what he had seen, he yelled as loudly as he could. He could feel the adrenaline rushing through him as he tensed up for action. He didn't know what to do, but he knew he had to move now!

He screamed, "Rachel, are you all right?"

"I think so."

Pieces of the house were now falling from the sky and hitting the limousine.

Rachel gasped. "The children!"

Jonathon, with terror inscribed on his features, was out of the car, sprinting toward the explosion.

The driver scrambled for his cell phone. "911? The Biggs home just blew up! I don't know. We need help now!"

Rachel left the limousine and sprinted toward the now burning rubble. She was struck by a flying fragment from the explosion and collapsed, unconscious.

Jonathon reached what was left of the house and skidded to a halt. He didn't see any of the children in the wreckage. In shock and denial, he hoped they weren't there, but he knew they were dead.

He looked around for Rachel.

The driver was kneeling beside her, holding a wad of paper toweling to her head.

"Is she..."

"No," said the driver, "she just got knocked out. She's coming around slowly. I called 911, and they're coming right now. I told them that we were out back and that Mrs. Biggs was injured."

"Thank you," replied Jonathon as he turned and walked haltingly up the construction road in the direction of what moments ago had been their new house.

Chapter Five

Jonathon was on the phone with one of the deacons from the church. "Our friends at church have been wonderful. Thank you."

"This whole thing is a whirlwind," he said to Rachel as he hung up from his conversation. "We need some time alone."

Rachel was crying softly, remembering the words of their pastors at the funeral service for the Biggs children. "Pastor Doug and Pastor George did a nice job today," she said through her tears. "I'm feeling frustrated by all of this, and I don't know if it's all right for me to feel that way."

"As long as it's real, it's all right." Jonathon crossed the room and held her gently. The day had been difficult from the beginning. A dreary, depressing rain fell all morning and became constant and heavy in the afternoon. At first sight of the caskets in a row at the front of the sanctuary, Rachel felt light-headed and nearly passed out. Jonathon helped her to her seat. He was sure at the time that he was going to throw up.

There were times during the service that Jonathon felt comforted, but other moments he felt crushed. Rachel sat straight up without expression during the entire funeral. They stayed alone in the church until the caskets were each placed in the hearses outside. Jonathon and Rachel left through a back door and followed the ominous black line of vehicles to the cemetery.

The graveside situation was a disaster. The cemetery was wet and muddy. The pall bearers were slipping around on the sloppy sod barely keeping their balance. During the pastor's prayer, the rain changed from soft falling to hard driving. Afterwards, Jonathon and Rachel managed to graciously thank everyone personally. These friends did their best to help in a very hard situation. Jonathon and Rachel genuinely appreciated them but needed more comfort than they could give.

The ride home from the cemetery was filled with emotionally exhausted silence.

How will Rachel ever get through this? thought Jonathon with a sense of hopelessness. *How will I ever get through this?* He sat with his face in his hands, barely breathing for fear of sobbing in front of his devastated wife. He was fighting despair. When he closed his eyes, he pictured himself falling slowly backwards into a dark pit. He was afraid that he could go there emotionally at any moment. *I must be strong for Rachel!* he told himself. *If I fight this pain long enough, it will get easier.*

The funeral was highlighted on the news. As Jonathon watched the report, he was reminded about the mess their lives had become.

<hr />

Breslin Kline had reported six cases of mad cow disease—one on each ranch. He'd put a hold on the slaughter of any more Biggs cattle until the investigation was completed. He told Eli, "This is the worst situation I have ever seen." He was attempting to trace the origin of each cow purchased within the last three years. He had the infected cows slaughtered, their brains and spinal columns tagged and sent to the National Veterinary Clinic in Ames, Iowa, for confirmation and further testing.

Breslin Kline was being unusually quiet. He was giving very little information to the press and had instructed his people not to talk about the Biggs investigation at all. There had only been one confirmed case of mad cow disease in the United States, and that cow had been imported from Canada. The thought of six cows from six different ranches being infected at the same time was impossible for him to grasp. Adding to his dilemma was the fact that all the ranches belonged to Biggs International, and that every ranch owned by Biggs was affected. Biggs was one of the three largest providers of beef in America. His cattle were being consumed by people all over the country. Mad cow disease was always fatal to humans.

Breslin Kline had wondered what Biggs was putting in his feed at the ranch. His USDA team had investigated the feed distributor, and they were in the clear. The supply of food supplements on each ranch had been checked and was well within USDA requirements. How were these cows becoming infected? Was there a new way for mad cow disease to spread? What was really going on here and why? Breslin Kline was deeply concerned and had no answers.

"Maybe someone is out to ruin Jonathon Biggs," said Breslin Kline to no one but himself as he drove, exhausted, to his hotel. "If someone orchestrated this, he had to know that I would suspect foul play." He reviewed the situation in his mind. "Who are Biggs' enemies? Who would benefit the most from the devastation at Biggs International?"

Speaking out loud again to no one but himself, "All of his children died the same day that mad cow hit his ranches. Is it possible that they were a target too? Where do I go from here?"

⇒➤●◄⇐

Eli Moore had been steering Biggs International through its worst crisis ever. Jonathon hadn't displayed any interest in the company since the funeral two weeks ago. The memorial service received national attention from the media. The press continually pursued the mad cow issue, and Biggs stock had fallen sixteen dollars a share. Eli knew that things would get worse.

"Listen, Jonathon, I know you're hurting right now. I can't imagine what you're going through. But I have to ask you to help with this." Eli knew he had to be direct. "When we sold margin calls on our existing stock to buy the Argentina ranch, we anticipated that our value would go up. It's gone down sixteen dollars a share in two weeks. When the option holders exercise their calls, we won't have the money to cover. Jonathon, Biggs International will go broke! We need to come up with a media blitz to reestablish our credibility in the marketplace. The public needs to see you back at the helm solving problems and projecting an optimistic future. You need to come back to work right away!"

"Eli, I trust you to run the show," Jonathon stated blandly.

"Jonathon, we need you!" Eli asserted.

"Rachel is depressed, and I have to focus on her right now," Jonathon said flatly.

"I know that, but if you don't step in here, you will lose everything!"

Chapter Six

"A stroke?" queried Rachel as they sat by the pool three weeks after the funeral.

"Probably." Jonathon's voice and expression were dull.

"What makes you think it's a stroke?" Rachel treated Jonathon's latest issue with some irritation in her voice. He had been coming up with feigned illnesses since two days after the funeral.

"Left hand is numb. Spasms in the left arm and no strength in that arm. Left thigh is weak, and it is painful to walk. Can't focus thoughts very well."

"It could be a heart attack!" Rachel exclaimed mockingly.

"No chest pain."

"Maybe we should ask a doctor." Now she was serious.

Jonathon turned his head away. He had been avoiding conversations for the last week. The wet April weather had turned into an unusually warm May. The last day or two, he spent most of his time sitting out by the pool, letting his mind wander. "Why not just let it run its course and see what happens?"

Rachel walked around him and made direct eye contact like a mother making a point to her child. "Jonathon, that's the dumbest thing you've said in a while! You've been on the couch for three weeks, sleeping and watching television. Why don't you do something constructive today? Hey, you could go to work—try to save the company. Chapter II doesn't mean you have to let it go into bankruptcy."

"The kids are all dead. The ranches are all in trouble. We're about to lose the company. Our debts are too great to even talk about. And, to top it all off, we're living in your parents' guest house!" Jonathon was sobbing with grief and shouting angrily at the same time. "I know that God doesn't want to destroy us. I know He helps people through tough times, but I just don't seem to be grasping what He wants me to get out of this. I still trust Him, but I don't get it."

"Go ahead and trust Him. I don't!" Rachel's anger had welled up inside of her, and she was on the edge of losing her self control. This was happening a lot lately. Jonathon had been very strong and comforting after the death of their family. He had refused to get involved in the business and had focused on comforting and encouraging Rachel. Two days after the funeral services, he wouldn't get out of bed. He said he was tired and needed to rest. That was three weeks ago. Rachel had tried to convince him to see a doctor or a psychologist, but her efforts were met with displays of sobbing anger. She had transitioned from sorrow to anger herself and wanted desperately to lash out at someone. She chose to be mad at God.

"The farms, the business, the house … He can have it all! But how can you trust a God who would take our family?" Rachel spoke with gritted teeth. Her eyes were wide open and filling with tears when she threw her head back, pinched her eyes shut, and glared at heaven. "Jonathon, you need to get up and get going!"

"I can't," he stated evenly.

"You can't, or you won't?" she sobbed and shouted at the same time.

"Both." His voice was sad. He wanted to get back into the mainstream of life but couldn't get himself to care anymore.

"Jonathon, is there room on that lounge chair for you to roll over and die? Talk to God, thank Him for killing our family, and then roll over and die!"

"Don't give up on God, Rachel." Jonathon said softly into her angry outburst.

"He's given up on us! The police and fire inspectors insist that the explosion was an accident, an unfortunate coincidence! Breslin Kline suspects that the mad cows were infected intentionally, but he's baffled. God is not even helping us discover what really happened. He's uninvolved. Well, I'm about to get involved." Rachel moved decisively toward the door.

Jonathon was surprised at the determination with which she spoke. "What are you going to do?"

"Stay by the pool, and listen to the news!" she shouted over her shoulder as she walked out the door.

Rachel grabbed her car keys as she left the house. She threw the car door open, sat down, and then slammed it shut. She impatiently rammed the key into the ignition switch, started the car, and squealed the tires all the way out of the driveway. When she had turned the corner, she pulled over and collapsed, sobbing on the steering wheel.

<hr />

Eli's secretary slipped quietly into his office, gently closing the door behind her.

"Mr. Moore, Mrs. Biggs is here. She is in Mr. Biggs' office, asking Maggie a lot of questions. I thought you should know right away."

Eli Moore leapt to his feet. "Thank you, Joan. I'm on my way."

Rachel was sitting at Jonathon's desk with a legal pad in front of her. Maggie, Jonathon's administrative assistant, was sitting across the desk with a notebook computer on her lap, typing furiously as Rachel gave her directions.

As Eli walked down the hallway to greet Rachel, he decided to act calmly no matter what happened. He strolled casually into Jonathon's office.

"Rachel, it's good to see you." Eli walked around the desk, bent over, hugged Rachel, and kissed her on the cheek. "What brings you here?"

Rachel thanked Maggie and dismissed her.

"Eli, too much has happened too quickly for any of these disasters to be accidental. No one seems to be making any headway toward solving the mysteries behind these terrible events. I intend to break down the roadblocks and get to the bottom of things."

"Have you talked to the police recently?" Eli asked carefully.

"Yes, the detectives, the fire marshal, and Breslin Kline. They have nothing but suspicions. Breslin Kline is being evasive." Rachel was terse in her answer.

"Frustrating, isn't it? How can I help, Rachel?" Eli spoke kindly. Rachel Biggs was a very special person to him. He was now concerned about her well-being.

"I'll be coming into this office every day, looking into the business issues here at Biggs. I want to find out who stands to profit from the demise of the company. I'll also be visiting the ranches asking questions. You can help me by making sure that I get everything I ask for and instructing Maggie that she works for me."

"Rachel," Eli said compassionately, "I understand your frustration. But do you really think you can find answers that the professional investigators haven't uncovered yet? I would rather you help Jonathon get through his troubles. I'll continue to manage things here, and we'll let the professionals do what they are trained to do."

"Eli," Rachel said pointedly, shaking slightly, "I understand your concern. But I am going to shake the bushes. The only thing I haven't lost is my husband, and he's an emotional disaster. Taking care of him is easy. He just lies around by the pool all the time. I have nothing to lose, and I'm royally angry about what I have lost; so I'll be looking at this from a different viewpoint than everyone else. Somebody did this to us, and I will find out whom, and when I do, there will be hell to pay!"

"Anything you need, I'll do it, Rachel." Eli wanted to end this uncomfortable conversation on a positive note.

"Thank you, Eli." Somehow her thanks sounded defensive.

Breslin Kline was sure that something subversive had happened at the Biggs' ranches.

"I see no possibility that only the Biggs' ranches could be infected. Mad cow disease takes years to manifest itself."

Kline was talking to Miles Masterson, the chief investigator for Bills and Masterson Cattle Certification, Incorporated. Miles was a confident problem solver. He prided himself on his ability to take impossible situations into the realm of the possible. He was not an imposing figure, standing at five foot ten and carrying one hundred and seventy pounds on his medium frame. Some suspected that he had served as a covert CIA agent earlier in his life. In his late thirties now, he was in superb physical condition and exuded a sense of self-assurance, which left him calm in every situation.

"Research scientists inject the virus into the brain stems of rats. The disease is manifested very soon after the injection and deterioration is rapid. I wonder if someone injected Biggs' cows intending to ruin him in the cattle industry," Miles offered.

Breslin Kline countered, "What would Biggs have to gain from this situation? Is there something we don't see that would motivate him to infect his own cattle? I know he's insured against mad cow disease. Is Biggs International secretly in trouble financially? What if Jonathon Biggs has created this scenario as a way to hide something within the company? You know, distract people from looking inside by creating a diversion outside. The culprit acts like a victim. I'll bet this whole thing is tied to Biggs' purchase of that Argentina ranch. Maybe he overextended the company's resources, needs to cover it up and receive an insurance settlement for lost revenue later."

Kline still didn't trust what he termed as "the upper crust." He was convinced that wealthy people manipulated situations for their own gain.

"Biggs International has filed Chapter 11 bankruptcy already," Miles said. "There's no doubt in my mind that Biggs will lose control as the majority stock holder soon. Jonathon Biggs is living with his in-laws after losing his family and new home in a freak accident. He isn't even trying to save the company. He hasn't been to the office since the death of his kids. He's practically broke and presently owes a lot more than he has the ability to pay. It doesn't appear that he has gained anything. He has lost it all!"

Breslin Kline reluctantly agreed for now. He had to admit that everyone at Biggs International had been exceptionally responsive to him. They had given him everything he had requested. Still, he was naturally suspicious. "What if we're only seeing what Biggs wants us to see? Margining his stock to purchase a ranch in Argentina was a risky move. The mad cow situations must somehow be connected with Biggs buying the Argentina ranch."

"Jonathon Biggs is the cleanest man in America," Miles said. He was becoming intense, as he was about to draw an important conclusion. "There is nothing in his personal or professional life that indicates dishonesty or deceit. There is no dirt on Jonathon Biggs. Someone wants to destroy or take over his business. Who would gain from that? And why would they make their agenda so obvious? Selectively infecting only Biggs' cattle is not exactly subtle. Infecting one cow on one ranch would have had a profoundly negative effect on Biggs International. Infecting one cow on each ranch is overkill—not necessary to position Biggs for a takeover attempt. Casting public suspicion on Jonathon Biggs could have been easily accomplished without going to these lengths. No, someone is out to destroy Biggs International, and for some reason, they want to make it obvious."

"Any perpetrators would obviously profit from Biggs' demise," Kline said. "Everyone will know who they are, and they shouldn't be hard to prosecute. This has to be an inside move." Breslin Kline was beginning to entertain Miles' theory.

"Can you prove that the cows were injected with the disease?" Miles asked.

Breslin caught himself shrugging his shoulders. "No, we have the brains and spinal columns and have verified the disease in each cow. But at this point, I don't think we could find the penetration point, if they were injected."

"So you can't prove anything?"

"No." Kline shrugged again. He didn't like this feeling of uncertainty. It was out of character for him, but he couldn't get rid of it.

"There is something lurking under the obvious. We must uncover it." Miles' investigative curiosity was showing.

"Miles, I know you're an independent investigator, but would you be willing to share information as we go along?"

"Definitely." Miles shook hands with Kline.

"You know that Biggs can't pay you for your work. He's broke," Kline said as he shook Miles' hand.

"I know."

"You will have no billable hours, you'll have to pay your own expenses, and you won't be able to take on any other projects until this is completed. This is going to be an expensive venture for you. So why continue?"

"Integrity. I'm convinced that Jonathon Biggs is a man of integrity. I want to know why someone would take these measures to ruin him. I'm doing this for the sake of a good man's reputation." Miles smiled, but negativity lingered in the air.

"I hope you can handle disappointment."

Miles Masterson and Breslin Kline parted company.

Chapter Seven

"Maggie, I'm wondering about something." Rachel Biggs was friendly but straightforward.

"What is it?" asked Maggie carefully.

Rachel had enjoyed a good friendship with Jonathon's administrative assistant since Maggie had come to work at Biggs International six years ago. Maggie was a highly sought after executive assistant. Jonathon hired her out of a difficult situation in an overseas company. She was in her early forties and attractive in a professional way. Maggie was personable and easy to like. She cared about other people and had an amazing mind for detail. She and Rachel Biggs connected immediately. They were in the habit of getting together for lunch twice a month to talk.

"I feel like you're holding back on me when I ask for help in the office," Rachel said with gracious directness.

"How is that?" Maggie was taken aback.

"You are slow about giving me the information I ask for, and I know that you are reporting my activities to Eli. I just wonder if you really want to help me get to the bottom of this or not." Rachel's friendliness had worn off, and she was becoming confrontational.

"I am loyal to Jonathon!" Maggie was offended at Rachel's comments. "With him out of the office, I answer directly to Eli. Eli should know what you're doing, because he is loyal to Jonathon too. The problem is that you are not telling him what you are thinking or doing. I don't think its right for you to come into Jonathon's office and make demands on us without explanation or authorization from Eli. I'm thinking about leaving the company because I don't want to be caught in the middle. In these situations the person in the middle always loses. Eli is trying to keep Biggs International on its feet. Having you around the office is an extra strain on him and a distraction from his business responsibilities," Maggie blurted out.

"Do you think Eli has anything to hide?" Rachel wanted to get as much information as she could from Maggie before she shut down or walked away.

"No!" Maggie was sure of her answer.

"Is it possible that he is working with someone on the outside to take over and break up Biggs?"

"No!" Maggie felt like she was in a courtroom.

Suspicion filled Rachel's words. "Has he told you to report all of my activities to him?" "Yes," Maggie said defensively.

"Has he told you to stall when I ask you for information or help?"

"Yes."

"Does any of this bother you?"

"This whole thing bothers me, Rachel!" Maggie was crying softly as she spoke. "We've been friends for a long time. I've also been a loyal and dedicated employee at Biggs. I don't know what is going on anymore, but it stinks! I think the company is going under, and I can't help stop it. I know you have lost your family and must be devastated—I don't blame you for trying to solve this puzzle—but I also don't know what my role is."

Rachel reached across the table and held Maggie's hand. She squeezed with desperation. "Help me, Maggie!" Rachel was tearful but intense. "These events are connected. Someone is trying to destroy us—not just the business—but us personally. The mad cow situation happens, then my kids are killed in a 'freak' accident, and Jonathon is taken ill and won't see a doctor. These things can't be coincidence; they are connected in some way, and I will find out how!"

"Bad things happen in threes." Maggie shrugged.

"That's ridiculous, Maggie, and you know it! Will you help me or not?" Rachel was pressing for a decision. "Tell me right now, so I won't have to wonder where you stand."

"But what about the business?" Maggie was overwhelmed with choosing Rachel over Eli and Biggs International.

"This isn't only about the business; it's bigger than that. It's about someone trying to destroy Jonathon Biggs. You just said that you are loyal to him. Are you in or not? Yes or no?"

"I'm in. What do you want me to do?" Maggie realized that it was fruitless to fight with her friend.

"We need to find out what Eli is up to. He's been quietly buying stock and adding it to his portfolio. He may be part of a conspiracy to take over the company. Can you look through some of the papers in his office and see what he's doing?"

"I think so, but I'll have to be careful." The thought of investigating Eli was beyond her ability to understand.

Rachel squeezed her hand. "Maggie, it's good to have you helping me."

"Jonathon, what happened?" Rachel walked into the family room and saw her husband lying on the couch, holding a bloody towel to his head. Rachel gently moved his hand and the towel away from his face. He had a large gash over his right eye, which was swollen shut.

"I was walking into the bathroom, got dizzy, and fell. My head must have hit the sink and knocked me out on the way down. I came to on the floor, bleeding all over the place. The blood makes it look more serious than it really is, but I probably need stitches."

"I'm sure you need stitches. Let's go to the doctor right now." Rachel knew that their family doctor would see him with short notice. She also knew that Dr. Delcoma would be discreet.

They arrived at the back door of the medical office building and took the service elevator upstairs. They were met by a nurse, who escorted them into an examination room and prepared Jonathon for the doctor.

"That's a nasty cut, Jonathon. It's going to require some sewing, probably eight to ten stitches." Dr. Delcoma casually picked up a syringe to numb the area. "How did this happen?" After hearing Jonathon's explanation, the doctor asked if he had noticed any symptoms leading up to this. Jonathon said, "No."

Rachel said, "Yes! He's been lying around for nearly a month, depressed and uninvolved with life. He's turned into a blob since the funeral."

Dr. Delcoma insisted on giving Jonathon a complete physical on the spot and ordered a blood test. He also talked to Jonathon about taking Zoloft to help with the depression. "I have a friend who is an excellent psychologist, and I'm sure I can get you in tomorrow."

Jonathon submitted to the physical and blood work and promised to think about taking the Zoloft and seeing the psychologist. Rachel took the prescription hoping that Jonathon would give in.

"Does Jonathon have any close friends who could spend time with him? He needs to talk about how he feels to someone other than you," Dr. Delcoma advised. "He may not want to cause you anxiety by telling you what's really going on in his gut."

Rachel decided to take the doctor's advice. She made a mental note to call a few of Jonathon's closest friends and share his situation with them. Jonathon had been aloof with everyone since the funeral. When his friends called, he acted as if he were doing fine. He would be upset with her if she invited them over to talk, but on the other hand, she couldn't sit by and do nothing while he drifted more deeply into depression each day.

The doctor continued, "I don't see anything wrong on the surface. I'll know what the blood tests say in a day or two. I'll call you."

Rachel took Jonathon home, and he lay down on his lounge chair by the pool, as if he had never left it.

Maggie was in Jonathon's office talking to Rachel at nine the next morning.

"I found something!" Excitement and fear were in her voice.

"Already? What is it?" Rachel whispered, even though they were alone in the room and the door was closed.

"I stayed late last night and went into Eli's office. I found a proposal from a major American cattle broker offering to buy as much beef as we can ship from the Argentina ranch. The price is fair and the contract covers the next three years with options to go five. There's enough revenue there to rescue Biggs International."

"What is the date on the proposal?"

"It is five weeks old."

"What would happen if Eli publicly announced that he had a deal of this magnitude?" Rachel sensed that her suspicions were becoming reality.

"The stock would stabilize and begin to climb out of the hole we've been in. Jonathon could probably cover his margins, and Biggs International could survive," Maggie spoke slowly and deliberately.

Rachel and Maggie stared at each other in disbelief. "I wonder why Eli isn't talking about this. We need some positive news now!"

Maggie was angry. "Let's confront him!"

"Not yet," Rachel said. "We need more information."

"I'll look around some more this afternoon. Eli has a golf outing and won't be back in the office until after noon."

Chapter Eight

"I don't mind if you sit in, but I will have to conduct the interview."

"I'm good with that. We'll be there in about ten minutes," Breslin Kline responded to Bob Holcroft, the FBI inspector's, comment. He had called Holcroft last week to discuss a possible conspiracy at Biggs International. The FBI agent was very interested in getting involved after he was brought up to date on the situation. Breslin Kline had a reputation as a tough, exacting investigator who didn't miss anything. Holcroft was anxious to work with him. They had decided to start by interviewing Jonathon Biggs. They were surprised when they called for the appointment and found Jonathon to be cooperative. When asked if he wanted his lawyer present, Jonathon declined.

"Mr. Biggs, do you have a theory as to how or why only your ranches have been infected with mad cow disease?" Bob Holcroft began the interview.

"No, I don't." Jonathon had decided to keep his answers short and concise.

"Tell me about your new acquisition in Argentina," Holcroft continued questioning Jonathon in a rapid-fire style.

"I bought another ranch. We're trying to get into the South American market," Jonathon answered with no emotion.

"Didn't you margin most of your stock in Biggs international to get the money for the purchase?"

"Yes."

"Wasn't that risky?" Bob Holcroft was confused by Jonathon's apathy.

"No, it was the best move for us. We have margined our holdings before to purchase other ranches. It simplifies the process and minimizes bank involvement, since we borrow against ourselves. Biggs International has shown consistent stock price increases for the last fifteen years. Our largest drop has been twelve cents. Historically, there was no risk for us."

"Unless something catastrophic happened. Like mad cow disease?" Holcroft was pressing Jonathon Biggs.

"Yes, unpredictable." Jonathon's apathy continued.

"What are you doing to help Biggs International recover?"

"My vice president, Eli Moore, is running things for now." Jonathon seemed disinterested.

"Is he staying in touch with you?" Holcroft pressed.

"Occasionally, but I'm not involved at this time. I'm sure you know that my children died in an explosion at our home. I'm taking some time off to recover from that."

"How well do you know Eli Moore?"

"Very well. He came to live with our family during his sophomore year of high school and stayed through college. He worked for Biggs part-time during his college years, and I hired him full-time when he finished his MBA."

"What were the circumstances surrounding his moving in with your family?"

"His mother was killed in a boating accident. My wife, Rachel, was out on our boat with some friends that day, and she rescued Eli from the wreckage. His father was taken into custody on the spot by the sheriff for operating his boat under the influence of alcohol. He was also charged with manslaughter. Eli was upset and alone, so Rachel brought him to our home. Since the accident occurred on a Saturday morning, they couldn't arraign Eli's dad until Monday morning. We kept him for the weekend. When Eli's father posted bond on Monday, he disappeared, and no one has seen or heard from him since. Rachel and I went to social services and became Eli's foster parents, and he became part of our family. We wanted to adopt him, but Eli always hoped that his father would show up. We just raised him as if he were one of our own children. Rachel said that God had given us so much that we ought to share it with someone in need. Eli has been an exceptional person, and we are blessed that he is part of our family."

"Do you trust him?" Holcroft knew that his question was ludicrous.

"Implicitly," Jonathon answered without hesitation.

"Would Eli try to take over the company?" Breslin Kline cut in.

"I doubt it. He's already the executive vice president, and I'm grooming him to be president and eventually CEO. He's going to have it all anyway." Jonathon laughed at the absurd suggestion that Eli would want to harm him.

"Your wife, Rachel, has been working at Biggs lately. She's using your office. What is she doing there?" Breslin Kline still did not trust wealthy people. He was searching for Rachel's ulterior motive.

"Rachel believes that someone is trying to destroy us. She is trying to figure out who and why. She also thinks that the explosion at our new home was no accident and that our children were murdered. She is convinced that there is a connection between the mad cow disease and the deaths of our children."

"Do you agree with her?" The FBI agent jumped on Jonathon's answer.

"I don't know. Right now, I'm just trying to get through each day." Jonathon's response was that of a weary man.

"Thank you for your time, Mr. Biggs."

"Right." Jonathon left the room and walked outside by the pool. The warmth felt good on his face. He decided to stay outside for a while, so he settled into a poolside lounge chair. He was glad for the unseasonably warm weather this May. "Maybe I'll get a different perspective on things out here," he prayed.

The only time Jonathon felt at peace was when he prayed.

He wasn't sure why, but he didn't blame God. Rachel was angry and doubting, but for some reason, Jonathon wasn't. He didn't fault Rachel for her resentment toward God. Her skepticism was normal for someone grieving the sudden loss of her children. Jonathon was hurt and confused, so he sat by the pool and prayed, hoping that God would help him sort it out.

Breslin Kline and Bob Holcroft watched Jonathon Biggs wander outside and let themselves out.

"That is one devastated man," Breslin Kline said in a low voice.

"Breslin, do I detect sympathy in your voice?" The FBI agent laughed slightly.

"Absolutely not!" Breslin Kline lied.

<hr />

Rachel Biggs was fuming. She was angry anyway, and this latest development added fuel to her frustration. Maggie had told her that Eli was going to be interviewed by the FBI and USDA inspectors. Rachel decided that the interview would be a good time to confront Eli about not announcing the three-year beef contract for the Argentina ranch. She was going to pin him down and get some answers.

Rachel had waited at the conference room door for the investigators to show up. When she informed them that she would be taking part in the interview, they bluntly told her that she would not be involved. She became demanding, and they dismissed her without further explanation. Rachel paced the hallway outside of the locked conference room for a full half hour, after the doors were closed. She was now walking back and forth in Jonathon's office, upset beyond tears. The intercom buzzed.

"Maggie, I don't want to be disturbed!"

"Mrs. Biggs, Mr. Kline and Mr. Holcroft are here and want to talk with you."

"I'm not available," Rachel shouted at the intercom.

"Mrs. Biggs, they want to set up an appointment to interview you."

Rachel exploded out of Jonathon's office into the reception area. She planted herself directly in Breslin Kline's face.

"Your investigation is a joke! You call yourselves 'professionals,' but you don't have a clue about what really happened. This company is being destroyed and my husband along with it. My children have been murdered, and the police call it an accident. Someone is trying to destroy us, and they are succeeding, because of your incompetence. I know more about this case than both of you. If you want to talk to me, get a court order and inform my attorney. Better yet, why don't you spend your time solving these crimes? Now get out!"

Rachel turned to Maggie. "If they're not gone in thirty seconds, call security and have them removed from the property." She closed the door to Jonathon's office hard, leaned against it, and slid sobbing to the floor.

Breslin Kline and Bob Holcroft left quietly. They were both annoyed. They had met with Eli Moore and the Biggs International corporate attorneys for three hours and walked away with very little information. They learned enough, however, to make them highly suspicious of Eli and wondered if he had established an inside conspiracy to take down Jonathon Biggs. They discovered that Eli had visited each of the six ranches two weeks prior to the mad cow discovery. He habitually visited each ranch only twice a year, and this tour was unscheduled. Eli claimed that he was making the rounds at Jonathon's request to explain the Argentina purchase to the ranch managers personally and to assure them that the company was secure.

"That is one angry woman!" Breslin Kline stated softly as they exited the building.

"Mama Bear Syndrome. Everything she holds dear has been ripped away from her."

Chapter Nine

Jonathon's depression had reached an all-time low. His blood tests had come back normal. Dr. Delcoma was sure that he was suffering from stress and anxiety and warned Jonathon that physical ailments could result from his stress. Jonathon thanked him for the information and returned to his new place, the lounge chair by the pool, to lie around. "If I'm going to be miserable, I might as well get a tan," he had told Rachel.

Now he had shingles. He couldn't seem to get comfortable. He put some ointment on the problem areas, but the relief was minor. Rachel was home every evening at six. She had asked him to pick up around the house and do a few chores, which he did. Rachel was trying to coax him into going for walks with her. When they did take the occasional walk, he tired quickly and retreated back to the poolside. He was still putting off seeing a psychologist or taking medication for his depression. April had been a nightmare, and in May it was continuing. "The only good thing," mused Jonathon Oliver Biggs, "is weather in the seventies and this comfortable lounge chair."

Tuesday, the six-week anniversary of the explosion, three men came to visit Jonathon. They had been called by Rachel, even though she knew that Jonathon would be upset with her. Rachel was taking Dr. Delcoma's advice and trying to involve other people in Jonathon's life, hoping that they could help him. The three men were good friends who had long relationships with

Jonathon. Rachel knew that they would have his best interests at heart and do their best to encourage him.

Miquel Sameros was a rancher from Portugal. He had worked at Biggs for ten years early in his career. Jonathon and Miguel had become good friends while working together in the mail room at Biggs International. Their families vacationed together often, and they had remained close over the years. Fifteen years ago, Miguel and his father started a cattle ranch in Portugal. Jonathon and his father had helped him in the early years. The Sameros Ranch was now very successful.

Doug Lister was the Senior Pastor at Jonathon and Rachel's church. Jonathon had known him since he came to the church four years ago. Before he became a pastor, Doug had developed a nationwide credit rebuilding business for people with financial problems. At forty, he decided to become a minister. His life goal became, "to help people realize God's purpose for them and live it!" Doug had made enough money at forty to last him two lifetimes. He served at the church gratis, returning his salary to their ministry to the needy. He and his wife, Millie, were regulars at the Biggs family gatherings. They were the first to arrive on the scene after the explosion and had worked tirelessly to help Jonathon and Rachel. Jonathon had been avoiding Doug for the past two months, making excuses to not spend time with him.

Ron Milliken was the CEO of Milliken Investment Strategies. He began investing in gold while in college and had a knack for making money. He was an independent thinker and worked well as an entrepreneur. Jonathon and his father were the first to invest with Ron and became trusted business advisors. Jonathon was on the board of directors at Milliken Investment Strategies. He and Ron had been good friends since college, and he visited the Biggs every time he was in town. Ron had remained single and traveled around the world from adventure to adventure.

"Jonathon, why are you lying around? You should be working, pulling things back together. What is going on in your head?" Ron Milliken got directly to the point of their visit. "We're here to help you!"

Jonathon was irritated by their intrusion. Still, he responded with a tired half smile and a nod.

"I'm tired. I've been knocked down and don't want to get up. I'm hoping to wake up one day and have everything back the way it was."

"How can we help? It's not like you to be out of the action. I think backing away from life is only making your situation worse. You aren't designed to sit on the sidelines; you're a player—so play! Even if you have to play hurt—play!" Ron's upbeat aggressiveness wasn't working on Jonathon. Ron was an influential motivator who knew how to move people.

Jonathon reached for his iced tea. He sighed but said nothing.

"Being lazy doesn't become you. You solve problems by getting in there and working out the tough stuff," Miguel Sameros interjected.

"I'm not lazy; I'm tired," Jonathon corrected him.

"You're not tired, you're de-energized," Ron jumped back into the conversation. "Getting back into the action will recharge your batteries. You need to grab hold of a good challenge, dig in, and make things happen."

"I can't even grab hold of life as it is—don't need any more stress."

Miguel spoke with gentle firmness, "You have lost almost everything. The most painful loss must be your family. I know that in time you will work through the pain. In the meantime, you have a business that's in trouble and needs your expertise to stay afloat. Many families rely on you for their incomes." To Jonathon, Miguel sounded condescending.

"Thanks for the review," Jonathon said with sarcasm.

"You helped Eli through the most difficult times in his life. You gave him a new life, an education, and a future with Biggs. He's down there alone trying to salvage this mess. You can't leave him unsupported—he's family to you." Miguel's intensity was obvious.

"Eli is family, and he'll do just fine. I trust him." Jonathon waved his hand, dismissing Miguel's concerns.

"What if he's in over his head? What if he can't rescue Biggs?" Ron Milliken was hoping that something they said would get to Jonathon.

"Then he can join me at the pool. We'll get a tan, drink some iced tea, and feel like crap together." Jonathon's sarcasm was increasing.

"Jonathon, you helped me start the ranch and taught us how to succeed. You even sent us our first customers. I remember when you and your dad gave me fifty thousand dollars to purchase livestock. When I tried to pay you back, you told me to use it to help someone else get started. I'm here to help you get restarted. What can I do?"

"Thanks for coming." Jonathon was dismissive.

"I'm not leaving. I didn't come here to be shrugged aside. I came to help somehow. I'm not sure what I can do for you, but I'm sticking around until I figure it out." Miguel was determined but not frustrated.

"Can you tell us how you feel about us being here?" Doug intervened, hoping that Jonathon would talk and reveal something about his inner struggle.

"I didn't invite you," Jonathon said pointedly.

"I know, Rachel did. She is very concerned about you. Look at this from her point of view for a minute. She has lost her entire family—except for you. She feels like she's losing you too."

"I'm still here," Jonathon spoke without emotion.

"Your body is here, but your heart isn't," Pastor Doug said softly.

"Yes, it is. It's just broken right now—shattered into little tiny pieces. I can't even figure out where each piece fits. I start with one piece and try to match others to it, but they don't fit right."

"Maybe you ought to let God rebuild your heart. He knows where the pieces fit," Pastor Doug suggested.

Sarcasm oozed from Jonathon's voice, "That sounds very pastoral! How does it work in real life?"

"Trust and surrender—stop trying to fix it yourself. Just start living one day at a time—or maybe just one hour at a time."

Jonathon thought, *If I didn't know better, I'd think that you guys were coached by Rachel.*

"I don't know why this happened or how!" Jonathon was agitated, speaking with hushed intensity. "I've always tried to be fair and honest. I've been successful but haven't become a snob about it. I want the people around me to succeed and have good lives. If Biggs fails, I can live with that. But my kids, that's way outside of my ability to cope. I've lost most of what I care about. I couldn't protect them. All I could do was watch. There were only a few, small body parts left. There wasn't hardly enough left of my kids to bury! What did I do to deserve that?" Jonathon was loud now, speaking with infuriated desperation. "I'm waiting for an answer, and it's not coming. I'm listening, but none of this makes sense. Don't tell me that God will comfort and strengthen me. I want this pain to stop, but it doesn't. It's dull most of the time, and then all of a sudden, it jabs into my soul and rips me up all over again. If I stay really still inside and don't scream or cry, it settles back to dull again. Containing my emotions keeps it in the dull mode most of the time. But then Rachel comes home angry, and I see what this has done to her. There's a stick of dynamite in my gut, and I know that it's going to blow me apart any minute. I brace myself for the explosion, and it doesn't come—but I know it will blow soon—maybe tomorrow. When it does, I'll be completely destroyed with no hope of recovery. The fuse is lit and burning down. I ask God to take it away or at least to put out the fuse, but when Rachel comes home, its still there." Jonathon paced around the pool while he was talking, creating distance between his visitors and himself.

"You have no idea what its like to be me right now."

Jonathon turned away walked toward the house.

Ron stood and began pacing on the pool's edge across the water from Jonathon. "You're right, but we still want to help. Tell us about the Argentina deal."

Jonathon stopped and turned slowly to face his friends. "It was a great opportunity. There is plenty of land, and it's priced right. Labor prices aren't bad either. We could be shipping beef all over the hemisphere. The ultimate goal was to grow the Argentina ranch to the point where it could support a complete processing plant. We could run the whole process and ship the beef ourselves: a ranching operation managing everything from A to Z. We wouldn't be at the mercy of the middle man anymore. In three years we could have five refrigerated jets flying beef to our own distributors all over Central and Latin America. Expanding from there would be simple. We could set up our own processing plants in the USA and ship using leased jets and our own distribution network." The words were now spilling out of Jonathon's mouth, as if a dam had been opened.

Ron and Jonathon were both standing by the shallow end of the pool. "Did you see the Argentina deal as a necessity for the future stability of Biggs International?" Ron was making direct eye contact.

"Was it necessary? It was the next step to secure our future in the marketplace. But the Biggs ranches were doing well without it. I think we saw it as just the next step."

"Tell me about the financing part of the deal." Ron maintained eye contact with Jonathon.

"I margined most of my stock. I wanted to finance the deal myself. With future purchases like jets and processing plants, I didn't want to overextend our borrowing power for the second and third phases of the project. The risk was minimal. We know how to do ranching, so phase one seemed like a good time to use our own money. We would finance the higher risk aspects of the plan later. Now my margins have been called in, and Biggs is in trouble financially because of the mad cow thing." Jonathon put his hands in his pockets and walked toward his pool chair.

Doug jumped into the exchange. "Have you thought that maybe you wanted too much? I mean, you already have the most lucrative ranching set up in America. Looking back, do you think you may have become greedy?"

"Absolutely not! This is good business. Growing with the

opportunities is smart leadership. Our stockholders, employees, and customers all benefit from this move. I'm not trying to rule the world's cattle industry! I do, however, want to manage my part of the industry well. We have been at the mercy of the middle man for years. If we can become our own middle man, then we have greater stability for the future." Jonathon sighed as he dropped heavily into his chair.

"Would you have done whatever it took to make this deal work?" Doug asked skeptically.

"I was and am convinced that this is the best next step for Biggs—so, yes," Jonathon answered.

"Jonathon, I ask this as a friend who wants to help you recover from tragedy. Making this deal, have you done anything questionable?" Ron Milliken looked around for affirmation from the other men. No one spoke.

"What do you mean?" Jonathon got up from his chair and began walking away from them toward the deep end of the pool.

"For the sake of the business, have you done anything illegal or unethical?" Ron pressed.

"What? Me? Are you crazy? I'm Mister Clean!"

————⋙•⋘————

After his conversation with Miguel, Ron, and Doug, Jonathon had gone swimming. He felt better having vented his feelings to his friends. Their visit had been hard but beneficial. He wasn't sure how he felt about some of the things they said but was glad that he spoke out. His integrity was intact whether they thought so or not.

Chapter Ten

"Rachel, meet me at Phil's Coffee House at two this afternoon," Maggie whispered into her cell phone. She had been watching Eli's movements through the office for the past few weeks. She voiced her observations to Rachel on a daily basis. At first, she wasn't sure that Eli was capable of hurting Jonathon Biggs, but she had since changed her mind. She had been influenced by Rachel's constant distrust of Eli. She had also seen him keep Rachel at a distance and only give her information when she specifically asked for it. Maggie was confounded by Eli's attitude.

"For someone leading a company that is in deep trouble, he doesn't seem very concerned," she had told Rachel last week. Maggie had become very suspicious and begun looking for opportunities to check up on Eli. She had only been able to pick up bits and pieces, until the day she found a list of passwords on a card in his desk drawer. At first she felt fearful about going through his desk, and it took all the nerve she could muster. Maggie didn't act on the passwords for almost a week. She wasn't sure that she wanted to know the truth anyway. She hadn't mentioned the passwords to Rachel. She didn't need that kind of anxiety. Rachel was very nervous and aggressive. Maggie was afraid that she would jump to conclusions without substantiating them. Rachel was on a mission to prove that the mad cow incidents and the deaths of her children were connected. She needed someone to blame and then destroy. It seemed that she had chosen Eli.

It was now two o'clock. Maggie walked into Phil's Coffee House. She strolled directly to the counter and ordered a two-shot, caramel latte. Rachel was seated at the window, watching with interest. When Maggie got her coffee, she moved deliberately to the corner farthest from the counter and sat with her back to the corner, facing the room. Rachel got up, ordered the House Blend, and made her way casually over to Maggie's table.

"How can you drink caramel lattes and stay in such incredible shape!" Rachel teased. She knew Maggie worked out relentlessly and was proud of her conditioning regimen. "What's going on, Maggie?"

"I did something that I thought I'd never do. I went through Eli's desk and found a list of passwords for his computer." Maggie was speaking softly but quickly. "I stayed late last night and checked out each one. I found some very damaging information about Eli's activities lately."

"I knew it! He's in the middle of this thing, isn't he?" Rachel's response was almost exuberant. For the moment, being right about Eli gave her a sense of satisfaction.

"I wanted to meet you here, because I am concerned about your reaction. At this point, I want you to promise that you won't do anything with what I tell you. We must proceed carefully—there's a lot at stake here. Do I have your word?" Maggie was clear about being in control.

"You can trust me to do what is right." Rachel tried to maintain the upper hand in the exchange.

"Not good enough. I need your promise." Maggie wasn't good at being assertive with her boss's wife. But she was determined.

"You said that you would cooperate with my investigation. Do you think I would do anything that would make it worse?" Rachel pushed back.

"Yes, unintentionally—but yes. Rachel, you are on the edge right now. This information will throw you over, and you will be out of control. I've been watching you change. You want someone to pay for what has happened. You don't trust anyone, and your anxiety level is sky high. I don't think that you are able to make good decisions about what I have to share, so I'm asking for a guarantee. I am in the middle of this, so I'm going to have control; or you get nothing else from me. I'm the one at risk here." Maggie wasn't giving in.

"That was harsh. I don't know what to say." Rachel did her best to look hurt, appealing to Maggie's sense of compassion.

Maggie got up and gathered her coat and purse. She headed toward the door. Rachel didn't move until she was in the parking lot.

Rachel caught up as Maggie was getting into her car. "I promise, Maggie."

"Get in."

———<><>———

"What do you think of his condition?" The inquiry was matter-of-fact. Both men were enjoying the imminent destruction of Jonathon Oliver Biggs.

"Jonathon Biggs is done. He's sick and depressed. His marriage is a time bomb waiting to go off. He's permanently damaged. He'll never be on top of things again." The man in charge was decisive.

"You're really enjoying this, aren't you?" His assistant sounded pleased with himself.

"Oh yes, I appreciate it when a good plan comes together for someone's destruction!" The sinister comment elicited scornful laughter from both parties.

"What about Eli Moore?"

"He'll go down with the ship." The thought was tantalizing to the leader. "The collateral damage will drown him for sure. He's a sharp business man but won't be able to handle the scandal or the emotional baggage we're laying on him!"

"I feel good about the way this is working out."

"So do I!" His statement was accentuated with pleasure at the idea that Jonathon Oliver Biggs was facing self-destruction.

———<><>———

Jonathon was coming out of the shower when the phone rang. It was Dr. Delcoma asking him to come in and talk. While he was at the doctor's office, the nurse took more blood to confirm Dr. Delcoma's conclusions. The confirmation would take three days.

"On the surface it appears to be a simple staff infection but is really a very rare strain of a virus. Most blood tests miss it, but I had them look again because the combination of your symptoms didn't make sense to me. It's like you have mono without the discolored eyes and temperature," Dr. Delcoma told Jonathon.

"I have been feeling like I'm in slow motion, unable to manufacture any energy."

"This virus plus the emotions of your grief have you wanting to check out on life. I still think you need counseling, Jonathon." Dr. Delcoma was gracious but definite.

"How long will the virus last?" Jonathon ignored the counseling comment.

"I'm not sure, but the consensus of viral specialists is around ninety days or so. You should be feeling physically better gradually very soon. I'm serious about the counseling, Jonathon. I can set it up for you today." The doctor was still gracious but firm.

"I'm relieved to hear this. I thought that I was going crazy. Do I need any medication?"

"No, just eat well, and ride it out." It was obvious that Jonathon wasn't ready to deal with counseling.

"Thanks, Doc." Jonathon shook his hand and left the office.

Jonathon was anxious to tell Rachel about the virus. He hoped the news would sooth her anger and help to calm her down. Jonathon called her cell phone, but she didn't answer. He left her a voicemail to come home immediately, that he had something good to tell her.

Rachel's cell phone rang as she got into Maggie's car. Without looking at her caller ID, she touched the *ignore* button. If it was important, they would leave a message.

"Maggie, you have control," Rachel conceded, because she needed Maggie's information to trap Eli.

"Thank you." Maggie sighed. "I found a list of passwords to Web sites and folders in Eli's desk drawer. I discovered that he has been buying large quantities of Biggs stock both in his name and Debra's."

"How much has he purchased?" Rachel fought her emotions and managed to stay barely under control.

"I'm not sure exactly, but he's spent at least seven hundred fifty thousand dollars himself and another five hundred thousand for Debra. Between the two of them, they control one hundred and forty thousand shares. That doesn't include Eli's previous holdings, options, or bonuses."

"That rat is trying to take over Biggs. He's taking advantage of Jonathon's trust and betraying us. I need to confront him immediately. I wonder if Debra knows what he is doing. Thanks, Maggie." Rachel was angry. Her adrenaline was getting ready for a confrontation.

"Hold on!" Maggie grasped Rachel's arm firmly. "Rachel, you promised not to do anything. Walk away from the edge, and settle down. We can manage this carefully and do our confronting at the most opportune time."

"How about now?" Rachel demanded. Her eyes were aflame with resolve.

"You promised!" Maggie's voice went up in volume. "You and Jonathon talk about integrity all the time—show some now, and keep your word to me." Maggie was expecting Rachel's response and had rehearsed her part well.

"Okay, you're in the driver's seat." Rachel backed down, but Maggie sensed that it was only temporary.

"Thank you." Maggie released her grip on Rachel's arm and leaned back into the seat. "If you do anything without my approval, I'll deny all of it and make sure that you never find my evidence," Maggie threatened. She wanted Rachel to know that she would decide how and when to use the information on Eli.

Chapter Eleven

Miles Masterson punched speed dial one on his cell phone. He felt a need to reassure Jonathon Biggs that this case was his highest priority.

"Jonathon, Miles Masterson, how are you feeling?" Miles' concern was genuine.

"A little better every day." Jonathon was surprised at his positive response.

"I'm checking in with our findings so far. This is the most difficult situation I've seen in my career. But I do have a few things to tell you."

"Thanks for working on this. I appreciate your help more than I can say." Jonathon meant what he said.

"I'm certain that your cows were infected through an injection into their spinal columns through the neck. Unfortunately, putting them down and taking out their spinal columns for testing has destroyed any possibility of proving my theory. I am absolutely convinced that someone is out to destroy Biggs International. Actually, Jonathon, I think that someone wants to destroy you. You don't have many enemies, and the ones you do have checked out fine. I'm beginning to think that there is someone we don't know about who is attempting to ruin you. If that is the case, then there are people being used to carry out the wishes of whoever wants you destroyed. Some of the people being used may be people that you know and trust. I've assigned private investigators to check out those around you just to see if anything unusual is going on in their lives."

"You're looking into key people on my leadership team?" Jonathon was shocked. He hadn't considered this possibility. He had always surrounded himself with trustworthy people. Disloyalty was unthinkable to him.

"Yes, and some of their relations as well. For example, my investigator checked out Debra Moore, Eli's wife. We have seen her meeting with an unknown man on at least four occasions, twice at a hotel downtown. We haven't been able to get a good enough look at the man to identify him. It may be an affair— or it could be something related to Biggs International," Miles reported.

"Debra Moore?" The surprise in Jonathon's voice was obvious to Miles.

"Yes," he said with no emotion in his voice.

"She has nothing to do with the company. She's married to Eli and loves to attend social functions. She has always seemed positive about her husband's role at Biggs. Their marriage is a little strained at times but not in trouble. I don't see how this relates to Biggs." Jonathon was puzzled.

"It probably doesn't, but right now, it's all we have. I'll check in with you in a day or so. Get well, Jonathon." Miles paused, waiting for Jonathon to close the conversation.

"Thank you, Miles. Your help is appreciated." Jonathon shook his head as he hung up.

"Debra Moore," Jonathon mused to himself. "Social climber, likes to live well, loves to shop, and wants to be noticed. Doesn't express interest in Eli's job, just in his paycheck and bonus package and his social connections. I hope their marriage is all right."

Jonathon's thoughts were interrupted as he heard the front door open and shut. *Rachel must be home,* he thought, *She will be glad to here my news about the virus.* He changed his shirt and went into the kitchen to greet her. He felt tired, but his mood was positive for the first time in weeks.

"Do I know you? Where's Jonathon?" Rachel may have been teasing, but her tone was too blunt.

"I have good news." He smiled. She hadn't seen him smile in a very long time.

"Have you kidnapped my husband? He's the one who sits out by the pool all day and never gets in. He's unshaven and showers only when I nag him." Her tone was getting lighter.

"I saw Doctor Delcoma today." Jonathon was leading her into the conversation.

"Did he give you a happy drug? You seem different." Rachel was wary.

"He redid my blood test and found a rare virus. He says it makes you listless like mono without the other symptoms. It takes around ninety days to work through your system and then you gradually feel better. They took some more blood today to confirm his findings." A little of the old Jonathon was showing through as he talked.

"Finally, someone has a breakthrough!" Rachel suddenly shifted to sarcasm. "You know, Jonathon, you have been hard to live with since that night. I've felt like you're not my partner anymore. You won't let me into your world, so I've created one for myself; and I like it."

"I expect to feel a little better every day, and soon I'll be fine. I went for a swim today after I met with Ron, Miguel, and Doug. By the way, thanks for asking them to come over." Jonathon took two steps toward Rachel and hesitated. He wanted to hold and reassure her, but he sensed her frustration so he stopped short.

"I asked them over a month ago to come and see you." She spat out the words.

"Well, it probably took them a while to get together. They came as a group. I shared a lot with them, and I think it helped." Jonathon was determined not to drift back into negativity.

"It's good that you could get some of the things off your chest with your friends that you can't say to your wife." Rachel's sarcasm was turning to anger. Jonathon began to feel the need to withdraw. His mood was going from positive to fearful. He felt like going back to the pool. He knew that responding to Rachel's comments would cause an argument. He had been through this scene before. She was angry and looking for a reason. She would pick something out of their conversation to use as a catalyst for a hostile exchange of words. He decided to respond, even though he wanted to flee to the safety of his pool chair.

"I'm sorry. I know that I've made life hard for you." To Jonathon, this seemed like the least-abrasive approach.

"Yes, life has been hard for me. My kids were murdered. My new house was blown up. My husband's business is a mess. We're living in my parents' guest house, and you just lay around feeling sorry for yourself, while whoever did this to us is walking away laughing. I'm going to turn over every stone until I find out who is responsible, and when I do, they are going to pay … and pay … and pay." Rachel was now moving toward the front door, while Jonathon stood and stared at her. "I'm going out."

"I was hoping that we could spend some time together tonight," Jonathon said softly.

"You've been disinterested for three months, and now after talking for five minutes, you think that everything will be fine?" Rachel had turned from the door and was heading toward Jonathon with her finger pointed at his face. Everything within Jonathon Oliver Biggs wanted to withdraw. He had become accustomed to the gloomy cave of depression he had been in for the past three months. Somehow he knew that if he didn't stand up to her now, he would lose her forever. Living separate lives while being married was something they had agreed not to do years ago. They were in life together no matter what.

"Rachel, we're in this together." Jonathon took a firm but gentle approach.

"Together? Where have you been while I've been working on solving this mess? Checking out on me when I need you the most doesn't communicate togetherness." She was in his face, pointing the finger. "Have you been to the office? Have you talked to the USDA? Have you returned Eli's calls? Or Maggie's? Have you looked into building another house so we have a place to live that's our own? Have you shown any personal interest in what I'm doing or how this is affecting me? Have you given me any affection besides the occasional, obligatory hug? Let me answer all of these questions with one word, *no!*" Rachel's grief and frustration gushed out.

Jonathon's eyes were getting wet. He wanted his cave. There was a certain unexplainable peace in his depression that, although painful, was predictable. He could live with the dull throbbing hurt, because he knew that getting involved in life again would cause a stabbing, ripping pain that he couldn't handle. As Rachel talked, he could feel the knife going slowly into his soul and knew he couldn't turn away from her.

"I've been sick, depressed, and withdrawn. But I'm back now. I'm not better, but I'm back. It will take a while for me to heal up physically, and I don't know that I'll ever be the same emotionally or spiritually; but I am here for you now, Rachel. I'm sorry with everything I am that I deserted you when you needed me. This grief thing is uncharted territory for us, and I haven't handled it well." Jonathon reached out and gently took her hands in his.

"And you think that I have?" Rachel blurted tearfully.

"You've done much better than me. You're out there trying every day. Hurting but trying to help. You have a courageous heart. I admire you for being the woman you are even in the midst of the worst possible pain anyone could ever experience." Jonathon looked into her tear-filled eyes and spoke from his heart.

"I'm really angry inside." Rachel tried to wipe her eyes, but the tears wouldn't stop. She sighed long and hard, as if to release her anguish and open her heart. "If I don't do something, it will overwhelm me, and I'll self-destruct. The investigation keeps me from losing my sanity." She stood in front of Jonathon, wet face to wet face, as two broken people became open to each other. Jonathon took her in his arms and held her gently. He raised his hand to her head and softly stroked her hair. He began to weep softly. She responded by setting her hand on the back of his neck and pulling him to herself. She began to sob, softly at first, then uncontrollably. The dynamite in Jonathon's gut was gone now. He no longer sought to withdraw in dull pain. His pain came out of his innermost being in a tsunami like flood that completely enveloped him. He was overwhelmed by anguish mingled with release.

There they stood; two broken people clinging to each other. Shuddering in sorrow and sobbing with relief as their separate pains bound them together as one. Jonathon knew the hurt that was Rachel's, and she knew his intimately now. They were together again, soul mates.

Chapter Twelve

"Good morning, Ed. I would like to check the sign out log for last evening please."

"Yes sir, Mr. Moore." The security officer turned the page back to the previous evening. Eli scanned the log sheet quickly and saw nothing out of the ordinary.

"Thanks. Ed, how would I get a record of the keycards used last night to open offices?"

"Just sign this authorization sheet, and I'll have the information processed and send you an e-mail."

"How long does that usually take?" Eli signed the form.

"About an hour."

"Good. Thanks, Ed, I appreciate your help."

"No problem, Mr. Moore."

Eli strolled back through the lobby toward the elevators. Something wasn't quite right. When he arrived at his office early that morning, something had changed. He was a very orderly person. Before he left his office each evening, he cleared his desk, placed his remote keyboard in the middle drawer, and pushed his chair against it. This morning his chair was at a slight angle, and his keyboard wasn't straight in the drawer as he had left it. Details were Eli's life. He took care of the details so that Jonathon Biggs could manage the big picture. Someone had been in his office. He thought that the custodian may have carelessly moved the chair while cleaning. She had done this once before, and Eli had called her in and demonstrated how he wanted his chair set against the desk. The custodian had left his office in perfect order since then, and that was two years ago. He hadn't noticed anything missing from his drawers, which were locked every night before he left. The lock on his drawer didn't appear to have been tampered with. He decided to wait for the key-card log.

The buzz of the intercom disrupted Eli's thoughts. "Yes?"

"Inspector Bob Holcroft from the FBI is here to see you. He has four agents with him."

"Thanks. Send them in." Eli punched the intercom button with his index finger, walked across his office, and opened the door to greet the FBI inspector. "Good morning, Inspector Holcroft. How can I help you today?"

"Mr. Moore, I have a court order to search the offices at Biggs International. It includes examining your computers." Holcroft was direct.

"May I see it, please?" Eli was surprised but spoke matter-of-factly. Holcroft handed the document to Eli, who picked up his phone. "Get me the legal department, please." He scanned the document with his eyes while he waited. "Matt, this is Eli. Could you come to my office right away? Thanks."

Eli looked up at Bob Holcroft. "Our chief attorney is on his way up to examine this document. Please be seated, and tell me what you're looking for."

"As you know, we've been working on outside leads and have turned up nothing. So, we have decided to do an internal investigation," the FBI inspector clarified. "It's nothing unusual for us, although it is inconvenient for you. I brought two of our most capable computer experts to help, so we don't have to remove your computers from the premises, unless we find evidence in them."

"I'm assuming that our lawyer will find your search documents to be in order. How would you like to proceed? Please be as specific as possible." Eli wondered if they had already been in his office last night. He decided that asking would make them think that he was hiding something.

"We want to examine Jonathon Biggs' office and computer as well as that of his administrative assistant. We want to do the same with yours."

"Anything else?" Eli didn't like this but reminded himself that Jonathon would want him to cooperate. Jonathon was above reproach and wanted Biggs International to operate with integrity in every area. His approach had endeared him to his employees and customers as well. Eli wanted to lead like his mentor.

"No, that's it for now." Bob Holcroft spoke as if he were bored with the whole process. He was a man of action and didn't enjoy many of the tedious duties of an investigation.

The chief attorney arrived and verified the FBI documents. He assigned two lawyers to each office to observe and take notes on the search. He took Eli aside and asked if there was anything he needed to know. Eli assured him that he was up to date on the situation and thanked him for his help. The attorney returned to his office and called Jonathon Biggs.

"Jonathon, the FBI showed up this morning with a court order to search headquarters. They specifically want to search your offices and examine your computer and Maggie's. They are doing the same with Eli's office. They brought their own computer people with them. They said that they won't take our computers off the premises unless they find something suspicious. What's going on? I can't protect you if I don't know anything."

"Thank you, Matt, but we don't need protection from the FBI. Let's cooperate with them." Jonathon's confidence didn't calm the attorney.

"We are, but I get the feeling that they are looking for something they already know about."

"Or think they know about. We have nothing to hide. If there is something out of order, they will find it, and we'll check it out. Thanks for your help, Matt."

Jonathon hung up and crawled back into bed next to Rachel. He pulled her close and held her. He prayed silently for strength.

"What was that about?" Rachel looked at him with wide-open, expectant eyes.

"That was Matt, the chief attorney at Biggs. The FBI arrived this morning with a court order to search the premises. They're going to look through my office and Eli's."

"Are they going to confiscate the computers?" Rachel sat up suddenly.

"Not unless they find something suspicious. Why are you interested in the computers?" Jonathon asked.

Rachel popped up out of the bed. "Let's get dressed, and I'll make some coffee. I have a lot to tell you."

Jonathon suddenly realized that silently praying for strength was going to become a regular activity.

⇒➤●◄⇐

Over coffee in the kitchen, Rachel brought Jonathon up to date on everything, including Eli's recent stock purchases. Jonathon's eyebrows were raised when she told him about the three-year contract with the Argentina ranch.

"I've been thinking that buying that ranch was a bad idea. Now I wonder if it will be the only thing we have going to rescue Biggs International." Jonathon questioned Rachel about her suspicions toward Eli. "What made you suspect him to begin with?"

"I don't know. He was obviously taken aback when I showed up at the office. Cooperation didn't come easily for him, and he told Maggie to stall me. He has her reporting directly to him about everything she sees me doing." Rachel wasn't angry anymore. As her emotions cleared, she was less suspicious of Eli.

"So he's surprised when you show up at the office. Maybe he thinks you might want a big say in the business. He might think that he's protecting the company. I don't know. But he's always been loyal to the family and the business." Jonathon was sure about Eli's character.

Rachel didn't want to believe what the facts seemed to say about Eli Moore. She had raised him through high school. He was like her son. She thought back to the day they brought him home from the lake. He was broken and afraid. Rachel and

Jonathon decided just to love him and try to help him. The first six months that Eli was with the Biggses, he asked about his dad often. He was devastated by his mom's death and then hurt again by his dad's disappearance. When Jonathon asked him if he wanted to make living with the Biggses a permanent situation, Eli wanted to know if this meant that his dad was gone for good. Jonathon answered him honestly and asked Eli to be part of the Biggs family. Eli was thrilled. He didn't mention his father after that but was an excellent son to the Biggses. Rachel wondered if the trauma in his life at age twelve would cause him problems later.

"Maybe someone else is influencing him," she said simply.

"Like who?" Jonathon queried.

"I don't have any idea. All I know is that he is buying stock in his and Debra's names and that he is sitting on a huge deal that could rescue the company."

"Miles Masterson called me about Debra today. He said that she had met four times with a 'mystery' man. Twice at a hotel. He thinks she may be having an affair. They haven't been able to identify the man yet. When they do, we'll know more." Jonathon wondered if Debra was involved somehow. She loved money and attention and seemed never to have enough of either.

"I've always felt that there was something wrong with that marriage. Poor Eli, does he know?" Rachel was surprisingly sympathetic.

"I don't know. Now you're feeling sorry for the guy you think is out to destroy us?" Jonathon laughed at the irony of it all.

"We love Eli. He's family, and I can't imagine him doing any-thing on his own to hurt us. But what if he can't keep up with Debra's lifestyle demands? What if he messed up during a time of weakness, trying to rescue his marriage? Good people do dumb things when they get desperate."

"True enough, but I hope that you are completely wrong."

"Me, too. Me, too." Rachel sighed.

"I'm going to lunch. You have my cell number if you need me." Eli told Bob Holcroft as he left the office.

As soon as Eli was out on the sidewalk, he called Debra. "Meet me at Carmen's Bistro on Fifth Avenue and Third Street in twenty minutes. No questions."

Debra followed Eli's call with one of her own. "He wants to meet me in twenty minutes. He didn't give me any explanation over the phone. This is so unlike him. Spontaneity is not in Eli's repertoire of characteristics."

"Where?" The voice was demanding.

"Carmen's Bistro on Fifth Avenue and Third Street."

"I'll be watching."

<hr>

Eli was seated at a window seat inside the restaurant when Debra arrived. Eli knew that she would have a salad with Italian vinaigrette dressing on the side. She didn't like eating where regular people ate. She called them the "lunch crowd" and preferred to eat at the more elite places. She would be irritated that he chose this place to meet.

Debra arrived and sat down. She kept her coat on and placed her purse carefully in her lap. "These places are never really clean," she commented.

"Debra, I need to tell you something important. The FBI came into the office this morning with a search warrant." Eli's voice was low but intense.

"So what? Biggs is the cleanest company in the world. They won't find anything, because there is nothing to find," Debra responded in her typical fashion. Throughout their marriage, whenever Biggs International came up, she shrugged off the conversation.

"Nothing illegal but something that may cause suspicion. Remember when I had you sign some papers a while back so that I could open a stock trading account for you?" Eli leaned forward, speaking in hushed tones. He wanted Debra to pay close attention to the conversation.

"Yes, you said something about diversifying our investments." Debra was still not interested.

"Well, I've been buying Biggs stock in your name and mine," Eli admitted.

Suddenly, Debra was paying attention. "How much?"

"A lot," Eli whispered.

"Exactly how much? Give me a number," Debra stated.

"Five hundred thousand dollars worth in the last ninety days."

Debra's mind was engaged in the discussion. Her love of money caused her face to become flushed. "Half a million? Where did you get that kind of money?"

"I sold other stocks. I also purchased seven-hundred-and-fifty-thousand dollars for my own account." Eli informed her cautiously.

"Why are you buying all this stock now?" Debra retorted in a loud whisper.

"Jonathon has lost his grip on the company. I know that we will recover from this mad cow situation, but I'm concerned that Jonathon won't have anything left financially at the end of it all. I bought the stock to give to him when this is over. He'll need it to recover."

"You are going to give Jonathon Biggs over a million dollars worth of our stock?" "Yes," Eli said simply.

"That is the most ridiculous thing I've ever heard! Jonathon Biggs has taken advantage of you for years. You are the brains behind that company. If it weren't for you, he'd still only have two ranches. You told him not to do the Argentina deal, but he didn't listen. He did this to himself. You don't need him. You never did. He knew how intelligent you are, so he took you in and paid for your education in order to take advantage of you later on. You have made millions for him. Sell the stock and quit Biggs International. Start your own company." Debra's words were condescending. She was good at making Eli feel as if he were wasting his life at Biggs International.

"I can't do that. They are my family," Eli said sharply.

"And what am I? Your loyalty to them borders on stupidity, Eli. Sometimes I think that you are more loyal to them than you are to me. Wake up and move on." Her harshness was stronger than usual.

"Debra, the FBI is going to find my stock records today. They will become suspicious of me. I'm clear of guilt, but they don't know my motives. We could be under scrutiny for a while." Eli spoke slowly and cautiously. He didn't want to experience her wrath at its fullest.

"Great, now you're going to get into trouble because you are loyal to the Biggs! Will this hit the news?" Her hard sarcasm was not unexpected but hurt nonetheless.

"I'm not sure." Eli hung his head as if he were a young boy who had done something foolish.

"Oh, this is fantastic, Eli! I'm going to be ruined in this town because I'm married to you! Thanks for messing up my life!" Debra reached the pinnacle of her ire. When she acted like this, Eli's stomach churned with anxiety. There was no peace in his marriage, and he didn't know how to fix it.

She was out the door and down the sidewalk before Eli could respond.

He shrugged at the waiter and left a twenty dollar tip on the table, even though they hadn't ordered anything. As Eli walked out of the restaurant, his cell phone rang. The caller ID said that it was Debra.

"Hello," Eli said tentatively. "Where are you?"

"I just walked into the bank down the street. I'm opening an account. Sell my Biggs stock now. I'll call you when I'm finished here and give you my new account number. I expect you to have the five hundred thousand wired to my account today," Debra ordered.

"I can't do it that fast!" Eli was in shock.

"Sure you can. You're Eli Moore, the brains behind Biggs International. Make it happen!" The phone went dead.

Chapter Thirteen

"Keep walking, Debra." A man came alongside her as she left the bank. She had her cell phone out and was about to call Eli with the wire transfer information. She calmly closed the phone and dropped it in her purse while she continued walking down the street.

"I knew that you would be waiting for me." She looked straight ahead as she spoke.

"I want to make sure that everything went well," he said as he looked over the people on the sidewalk to see if they were being observed.

"Eli told me that he has been buying stock in Biggs International in my name."

"No surprise. I gave you that information a week ago." Her companion liked to have the upper hand.

"I followed your instructions and told him to sell immediately. As soon as I call him, he will wire the funds to this bank account." As she spoke, Debra touched the man's hand affectionately and left a business card from the bank with the account number on it. "What's next?"

"Let's give the FBI a chance to think about what they've found. We'll give them another piece of the puzzle soon. I'll be in touch."

"I did love him, you know. He just couldn't keep up." Debra turned into a jewelry store while the man walked on.

Eli called his broker on the way back to his office. During high school and early in his college years, Eli had wanted a lifestyle like the Biggses.' He wanted the success and the marriage to go with it. He met Debra while studying for his master's degree in business. She was beautiful and fun to be around. She came from a wealthy family but didn't seem to flaunt it. He fell in love with her almost immediately. She moved in social circles much higher than anything he'd ever seen. While living with the Biggses, he rarely attended high-society parties. Jonathon and Rachel weren't that type. Their social life consisted of family and a few friends. Eli worked hard to romance Debra and to prove to her that he could provide for her lifestyle. At first, they were very happy. He was the young rising executive and was in awe of the connections she had through her family and friends. Jonathon Biggs paid him well from the beginning and moved him up the ladder of success quickly. It was obvious to all that Eli was a genius at business.

The fourth year of their marriage Debra became more and more demanding and was very concerned about her social status. She had worked on a couple of charity fundraisers with very prominent people and craved their level of influence. The most important thing in her life became her status as a society player. Eli knew that if he didn't accommodate her wishes, she would leave him. The media spin would give her sympathetic attention and improve her position in society. Eli arranged for the stock sale and the fund transfer. Biggs stock had gone up slightly in the last month, and the value of Debra's stock was now $525,000.

Bob Holcroft met Eli at the door to his office. "Mr. Moore," he said, "we're concerned about your recent stock purchases. It seems that you are buying as much Biggs stock as you can afford."

"Yes, I am," Eli spoke confidently. "Others have bailed out, but I'm buying in. Biggs will go up, and we will recover our losses. Have I broken the law?"

"Not to my knowledge. It's just curious that you are buying so much right now. We're satisfied here. We'll be out by the end of the day." Bob Holcroft was bored.

"Is there anything else you need?" Eli asked politely.

"No thanks, your people have been very cooperative."

"Excuse me, Bob, may I speak with you over here?" Holcroft was interrupted by one of the FBI computer experts. He excused himself from Eli and walked over to the desk where the expert was working. "It seems that Debra Moore just sold all of her shares of Biggs stock."

"When?" Holcroft's interest increased momentarily.

"Just now, sir."

"Mr. Moore," Holcroft addressed Eli as he was walking toward him, "did you know that your wife has just sold all of her shares of Biggs stock?"

"Yes, I made the call to the broker," Eli admitted.

"Why did you only sell her shares?"

"We discussed this at lunch, and she doesn't share my optimism about the company. She insisted that I liquidate her shares and wire the funds to an account at a local bank," Eli said.

"Mr. Moore, we may want to talk to your wife." Bob Holcroft believed Eli but wanted to end the day on an interesting note.

"Just tell me when and where, and I'll make sure that she's there."

"Thanks, but we'll contact her ourselves." Holcroft anticipated an intriguing conversation with Debra.

———⇒>●<⇐———

Jonathon was emotionally exhausted and still physically tired. He had tried hard today to focus on his conversation with Rachel. They had talked through coffee and lunch and were still talking as they prepared dinner. They had covered every topic from the beginning when he had first heard about mad cow disease at the Tucson Ranch. They had relived the news about each ranch being infected and the explosion that evening. They had talked about every one of their children and wept over the death of each one. As they talked about their daughter-in-law, Jane, they decided to call her parents and talk about how much they loved and enjoyed her. This had been their best day since the funerals, but also the most draining.

"Jonathon, I think we need to have another talk with the fire inspector. I really think he needs to look again. I'm sure that the explosion was intentional. I'm also sure that the mad cow disease and the explosion are connected to the same person or people who want to destroy us."

"I'll call him in the morning and get an appointment. It might be good for us to write down our questions and observations so that we don't miss anything when we talk to him." Jonathon was as convinced as Rachel that the ranch incidents and the explosion were orchestrated together. He was persuaded when Rachel pointed out to him that if the "bad guys" (Rachel's term) wanted them dead, they could have waited until everyone was in the house. She also pointed out that Jane's parents were also late due to car trouble. She insisted that the children were the target and that their deaths were designed to make Jonathon and Rachel live with a pain worse than their own deaths.

Rachel reluctantly agreed with Jonathon's idea to have a strategy meeting with a few key people. He suggested Maggie, Miguel Sameros, Doug Lister, and Ron Milliken. He wanted to include Eli as well. Rachel was adamant about not including him. After much discussion, they agreed to sleep on it and talk about Eli in the morning.

"If he is our enemy, let's keep him close. We can use the group to test him, and if he's dirty, we'll catch him." It was hard for Jonathon to talk about the possibility that Eli Moore would hurt them.

<hr />

The meeting with the fire inspector went well. After hearing Jonathon and Rachel's reasoning, he agreed to take another look at the situation. The remains of the house had not been cleared yet, so he agreed to go back to the property and see what else he could find. He would let them know when he was going and that they could come with him if they wished.

The strategy meeting met with mixed results. Rachel had conceded and agreed to let Jonathon invite Eli. Everyone seemed to be in denial when Rachel proposed that the mad cow events and the explosion may have been connected. Rachel was assigned to follow-up with Breslin Kline and see if he had another angle of approach to the investigation. Eli was going to visit the ranches and follow up on all personnel who had been on each ranch within three months of the time the infected cattle were discovered. Maggie was going to examine the employee roster to see who had been hired in the past year. If she ran across anyone slightly suspicious, she would let Jonathon know and he would get Bob Holcroft to check the person out. Bob Holcroft and the FBI were assigned to Jonathon. He wanted to convince Holcroft to come out to the explosion site with the fire inspector.

Ron Milliken and Miguel Sameros would quietly look for a buyer to purchase the European Manufacturing Division of Biggs International. The sale of the European Division would allow Biggs International to move out of Chapter 11 and provide enough cash flow to keep running for at least six months. Pastor Doug Lister was responsible to keep everyone in the communications loop. He was to check in regularly with each person and help with any snags they ran into.

During the meeting, Jonathon received a call from Miles Masterson:

"Jonathon, this is about Debra Moore." Miles was guarded as he spoke.

"I'm alone, go ahead." Jonathon left the room and went outside.

"She had lunch with her husband yesterday and left the restaurant in a hurry. She went down the street and entered First Bank, where she opened an account with one thousand dollars. Before close of business, a wire transfer was received from her broker depositing $518,000 and change. We secretly checked out her brokerage records and discovered that the money came from the sale of Biggs stock. It turns out that she has been buying large quantities of Biggs over the last three months. I don't know what this means, because she is selling prematurely. Unless she expects the stock to crash, she should have held onto it for a while," Miles reported.

"Her husband has been buying the stock. He must have told her about it, and she decided to cash it in." Jonathon recalled the details of his exchange with Rachel about the stock purchases. "Eli has also purchased $750,000 worth in his own name."

"That's good information, thanks," Miles said. "Our man followed her after lunch with her husband and waited outside the bank to see where she would go or who she would meet. Guess what?"

"The mystery man?" Jonathon anticipated Miles' answer.

"Right, he slipped up behind her like a pro and walked with her for about a block and a half. At one point, she held his hand. It looked romantic, but she was actually passing a paper to him. She peeled off into a jewelry store, and he went on from there. My man was right behind them when they split, and mystery man said something about another piece of the puzzle and that he would be in touch. My guy chose to follow him instead of her from that point. He walked two more blocks and caught a cab. My man walked past him as he got in and heard him tell the cabbie to take him to Upper Traynor Park. Isn't that the area where your house was?"

"Miles, Eli is here right now in the other room. I need to tell him about Debra. He should know." Jonathon didn't like to hold back information from his friends.

Miles explained to Jonathon that Debra Moore was seen going into the Downtowner Hotel that day. She had checked in under the name Dee Mott and paid in cash. She stayed about two hours and left. She went directly home from there. A rough sketch of the man she met on the sidewalk was created. He was wearing a coat with the collar pulled up, sunglasses, and a hat pulled down to the top of the glasses. Miles promised to send a messenger out to Jonathon's house at ten that night with a copy of the sketch.

He was looking for ideas as to whom it might be. No one was seen that looked like him coming or going from the hotel. He could have gone in and out a rear door or he could have arrived earlier and waited for her in another room. The possibilities were endless. "If they keep meeting, we'll get a positive identification. She has no idea that she's being followed. Tell Eli what you like but remember. If she catches onto us, we'll lose our advantage."

"Thanks, Miles. Your input is invaluable." Jonathon shook his head slowly as he processed this startling information.

"I'll send the sketch. Call me tomorrow."

"Good-bye, friend." Jonathon spoke with gratitude in spite of the difficult news he had just received.

"Good-bye, Jonathon. Stay well." Miles hung up.

Jonathon turned around as he closed his cell phone to see Eli standing in the half-opened doorway. Jonathon didn't know how long he had been there or how much he had heard. It didn't matter; Jonathon was going to tell him everything anyway. He still trusted Eli completely.

"Jonathon, when everyone leaves, I need to talk to you and Rachel alone. I have something very important to tell you," Eli said soberly.

"That's fine. Eli, I have something very important to tell you as well." Jonathon's voice shook slightly, as he considered how he would tell Eli about Debra.

The meeting broke up, and Miguel left quickly to make some calls. Maggie and Rachel committed to meet for coffee in the morning. Doug and Ron stayed around and talked to Jonathon about his health. They warned him to be careful about coming back at full speed too soon. They also questioned him about any business dealings he may have had over the years that may have caused someone to hate him. Jonathon insisted that his integrity was intact and reminded them that he had always been careful for others. He cited three instances where he had backed away from business deals because they would have ruined someone's business. "There are plenty of good opportunities to expand our business without harming people." Jonathon struggled to keep his emotional balance during the discussion. He felt like he had to defend his whole life to his closest friends. He prayed silently each time he felt the urge to retreat to the poolside lounge chair that until a few days ago had been his sullen refuge.

"I feel like I'm in court on the witness stand being grilled." Jonathon felt his assertiveness returning.

Pastor Doug leaned forward in his chair and looked compassionately into Jonathon's face. "Sometimes good friends must have hard conversations. It's part of trusting each other with who we really are inside."

"I'm not sure I can take anymore tonight." Jonathon trusted them to understand.

"We're glad that you can tell us where you limits are." Ron Milliken got up to leave and hugged Jonathon. "We want to help not hurt you." Pastor Doug did the same.

When the two friends left, Rachel came out of the kitchen with fresh coffee. She sat on the couch next to Jonathon. "How are you holding up?" she asked as she kissed him gently on his nose.

"This was hard, but I'm fine. I can't handle as much emotional stuff as I used to. We still have more to deal with tonight." Jonathon stood up and exhaled with a slight groan. "Eli has been outside pacing around the pool all evening."

"Why is he still here?" Rachel asked cautiously.

"He's been waiting for everyone else to leave. He wants to talk to us." Jonathon walked to the sliding patio door and opened it.

Eli walked into the room and sat in the overstuffed chair directly across from them. Rachel poured him a cup of coffee but didn't make eye contact.

"I'll go first," Eli started. He told them about his stock purchases and his motives. Everything he did was legal, ethical, and reported to the proper authorities on the stock exchange. He wept when he told them about Debra's response and the sale of the shares that were in her name.

"All I know is that the money is deposited in her account at First Bank. I don't know if she'll be home when I get there or not. She had pretty much let me know that unless I hold position and have status, she's through with me. I love her, but I don't want to play in her league. I can handle the financial part, but I'm totally uncomfortable and often disgusted with the phoniness and posturing for attention. I was going to give the stock to you as a gift when you came back into the office, but you haven't been there yet."

Sorrowful tears were pouring down Rachel's cheeks, falling on her folded hands. It looked as if she were begging. She was—for forgiveness.

"Eli, I'm so sorry that I misjudged you. You were acting strangely and being secretive toward me, so I thought you were part of the problem. Please forgive me for not trusting you. You are family and I doubted your heart. I'm ashamed for jumping to conclusions in my grief and anger and thinking badly of you."

Eli jumped to his feet and pulled her up by the arms. "I forgive you. You've been my mom through the toughest part of my life. I will never violate your trust. I'm sorry for the horrible pain you must feel losing most of the family. I understand your anger and distrust. I felt that way toward you and Jonathon after my father disappeared and you took me in. My mother was dead, and my dad was gone. I was angry and thought that even the people that wanted to help me were out to hurt me more. I understand, and I forgive you, Mom."

While they hugged, Jonathon slipped out to the poolside. He was amazed at the scene he had just witnessed. These people were dealing with the hardest of life's issues with compassion and selflessness. He was thankful as he walked over to the poolside lounge chair. He pointed at it and spoke with finality. "I won't be back. I'm through with you. I'm out of the cave, and I'm staying out no matter what!" With that, he picked up the lounge chair and threw it into the pool. When he looked up, he saw Eli and Rachel watching him curiously.

"What did we just witness here?" Rachel queried, laughing.

"I just broke up with my depression," Jonathon said painfully.

"You sound like you're really hurting inside." Eli looked concerned.

"My inside is fine. I just threw out my back."

It felt good for them to laugh again.

Eli and Rachel helped Jonathon to the couch. They agreed to talk more the next day. Jonathon wanted to tell him about Debra and the mystery man but wanted the evening to end on a positive note. The bad news could wait another day.

Chapter Fourteen

Miles Masterson arrived at ten o'clock in the evening.

Rachel answered the door, and Jonathon spoke to Miles from the couch. He had a heating pad on his lower back and sat up painfully. "I thought you were going to use a messenger to deliver the sketch."

"I decided to bring it myself and see how your conversation with Eli Moore went," Miles said.

"What's this about?" Rachel's suspicious edge was showing.

"The call I received during our meeting was Miles updating me on Debra Moore's activities. He suspects that she may be having an affair. Miles, please bring Rachel up to date."

Miles Masterson skillfully and completely laid out the details for Rachel. "Jonathon was going to tell Eli about Debra tonight."

"I didn't—too many other things going on. I'll talk to him tomorrow."

Miles slipped two copies of the sketch out of the manila envelope he was carrying. "We drew it up just as our man saw him. We included the sunglasses, hat, and raised collar. Not a great sketch, but maybe his lower face will tell you something—if there is anything to tell."

"This looks like ... " Rachel's voice tapered off.

"It really resembles him," Jonathon said tentatively.

"He has a common face. This could be someone who looks like him." Rachel looked at Jonathon with disbelief.

"And it's only the bottom half of his face; the sunglasses are hiding his eyes." Jonathon was sure, but he didn't want to be.

"It can't be him." Rachel laughed. "This is so strange."

"Any information you can give would help," Miles interjected, "even if it seems ridiculous. Remember, we have nothing at this point."

"This man looks somewhat like our minister and close friend, Doug Lister." Jonathon laughed out loud.

"But it isn't him. I'm sure." Rachel shook her head at the absurdity of it all.

"Does your pastor know Debra Moore?"

"Only from a few social and family events. Doug knows Eli fairly well and Debra as an acquaintance. She would probably recognize him on the street, as someone she had seen before. I doubt that she would remember his name." Rachel was trying to remember any contact the two of them may have had.

"How is their marriage?" Miles asked.

"A little shaky," admitted Rachel.

"Very shaky," corrected Jonathon.

"Maybe he's meeting with her to help with their marriage problems?" Rachel knew that their pastor did marriage counseling.

"Rachel, people who get marriage counseling don't meet at hotels." Jonathon had decided that in light of everything that had happened, anything was possible.

"The question is: are they sneaking around cheating on their spouses, or are they suspects?" Miles looked at Rachel and then Jonathon. They looked at one another other in disbelief.

"I'll check him out." Miles left the envelope on the coffee table and showed himself out.

Jonathon and Rachel said nothing for a full half hour.

"I'm sure that this isn't Doug." Jonathon was trying to reassure himself.

"Miles will look into it and come up empty." Rachel said with no conviction in her tone.

"You're right." Jonathon was weary. "We've had a long day. I'm sure we'll see things more clearly in the morning."

Neither one of them slept that night.

———❦———

"He's back!" her secretive whisper penetrated the silence.

"I know," his irritated voice retorted.

"What should I do now?" She sounded desperate.

"Just watch him." He didn't want her to lose her composure.

"We need to meet." There was a demanding sense of urgency in her voice.

"Not yet, I have to inform the Cleric. He'll give me instructions."

"Is there anything I can do while I'm waiting?"

"Keep track of everyone he talks to in person or on the phone. His movements may dictate our next move." He hung up and made his next call. The Cleric wasn't going to be happy to learn about Jonathon Oliver Biggs' improvement.

———❦———

Jonathon Biggs arrived at his office at nine in the morning. He was greeted with warmth and enthusiasm. His first activity was to tour the building and talk to the employees. It was evident to all that he was low on energy, but his presence still had a positive impact. Jonathon talked to each person he saw and thanked them for staying the course during rough times. He was optimistic about the future of Biggs International and let his employees know that their jobs were safe.

"We're not folding our hand; we're just reshuffling the deck."

Jonathon had only one meeting planned for his first day back. He and Eli were meeting in his office for lunch, and he planned on talking about Debra at that time. Jonathon wondered if telling Eli was the best thing to do. He decided that if it were him, he would want to know.

Jonathon checked in with Miles Masterson at eleven to see if there were any new developments.

"I'm meeting with Eli Moore at noon. Is there anything else I need to know?"

"No, nothing new. Jonathon, don't tell him about the sketch. If he goes to Debra, we want her to think that we don't know or care about the identity of the mystery man. Let him believe that we came across this as part of looking at everyone close to the leadership team at Biggs. He needs to think that we dropped Debra from our list of possibilities and that this is just collateral information."

"Got it." Jonathon was fine with this approach, as he was sure that Debra's situation was random and not part of the problems at Biggs International.

"Good. Let me know what happens. We're keeping an eye on Doug Lister, and we're still watching Debra. If he's the other man, we'll know," Miles said with confidence.

"Miles, is this necessary? I'm sure that this is a marital problem at most." Jonathon wasn't looking forward to his conversation with Eli.

"I always ask, 'What if?' in these circumstances," Miles said.

"What does that mean?"

"What if there's information we can learn that will help solve this puzzle? If we don't follow up, we could miss something." Miles was thorough.

"I'm sure that you're wasting your time," Jonathon said slowly and clearly. He wanted to discourage Miles from following Debra, but at the same time, he was curious about Doug Lister.

"If I am, then we'll move on to the next thing. I'll check back with you later."

<hr />

"Eli, every time we eat in, you order the same thing. The deli makes more than one sandwich, you know." Jonathon smiled at his young protégé.

"I know, but there's nothing like a good cheeseburger with

everything on it." Eli took a bite out of his burger, and it dripped all over his plate. "See, that's what I'm talking about! Good and juicy, not like—what is that?—chicken salad, tuna salad, or turkey salad? At least my cheeseburger has personality. What are we talking about today?"

"I have something difficult to tell you," Jonathon began carefully.

"As long as it's not another mad cow situation, I can deal with it." Baring his soul and forgiving Rachel had lifted a great burden from Eli. He was upbeat and relaxed. He was at his best when he was like this.

"It's about Debra," Jonathon said cautiously.

"What's going on with Debra?" Eli was curious but not apprehensive.

"As part of the investigation, Miles Masterson checked out everyone close to our leadership team. Debra, being your wife, was on their list," Jonathon proceeded, carefully choosing his words.

"So what did they do, follow her from store to store? I know where she is every day. I just follow the American Express trail." Eli's laugh was tinged with sarcasm.

"They came up with a piece of nonrelated information that I think you should know." Jonathon's voice took on a serious tone.

"Okay." Eli shrugged as he popped a French fry into his mouth.

"They saw Debra meeting with a man on a number of occasions at various locations." Jonathon knew that there was no good way to tell Eli what Miles had discovered.

"Like … where?" Eli's asked attentively.

"The Downtowner Hotel was one place. She checked in for a couple of hours, and he met her there at least twice."

Eli was suddenly irritated at the idea that someone was intruding into their private lives. "Why were they even following her? She has nothing to do with any of Biggs' issues."

"They didn't consult me before they followed her. Miles gave me this information as a friend. After what you told us last night, I thought you should know."

"I knew it! She's been drifting away from me for the last two years. A little at first, then more as her socialite buddies coaxed her into their world." Eli was upset but not angry. "I've been wondering when she would leave me. She's been telling me that I can't keep up with her lifestyle needs. I can keep up, but I don't want to. Who's the guy?"

"They don't know. He was very careful not to be recognized, and the investigator was only checking her out as a matter of routine. He didn't expect to find anything related to Biggs, so he wasn't very observant."

"Thanks for telling me. I don't know what to do with this information. Should I confront Debra or wait for her to tell me when she's leaving?" Eli sensed that the marriage was over.

"I don't know how to advise you. Eli, why don't you take the afternoon off and go for a ride in the country to clear your head. If you need company, I'm sure that Rachel would love to talk through this with you. I'll cover for you here. If anything comes up, I'll get you on your cell."

"Okay, thanks." Jonathon hugged Eli and let him out of the office.

Jonathon felt dirty. He called Rachel, and she promised to call Eli right away and help in any way she could. He then called Miles and told him about the exchange. He sat in his office and looked out the window for the rest of the afternoon. He went home tired at five.

⇒>●<⇐

"I think that Eli suspects that I'm meeting someone." Debra and her 'mystery man' were meeting in her room at the Downtowner Hotel. She had checked into room 213 at eleven in the morning. Unknown to her, the mystery man had checked into room 451 last evening and would stay there again tonight.

"But you're not sure?" The inquiry was cautiously delivered.

"I don't know. He hasn't said anything to me, but he's acting strangely. We had a big fight the other day at Carmen's Bistro, and I left him with the impression that I might not come home. He sold the stock as I demanded and deposited the money in my account at First Bank. I was sure that he thought I was setting up an account to take when I leave him. I think I overplayed my role." Debra's anxiety was obvious. "He seemed different toward me that night."

"How so?" He needed more information before he decided whether to give any measure of credibility to her concerns.

"He won't look me in the eye. He won't even touch me. Eli requires a great deal of affection. I thought that being amorous would ease the tension. He wasn't interested at all. I told him that I felt bad about the way I had treated him that day. He just shrugged, rolled over, and went to sleep."

"Has anything changed over the last two days?"

"He is withdrawing from me. I carry on every conversation with little or no response from him. It's like he knows that we're over, and he's just going through the motions until I decide to tell him." Debra wasn't concerned about ending her marriage, but she wanted to do it her way and in her own time.

"Do you think he knows about me?" Her companion asked thoughtfully.

"I think he knows that there's someone else. I doubt that he knows it's you."

"Will he try to find out?" He was thinking through the potential complications. Dealing with Debra Moore was difficult enough without adding her husband to the mix.

"No, in his mind it's over. We've been heading down this road for a while now." She spoke with certainty.

"Try to string him along. We need you to be in position to help him take the fall for all that's happened to Biggs International." He was careful to make his tone of voice sound like a strong suggestion. Giving orders to Debra Moore didn't work. She needed to have a sense of control, or he could lose her cooperation.

"How is that going to come about?" she asked, expecting an explanation.

"Remember when you told him that he should take a greater interest in what went on at the ranches?"

"Yes," she said proudly, "and he took my advice."

"He visited each ranch right before the Argentina deal went down. That was unusual for him, and it places him in position to become a suspect in the mad cow situation."

"No one suspects him," she said with certainty.

"We're not done setting the stage yet. We knew he was buying Biggs stock in your name. When you made him sell and give you the money, you made it look like he was doing something unethical that you didn't want to take part in. We're going to let that leak to the FBI later. Right now, it would be a good idea for you to begin telling your friends that you are concerned about Eli's behavior. Let them know that he has changed since the mad cow incidents. Tell them that he's anxious and uptight. He is short with you and argumentative. You're not sure if you should be afraid or not. Ask a couple of your friends if you can stay with them if you have to get out of the house on short notice."

"When we separate, I want people to feel sorry for me. I want to look like the courageous woman who tried her best to make the marriage work." Debra wanted positive attention from powerful people. It made her easy to manipulate.

"Do you recall our first meeting? I told you that we had different interests that could work out well for both of us. We get what we want and ... "

"I get Eli out of my life and look like a victim. Society loves the victim." She smiled her best social smile.

"Yes, society loves the victim. I'll be in touch. Do this part well, and Eli will do the rest for us." He was confident that she would follow through in every detail and be very convincing in the process.

Debra left first. He watched her through blinds as she left the lobby and walked out onto the street. As he returned to his room, he made a call on his cell phone.

"The stage is set, but we're going to need to move sooner than

I thought. I don't know how long she can keep Eli dangling on her string."

"How soon?" The voice was businesslike.

"Three days max." The answer was direct.

"Then we need to meet right away."

"I'm in room 451. Have the group here in two hours," Pastor Doug Lister ordered.

"I'll call the Cleric and tell him what we're thinking."

Doug Lister terminated the call and immediately dialed the front desk. He reserved room 174, two rooms down from the alley exit.

"I know that Jonathon Biggs has integrity. That's what makes him such an easy target!" Pastor Doug mused as he walked into room 174 to wait.

Chapter Fifteen

Two forty-five in the afternoon found two people waiting in room 451. Both the man and the woman had master-keycards to every room at the Downtowner. The hotel had become their regular meeting place. Their routine was simple but required patience. They would wait in the room, while Doug Lister made sure that they weren't followed. At four o'clock the woman received a call on her cell phone instructing her to go to another room. This time it was room 174. Ten minutes after she arrived, the man received the same instructions. Ten minutes after he arrived, Pastor Doug Lister walked into the room.

"Jonathon Biggs is back in play. He's fragile but functional. We need to hit him again." Doug began the meeting.

"Why don't we just kill him?" She was anxious to finish what they had started.

"The Cleric said no. Biggs is supposed to suffer. When we're done here, he will have destroyed himself." Doug knew how the Cleric operated. He liked to push people to their breaking point and beyond. The ultimate success occurred when the victim in a state of despair took his own life. "But we do need to kill Debra Moore. She is about to let her friends know that Eli is anxious and unstable. She's even going to arrange to stay with someone else in case life becomes intolerable at home. In three days, I'm going to tell her to call a friend and pretend that she needs to get out of the house quickly. She will slip out later in the evening, and we'll take her out on the way to her friend's house."

"Eli will be the prime suspect," the other man in the room said with confidence.

"Yes, they'll probably arrest him the next day." Doug was confident as well.

"That will get him out of play at Biggs International," she interjected.

"And put the whole weight of the company on fragile Jonathon," Doug added his sound bite to the rapid-fire conversation.

"He'll suspect Eli and Rachel will go to a whole new level of anger." She was enjoying the exchange. "The company will implode, and their marriage will explode!"

"Jonathon will go from depression to despair. He will be completely ruined inside and out." Doug could see the plan unfolding in his mind.

"Maybe he'll end up ... " the other man said in a hoarse hush.

"Taking his own life?" The woman laughed softly.

"Jonathon Oliver Biggs, dead by his own hand." Pastor Doug Lister laughed out loud at the prospect of performing the funeral service.

"How will we take care of Debra?" The woman brought them back to the subject at hand.

"The Cleric will take care of that. We don't need to know." Doug Lister rose from the edge of the bed and left through the alley exit. Within the hour, he had called the Cleric and arrangements were being made for the very public demise of Debra Moore. Society would remember her as a victim. Society has a short attention span.

———⟶⟶∘⟵⟵———

The fire inspector was waiting when they arrived at the site of the Biggs home. Jonathon and Rachel came together. Miles Masterson convinced Bob Holcroft to come also.

"Inspector Albright, this is my husband, Jonathon, and FBI inspector Bob Holcroft. Thank you for meeting us out here today." Rachel had visited the fire inspector soon after the explosion with her concerns. He had been kind and understanding in spite of her angry accusations of incompetence. She had since apologized and arranged for him to take another look at the site.

"This is an unusual situation. The mad cow situation on your ranches gives me cause to wonder if the explosion is somehow related. We haven't uncovered any evidence to substantiate my concerns, but we'll look again," the inspector said candidly.

"I received your report about the construction people who had worked on the house. They all check out. One of the carpenters had just been released from county lock-up for a DUI, but that's it. The delivery people also checked out." Bob Holcroft wanted to assert his presence as an investigator.

As Holcroft was speaking, another car arrived. Miles Masterson was driving, and his passenger was Breslin Kline.

"I called Mr. Kline and told him what we were doing. He is with the USDA and is exceptionally observant. With him is Miles Masterson, president of Bills and Masterson International Livestock Investigations," Bob Holcroft quickly explained.

Breslin Kline walked up to the fire inspector. "Breslin Kline, senior investigator, USDA," he said and showed his badge.

"I'm Miles Masterson; I invited Inspector Holcroft."

"And I invited Breslin," interjected Bob Holcroft

"Where do we start?" Jonathon Biggs was anxious to see what this group of top professionals would discover.

———⟫•⟪———

"They wanted to wait six months to make sure that mad cow wouldn't show up at the Argentina ranch," Eli explained to Jonathon Biggs over lunch in his office.

Jonathon was looking over the proposal from a large Central American beef distributor to buy from the Argentina ranch for the next three years. As soon as six months passed, the proposal would then become a contract with a possible extension of up to five years.

"This is good news. It will create the momentum we need to get past the mad cow problem." Jonathon was optimistic.

"I haven't gone public. I don't think we should, until it's a done deal." Eli was being optimistic but cautious.

"Good thinking. If something happened after we announced, the bottom could fall out fast," Jonathon added as he continued to look over the contract.

"I'm staying on top of this and keeping the relationship fresh, so they don't go elsewhere. I don't think that they could beat our per-pound price anywhere in this hemisphere, or Europe for that matter." Eli was working in his element.

"When do you leave to tour the ranches?" Jonathon was trying to keep up with his vice president's schedule, even though he fatigued easily.

"Next week."

"I think you should visit Argentina too. It would be good for them to see you. We haven't been down there much since we bought the place," Jonathon suggested.

"I'd like that. It would help me to have a good relationship with them. Their business culture is different than ours. Relationships and attention are very important to them."

Eli was anxious to get Biggs international moving in a positive direction once again. He also needed time away from what had become constant pressure from Debra. She wanted him to leave Biggs and pursue a more prestigious position elsewhere. She rarely talked about anything else anymore.

When Eli left the office, Jonathon called Bob Holcroft to check in.

"Has anyone heard from Breslin Kline since yesterday? He hasn't returned Rachel's calls. The way he left the building site I was sure that he was convinced that there was a connection between the explosion and the ranches," Jonathon inquired of Holcroft.

"He hasn't talked to me." Bob Holcroft was also convinced and was very vocal about the FBI's getting involved with the fire inspector to find any possible connections between the ranches and the explosion. Bob used the words *murdered* and *blown to bits* to assert the priority of the investigation. Rachel went to the car in tears, but Bob won over the fire investigator; and he gave top priority and put manpower at Holcroft's disposal. "I have a special cell number for him." Holcroft gave Jonathon the number, and Jonathon in turn promised to get back to him with details about their conversation.

Jonathon used the number that Bob Holcroft had given him. "Breslin Kline here."

"Mr. Kline, Jonathon Biggs. I've been hoping to talk with you about our findings yesterday. You seemed sure that there is a connection between the house and the ranches." Jonathon was searching for affirmation from the USDA inspector.

"I'm leaning that way but won't be able to follow up. I've been given an untimely promotion to national headquarters. It appears that I'll be training agents for the field." Breslin Kline said matter-of-factly.

"Why now?" Jonathon was surprised and disappointed.

"I don't know. Agents don't usually get promoted for not solving cases. We don't usually reward failure at the USDA." Breslin Kline's frustration was evident in his voice.

"Breslin, you have a well-earned reputation for being the best. You deserve the promotion. They're smart to have their best agent training people. Do well and thank you for your help." The words came out of Jonathon's mouth, but in his heart he wanted Kline to stay on the case.

"I asked them if I could finish this case, as I have new insight from my visit to your home site. They insisted that I go right away. I'm packing my things as we speak." Breslin Kline was as disappointed as Jonathon at this turn of events.

"Is it normal for them to pull a head investigator in the middle of a case?"

"No, and frankly, I don't understand. I'll go, but I don't like leaving before I'm finished. It's not my style." Breslin Kline was uncharacteristically open about his feelings. "If you need to contact me, please feel free to use this number."

"Thank you, Breslin." Jonathon felt like he had an ally. "Good-bye, Mr. Biggs"

—————>❈<—————

Debra Moore was shopping. She had been pleased with herself since her last meeting with Doug Lister. She was anticipating an advantageous end to her marriage. Good for her and socially beneficial.

When Doug had first contacted her three months ago, she recognized his face from a few family gatherings at the Biggses.' She tried to avoid going unless Eli was very insistent. Biggs family gatherings weren't exactly high society affairs. She had managed to feign illness often enough to get the point across to Eli that she wasn't interested in attending. She first met Doug Lister at one of the Biggses' birthday celebrations. She didn't remember which one, because it didn't matter to her.

When he explained his mission to her, she was surprised that a pastor was out to harm someone. She questioned him about it at their first meeting.

"I have to be their pastor to get their trust and respect. I don't want them to expect what's coming. My employer has me play various roles depending on the situation. This time, I happen to be a minister." He made it sound exciting and sinister at the same time.

"Kind of like deep cover for a CIA agent." Debra liked the idea of secret rendezvous and clandestine activities.

"Sort of like that. Now, tell me why you are unhappy with your husband. Maybe we can help each other." Doug spoke with great sincerity. Debra confided in him immediately.

Debra was self-centered and spoiled. She had told Eli that she hated him when he didn't give her what she wanted. She told Doug that she had married the wrong man and had grown to dislike him intensely. He wasn't in her league socially and didn't deserve her. She wanted to leave him but was afraid it would affect her status in her social network. She needed a way out that would endear her to the people who counted. Recruiting her was easy for Doug. He told her that his employer went after companies who had reached the pinnacle of success by devouring smaller corporations and leaving them bankrupt and desolate. If Biggs grew any bigger, they would crush the little guy who was just trying to make a living. Debra was so caught up in her own issues that she never asked Doug for details about himself or his employer. Her selfishness set her up to be used and discarded.

Debra was comparing two china patterns when a man slipped quietly beside her. He leaned over, acting interested in the plates. "Debra, it's time. Make your move tonight. Call your friend, and tell her how difficult it is at home and ask if you can stay for a few days."

"What about my things?" she said softly, looking straight ahead.

"Don't worry. Eli's going on a ten-day business trip next week. The day he leaves, you can go back home. Get a restraining order, file for divorce, and have all the locks changed while he's away. When he returns, he won't know what hit him."

"Tonight?" Suddenly, Debra was nervous. She had reviewed the plan in her mind many times, imagining various outcomes. In her imaginary scenarios, she was always confident and in control. Eli would squirm and concede easily. But now that it was time to act, that confidence within her didn't seem to be as strong.

"Do it, Debra, tonight or never." There was no room for discussion. This was the final word.

The man gracefully blended into the crowd on the sidewalk and was gone. Debra wondered why Doug hadn't come. She assumed that he didn't want anyone to think that he was having an affair with her.

Chapter Sixteen

Debra sounded frantic on the phone. "He has never gone this far before! He called me names that I can't even repeat. He screamed at me again about selling my stock in his company."

Debra had prepared her friend Yvonne well ahead of time for this moment. She was asking all the right questions. She had been primed and was responding better than Debra had hoped she would. Yvonne was oblivious to the fact that she was a pawn in Debra's plan. She was more than willing to help Debra get out of the house and seek help.

"Do you think he might hurt you?" Yvonne's anxiety oozed through the phone.

"No! Well, I'm not sure. He raised his hand to me once but stopped himself." Debra wept softly, as if she were uncertain as to what Eli might do next.

"Where is he now?" Yvonne's urgent tone told Debra that she was being believable.

"Upstairs brooding. I don't think he'll come back down tonight. Its nine-thirty, and he usually showers and goes to bed by ten." Debra added a sigh and a sniffle. Just the right amount of emotion to motivate her friend to act on her behalf.

"Should I come and get you right now?" Yvonne said protectively.

"No, thank you. Your coming to get me would just make him angrier. I'm going to wait until he's asleep and slip out. I should be there by eleven or so." Debra had played this scene as long as she could. She decided to end the conversation before Yvonne took action. That would come later.

"I'll stay off the phone, so you can call if you need me. If you feel threatened, call me, and I'll send Scott over to get you out." Yvonne's husband was a former college-football lineman who could be intimidating if necessary.

"I have to go. He's calling for me. Bye." Debra hung up hurriedly.

"She's really good!" Debra's executioner said to himself as he removed the earpiece he had used to monitor the call. He left the car quietly and stayed in the shadows as he made his way around the corner to the Moore's house. He had parked on a hill so that he could coast half a mile before starting the engine. He had decided to stand between two tall Italian Cypress trees next to the back door. He knew that she wouldn't go out the front, because the master bedroom was directly upstairs and Eli would hear her. The garage was not a consideration, as Debra had been parking her car on the street in front of the neighbor's house for the last two days in preparation for this moment. Eli was picked up and dropped off by a limo service and hadn't been in the garage. He positioned himself and waited. He was trained to be patient then to strike quickly when the opportunity presented itself. He had served the Cleric since leaving the Navy Seals six years ago.

The back door opened slowly and quietly at ten fifty-four. Debra felt the warm, humid June air as she slipped out of the half-open door. She was wearing beige slacks and a pastel green blouse. She carried a jacket over her arm. She turned her back on her slayer as she carefully pulled the door closed. He moved quickly up behind her. When she turned around, he slammed his fist into her throat, crushing her larynx. She gasped, eyes wide with surprise, as he pounded his knee into the bottom of her rib cage. Debra was stunned and couldn't draw in a breath. As she grabbed her throat, he picked her up over his head and threw her down head first against the cement stairs. She gurgled as she lost consciousness. He repositioned her on the stairs, making it look as if she had been thrown from the top step. The killer moved decisively, breaking her neck against the edge of the bottom step. Gently opening the back door, he took her jacket and silently slipped away in the shadows unheard and unseen.

At eleven thirty, Debra's phone vibrated in her jacket pocket. Her assassin smiled to himself. "Her friend is looking for her already. This will be the worst night of your life, Mr. Moore. Enjoy your nice comfortable bed tonight, because tomorrow you'll be spending the night in jail." He would deliver the cell phone and jacket to the Cleric as instructed. When the phone vibrated again, the killer laughed out loud with satisfaction.

⊰●⊱

Yvonne called Debra's cell phone for the second time with no response. She sensed that something was terribly wrong.

"It's one in the morning, Scott. Debra was supposed to be here by eleven. Something is wrong."

"They probably made up and are enjoying each other's company. Leave it alone, Yvonne. She'll call if she needs you."

"How do you know he didn't catch her trying to leave? Maybe he won't let her go."

"Eli Moore is not the monster she makes him out to be. He's a good guy under a lot of pressure. Everybody gets emotional once in a while. Maybe they needed a good fight to let off some steam. They're reasonable people. Let it be, and go to sleep." Scott was tired of the conversation. The Moore's had become Yvonne's favorite topic.

Yvonne began getting dressed. "I'm going over there right now."

"No you're not." Scott knew by her stubborn tone that she wouldn't let this rest until she did something.

"If you don't let me go over there, I'll call 911!"

"All right, I'll go with you." Exasperated, Scott got up and dressed.

Yvonne jumped from the car before Scott came to a complete stop. She ran immediately to the front door and incessantly pressed the doorbell. Scott, embarrassed, took his time parking the car. As he got out, he saw a light go on upstairs. Eli opened the front door as Scott walked up.

"Where is Debra?" Yvonne demanded as she tried to push her way past Eli. He blocked her from entering the house.

Eli was defensive and confused by Yvonne's aggressive behavior. "What do you want? And why are you at my door in the middle of the night?"

"I want to see Debra right now!" Yvonne demanded, looking at Scott for support. He looked at Eli and shrugged.

"I'm sorry, but you are not going to see anything but this door closing. Leave us alone, and go home, or I'll call the police." Eli slammed the door. As it closed, Yvonne began pounding on it.

Eli began to realize that Debra hadn't come to bed. When he went to sleep, she was watching television. It was still on in the family room. *She probably fell asleep on the couch,* he thought.

She wasn't there. "Debra, what's going on?" he asked in a normal tone of voice.

Suddenly, he heard a high-pitched wail coming from the backyard accented by a man's voice yelling. "Is it her? Is it her?"

Eli opened the back door to a scene that caused him to become dizzy. Debra was lying just as her killer had left her. Eli took the entire staircase in one leap. He checked Debra's pulse and found none. He began to administer mouth-to-mouth and noticed that her body temperature was somewhat cool. Scott was shouting into his cell phone telling the 911 operator what he was seeing. Yvonne began beating on Eli's back with her fists. He pushed her away, but she came back with a vengeance.

"She was leaving you tonight, and you hurt her. She is afraid of you. I offered to come and get her, but she wouldn't let me. Now she's hurt bad! Oh, please God, let the paramedics hurry, before it's too late," Yvonne blurted out.

The activity surrounding Eli was surreal. He continued to perform CPR as best he could, but in his gut he knew that Debra was gone. The longer he worked on her, the more blurred the evening became.

The police arrived first, and the paramedics were right behind them. One officer helped Eli away from Debra's body, while three others with Scott attempted to control Yvonne. The lead paramedic spent less than a minute checking Debra. He walked over to the officer with Eli and told him that she was dead. The officer called it in as a possible homicide.

Soon after, Yvonne calmed down enough to tell her story. Eli was handcuffed and informed of his rights. He asked the officer to call Jonathon Biggs and gave him the phone number. The officer said he would do that, after they went to the station for preliminary questioning.

"If you want me to answer any questions, you had better call Jonathon Biggs and ask him to bring my attorney. I won't answer any questions without my lawyer present," Eli said to the officer evenly. This was the worst of nightmares come true.

"We'll do this the way the detective says. Let's go." The officer put his hand on the top of Eli's head and directed him into the backseat of the squad car.

"This can't be happening," Eli muttered in disbelief.

But it was.

Chapter Seventeen

"I want them to hold Eli for a while. Whoever killed Debra needs to think they got away with it for now." Bob Holcroft was talking as Jonathon paced the floor furtively, rubbing his hands together. He was breathing like a long distance runner. He knew that if he let his feelings go, the depression would return with a vengeance. He stopped his mind in mid-thought. *The kids, the ranches, and now this... could my life be any more messed up? I can get through this. I have to hold on here. Trust God, and pray...*

"What do these people want? I'll give them everything if they stop killing people. I don't own anything worth killing over," Jonathon pleaded to no one in particular.

"Debra told her friend Yvonne that Eli was making a play to become majority stockholder. Yvonne says that Debra ordered Eli to sell her shares, because she didn't agree with what Eli was doing to you. Do you buy that?" Holcroft's words brought Jonathon back to the situation at hand.

"Absolutely not! I believe Eli's version. Debra was a social climber. Eli taking over Biggs would move her up the ladder. Eli isn't much of a socialite and barely tolerated her upper-crust antics. She was getting ready to leave him; it was just a matter of time. Somehow she is connected with the people who want to destroy me." Jonathon was sure that he was right.

"I agree. Let's let them hold Eli for a week and see if they get careless. Don't come into the office. Work from home for now.

I want the enemy to think that you're melting down again" Bob Holcroft looked into Jonathon's eyes unsure whether he would melt down for good this time.

"I can do that. I have to take over the Argentina beef proposal, so I'll log plenty of phone time." Jonathon decided at that moment not to let the looming feeling of despair defeat him.

"By the way, Jonathon, don't give out too much information to your friends. Some of them may not be your friends," FBI Agent Holcroft warned.

"I've known some of these people for years," Jonathon replied defensively.

The intercom buzzed as Miles Masterson walked into the room. "Mr. Masterson is here to see you."

"Yes, I can see that."

Miles Masterson closed the door firmly. "Doug Lister met with Debra Moore the day before her death. They met at the Downtowner Hotel room 213. She checked in again as Dee Mott and paid cash for the room. Lister checked into room 451 the night before under the name Ben Alan, and he paid with a valid Visa card. The address traces to somewhere in the mountains of Montana. He is at very least a messenger."

"Does he know that you've identified him?" Holcroft inquired.

"No, my man was very discreet." Miles was sure. "Lister is our first real lead."

"Are we talking about Pastor Doug Lister? The pastor at my church?" Jonathon said in disbelief.

"The same," Miles responded.

"This is completely impossible! How could he be so convincing? I've known him for four years. We have helped each other through some tough times." Jonathon threw his hands into the air. A wave of nausea came over him. "You can't be right about him." Even as Jonathon heard his own words, he knew that Miles was right.

Miles spoke softly but firmly, directly to Jonathon, "We don't know what is motivating him. Perhaps he has been threatened or blackmailed. He may even be a willing player. As long as we don't know his motives, we must assume the worst."

"That he planted himself in the church to gain my confidence so he could plot my destruction? I don't see how he could do that to us." Jonathon's frustration was turning into anger.

"We need to use him to our advantage. Do you have his cell number? We can monitor his calls and see what we learn." Bob Holcroft was planning as they talked.

"I already checked it out. He has a chip in his phone that prevents monitoring or tracing." Miles' words struck Jonathon like a sledgehammer. Miles continued, "Why would a minister have a cell phone that was secure? Doug Lister is a pastor, not a secret agent." Jonathon stopped his thought process again and tried to focus on the conversation between Miles and Bob Holcroft.

"The media is having a great time speculating about Eli murdering Debra. That should distract them for a while. In the meanwhile, let's concentrate on our leads from the explosion. How is Rachel doing with the fire inspector?" Holcroft asked Miles.

"They are tracing the origin of the explosion. They are also trying to find out who else may have been out to the building site that we may not know about. They have a few remote possibilities," Miles answered.

"I have a problem." Jonathon and Rachel had a dinner scheduled with Maggie, Miguel, Ron, and Doug Lister at a local restaurant in the city. "We're going to discuss the European Division among other things."

"Can you handle being around Doug without acting differently toward him?" Miles watched Jonathon's body language as he waited for the answer. Jonathon didn't slouch or look away in denial.

"I think so. I've been struggling with depression and fatigue lately, so no one expects me to be up—especially after a full day in the office following Eli's problems." Jonathon was trying to muster up his old sense of determination.

"Good. Can Rachel handle this?"

"I don't even know if I can handle this myself! Rachel will not be able to accept this about Doug. She will deny it before she believes it. Maybe I should wait until after we get home tonight to bring her up to speed. We won't have a chance to talk before dinner anyway." Jonathon couldn't believe that he was planning to withhold information from Rachel. He had never done this before. He felt guilty and yet knew this was the best decision.

"The Cleric wants us to hit Biggs again."
   "He's perched on the edge, ready for his final fall."
   "Let's give him a push."
   "What does the Cleric have in mind?"
   "He'll let us know soon"
   The two men were meeting in Doug Lister's office.

Maggie had arranged for a private dining room at the restaurant. She made sure that the atmosphere was good for conversation. She met Jonathon and Rachel at the kitchen door to avoid the press. Media people had been perched outside of Biggs International all day. Jonathon didn't care if his people talked to the media. He wanted to keep their frenzy going while he worked with Miles and Holcroft on the clues from the explosion.

   As Jonathon walked into the dining room, he looked around, wondering which of his friends he could still trust. The mood around the table was somber. Everyone expressed disbelief at Debra's death.

   Rachel had been in touch with Breslin Kline's replacement. "I'm disappointed that Breslin was transferred. This is the most inopportune time. We have some threads of evidence to follow up and really need his expertise."

   Ron Milliken was curious. "Didn't you have a hard time getting him to cooperate?"

   "Breslin is an eccentric perfectionist. That is what makes him the best investigator the USDA has. Once I tuned in to his personality, we were fine. Besides, I think he was starting to like us." Rachel was right. Miles and Rachel had slowly won Breslin Kline over. In their last conversation, Kline had told them that he was impressed by their commitment to find the truth.

Pastor Doug explained to everyone, "Right now, Rachel is focusing her attention on Greg Albright, the fire inspector. He says that the threads of evidence are thin but is convinced that a more detailed investigation will turn up something solid." As he spoke, Jonathon bristled, wondering about Pastor Doug's true intentions.

"It was a good thing that Breslin was there at the house. He turned up three key things that no one else saw." It was obvious that Rachel was unhappy that Breslin Kline was off the case, because she believed he was indispensable.

Maggie shared that she had followed up on all new employees and found nothing suspicious. She explained calmly, "I don't think our problem is coming from inside, unless it's on the ranches themselves. Cowboys are independent people who move around when they get bored or feel tied down. The ranch managers have given me a list of all the people that have worked for us for the last three years. Following them up is difficult because turnover is fairly high, especially among laborers. I asked Miles Masterson to help. He's done this before and has resources that the FBI wishes they had."

Rachel asked sharply, "Do you think someone hired in and waited for an opportunity to inject a cow with the disease?"

"That is possible," Maggie continued, unphased by the tension in Rachel's voice. "The injected version of mad cow takes about three weeks to manifest itself in lab rats. No one is sure how long it would take if a cow were injected. Miles Masterson's people said that it would take a minimum of three weeks and a maximum of eight. The incidents at all six ranches occurred over a three-day period of time. Here's the test scenario: If all six ranches had people on the payroll timed to inject cattle on all six ranches on the same day, the odds are astronomically against all of the injected animals displaying symptoms within three days of each other. Maybe they tested their serum on a few heads and knew that it could take between, say, three and five weeks to work. Maybe they added something to their injection that sped it up. The results, being this close together, are coincidental at best." It was obvious to everyone that Maggie had done her homework.

The intensity in Rachel's voice escalated. "Does the USDA have any conclusive information based on testing cattle?"

"According to Breslin Kline, rats have been tested with mad cow, but the USDA has never tested cattle," Maggie stated.

"Good work, Maggie." Pastor Doug nodded to Maggie and turned to Ron Milliken.

"We talked about trying to sell the European Division. Ron and Miguel give us an update." As Pastor Doug facilitated the meeting, Jonathon Oliver Biggs prayed silently for self-control.

"This is going to take some time. I've put out some feelers for potentially interested parties. Nothing to report yet, unless Miguel has something." Ron quickly deferred to Miguel.

"I've done the same thing. I may have an interested party, but he would have to put together a group of investors. He insisted that I talk with Jonathon privately and see if there is a mutual interest in working something out. Other than that, I have nothing," Miguel answered confidently.

"Jonathon, you've been spending time with the FBI and Miles Masterson. Is there anything new that you can tell us?" Pastor Doug nodded in Jonathon's direction.

"The FBI is working with local law enforcement on Eli's situation. I don't need to tell you that it doesn't look good. I'm sure for now that Eli is innocent, but Debra's friends are telling the detectives that she was afraid of her husband. This is almost too much to handle." Jonathon looked at Pastor Doug with tears in his eyes.

An uncomfortable silence followed Jonathon's remarks. Everyone concentrated on the food in front of them. Rachel touched Jonathon's knee to comfort him, unaware of what he knew about Pastor Doug.

Pastor Doug's wife, Millie, finally broke the silence. "We need to see the dessert tray. There are chemicals used in making desserts that produce a pleasant, carefree feeling! Three out of four psychologists recommend large amounts of chocolate."

Everyone laughed with nervous relief.

"Any time is a good time when you're with friends."

"That is true, Pastor Doug." Ron Milliken lifted his glass.

Later that night, Jonathon told Rachel about Pastor Doug.

Chapter Eighteen

"I stopped at Starbucks on my way over." Miguel Sameros followed Rachel into the kitchen and sat at the counter. "Would you like mocha, a latte, or a caramel macchiato?"

"Hard decision—Jonathon will want the caramel. Which do you like best, the mocha or the latte?" Rachel moved the caramel macchiato aside for Jonathon.

"It doesn't matter. I sipped all three on the way over." Miguel laughed.

"I'm glad you don't have cooties!" Rachel giggled as she took the latte.

"Hóla, Jonathon! Come on in before your coffee gets cold." Jonathon was cleaning the pool. He put the vacuum down and came into the kitchen.

"What's this?" He tasted. "I love the caramel macchiato at Starbucks. What, no whipped cream?"

"I thought you should start watching your weight." Miguel tapped Jonathon's stomach and smiled. Miguel worked out every day. Although he was five foot seven and slight of build, he prided himself in his personal conditioning program.

"Thanks for your concern. Want a Danish?" Jonathon played along. It felt good to have a light conversation.

"Sure, do you have a raspberry?"

Life seemed lighter when Miguel was around. He had an unquenchable spirit and loved to help people see the positive in every situation. He was a good man to have around during a crisis. He had committed to stay in town, until he was sure that the Biggses were able to recover. Jonathon put him in one of two condominiums owned by Biggs International. They were used for visiting VIPs. Miguel's wife, Felicia, was flying over tomorrow to spend the week with him. Theirs was a marriage much like Jonathon's and Rachel's. "Her name means 'happiness,' and she is my happiness!"

"Let's talk about this potential buyer for the European Division." Miguel changed the subject but not the mood. He had good news and was anxious to share it.

"I can't believe that you have something going already. You're amazing," Jonathon said with genuine admiration.

"I called my father and told him about our strategy session. He called me back two hours later and suggested that Sameros Ranches Incorporated buy your European manufacturing division. He feels that we need to diversify our holdings, and we have been looking to expand."

"How would a deal be shaped?" Jonathon was curious about his friend's proposal.

"Papa said that with your permission, he would have a private assessment done to determine the value. He would be discreet."

"Okay, what else?"

"We would put together an offer based on a three simple contingencies." Miguel sensed that Jonathon was positive about the possibilities.

"What would they be?"

"First, my father would have to put together a group of investors. He doesn't think that this would be difficult. He already knows of five men looking for opportunities to invest with Sameros Ranches. If he can deliver three of them, the deal would probably be doable."

"Second?" Jonathon was impressed.

"We would want you to be an investor with us. Your part would be five hundred thousand American dollars—not much considering that the total purchase will be around fifteen million."

"Right now, I don't have five-hundred-thousand dollars, and I don't expect to have that much any time soon," Jonathon responded with a shrug toward Rachel. She returned his shrug with a hopeful smile.

"I have checked, and you do have an investment that you could liquidate immediately, which would produce five hundred thousand American dollars." Miguel had a sly smile on his face. "Remember when you loaned us fifty thousand dollars eighteen years ago to start Sameros Ranch?"

"Yes." Jonathon sensed Miguel's excitement.

"When we tried to pay you back, you told us to pay it forward by helping a struggling business to succeed." Miguel was leading Jonathon and Rachel toward something very good.

"I remember."

"We invested that money in Sameros Ranches in case you or your family ever needed it. As you know, we have been very successful. Your fifty thousand is now worth five hundred thousand." Miguel threw up his arms, left the couch, and danced around the room with delight.

"You are kidding?" Jonathon and Rachel responded together with amazement and joy.

"No." Miguel laughed. "And Papa cashed you out yesterday. Here's a check for five hundred thousand American dollars!" Miguel handed Jonathon the check and danced around the room once more.

"Miguel, you are amazing!" Rachel and Jonathon were laughing, crying, and dancing all at the same time.

"I can hardly wait to hear the third contingency." Jonathon's words were choked with emotion. His sense of hope was rekindled.

"We want you to serve as chairman of the board for Sameros Manufacturing. We will provide you with a salary of $150,000 a year plus a bonus that will far exceed that, if we are successful."

"Thank you for your generosity. I don't know what else to say."

"May I give you some advice for the future?" Miguel put his arms around them both.

"You just delivered hope to us on a silver platter, so go ahead, advise!" Rachel was having fun with the conversation.

"When Eli gets out of jail. And he will soon. Make him the president of Biggs International. You serve as the CEO. That will cut your job in half and give you time to pursue other things."

"As long as you're moving people around at Biggs, who would take Eli's role? It's going to be tough to find the right person to fit that position."

"Papa was talking to someone who did some work for us about three months ago. I think he is available. He is very good and well acquainted with Biggs International." Miguel's tone of voice brimmed with laughter.

"Who is it?" Jonathon was becoming overwhelmed by Miguel's act of friendship. He felt his strength returning as they talked. He looked at Rachel and saw the sparkle in her eyes. Right now, he knew that they would make it through together.

"Miles Masterson," Miguel shouted triumphantly.

"Miles? He's the second man at Bills and Masterson. Why would he leave them? His name is on the company! He is perfect, but he wouldn't do it." Jonathon knew that Miles would be perfect. He had integrity, he cared for people, and he possessed the right temperament for the job.

"He and my father are very close. During a private dinner with Papa and me three months ago, he indicated that he was tired of traveling all over the world. Miles wants to settle down in one place and put down roots. He's ready to move, and he likes Biggs and admires you, Jonathon."

"Very interesting possibility. Tell your papa to move ahead full speed. Here's my check for five hundred thousand dollars as your first investor. There is a future for us!" They all danced again. This was a healing moment, and they enjoyed all of it.

Rachel walked over to Miguel and kissed him on the forehead. "Thank you, Miguel."

Chapter Nineteen

Bob Holcroft was craving a cigarette. He quit three years ago but still wanted one when he felt the pressure from an investigation. Holcroft was sitting in an interview room at the county jail. Eli Moore was on the other side of the table. Holcroft's large frame made Eli look small at six feet tall.

"Tell me how Debra was killed."

"I've repeated this at least ten times already." Eli was fed up with the constant questioning from the police, the prosecutor, his attorney, and now the FBI.

"Repeat it again." Holcroft showed no emotion.

"I don't know what happened. I arrived home from the office a little after six as usual. I use a limo service because of traffic in the city. I also like to make calls while I'm commuting."

"Go on."

"Debra was already home when I came in. She was pleasant. I was distant. She has been unhappy with me for a while. She says—said—I was unable to keep up with her social agenda. She fancied herself as a high-society player. I don't have much use for that stuff. I'm more of a family guy that likes to spend time with a few friends without the public looking in on my life."

"So you had different ambitions?"

"Different attitudes toward life are more accurate. Debra didn't care much about my career. My role was to provide the income for her life as a socialite."

"You came into the house…"

"Yes, we made dinner together. We had chicken with wild rice and green bean salad. We ate in silence. Actually, I was silent, and she talked about her day. She had been shopping, which is what she does most days, and bought a new set of china. It was going to be delivered next week, and she wanted to have some of her friends over for dinner to show it off."

"Who did she want to have over?"

"Yvonne and Scott, I'm sure you know them by now. Maggie and Frank, Maggie is Jonathon Biggs' administrative assistant. Bill and Marsha Hartmuth, Bill is the majority partner in a prestigious investment firm downtown. His wife, Marsha, is probably the most powerful woman in Kansas City. It has been said that even politicians can't raise funds without her endorsement. That's it in a nutshell." Eli stood up, indicating that the conversation was over.

The FBI agent continued the questioning. "How do Maggie and Frank fit into this group?"

"Maggie and Debra became friends about a year after Maggie came to work at Biggs International. She and Debra met at a dinner, which Jonathon hosts at the end of our annual corporate leadership retreat. They hit it off immediately. We went out with them as couple and had a great time. We became friends. Frank is an easy guy to like. He's a low-pressure type with a good sense of humor. Not big on socializing in groups. He is a freelance research scientist hired by major drug companies. They call him the "Bacteria Buster." Eli leaned forward over the back of his chair as he shared what he considered to be useless information.

"So you had dinner, then what?"

"We cleaned up and watched television for a couple of hours. We were both tired and felt like lazing around. Debra received one call during that time and made one call."

"Do you know who she talked to?"

"Yes, Yvonne called her, and then Debra called Joshua Mott. Joshua is the director of the Help Women Centers. They are a refuge for women in trouble. We donate to them. It's a very good organization. Well run and affective." Eli stepped back and leaned against the wall opposite Holcroft.

"Do you think that she was calling Joshua on a business matter or for personal help?"

"I don't know. I'm sure that the detective has talked to him already. Debra had no reason to ask for help from anyone. I am not a violent person. I don't anger easily and have never threatened Debra or anyone else. I'm a peaceful guy." Eli couldn't tell if Holcroft believed him.

"You watched television, Debra was on the phone twice, and then … ?"

"Right. I was dozing off in front of the television. Debra told me that I needed to go to bed. I went upstairs and took a shower. After I got into bed, I turned off the light and went to sleep. The next thing I know, the doorbell is ringing like crazy. I looked at the clock on my nightstand, and it was five after one in the morning. I went to the door and Yvonne started yelling, 'Where's Debra?' and trying to push her way into the house. She demanded to see Debra. I told her no and shut the door. Her husband, Scott, was standing off to the side. He looked embarrassed." Eli repeated the scene rapidly.

"What did you do next?"

"After I closed the door on Yvonne, I realized that Debra hadn't come to bed. I heard the television and went to see if she was asleep on the couch. She wasn't there. I called her name, and she didn't answer. All of a sudden I heard this high-pitched screaming sound coming from the backyard. I opened the back door and saw Yvonne running around the yard screaming and pointing. I looked down and saw Debra lying on the stairs. I got down to her, and she was unconscious. She didn't seem to have a pulse, so I began to give her mouth-to-mouth. The way she was laying there was unnatural. The police and paramedics showed up. I spoke with an officer, and a minute or so later the paramedic came over and told the officer that Debra was dead. He called it in as a murder! I've been here ever since." Eli was angry at the death of his wife and the fact that he was being held as the murderer.

"Where was Yvonne's husband, Scott, while you were on the steps with Debra?"

"He was in the yard somewhere. I think he's the one who called 911. I didn't kill Debra," Eli declared as if it should have been obvious to everyone involved.

Holcroft wanted to say, "I know" to Eli, but he didn't. Eli had to think that he was in the hot seat. If he knew that he was no longer a suspect, his demeanor would change and the real criminal might go deep into hiding.

Holcroft's cell rang. "Holcroft here," he said as he got up and walked away from Eli.

Holcroft left the room and walked down the hall.

"I guess this interview is over!" Eli kicked his chair across the room in frustration. The door clicked shut, and Eli sat on the table to wait.

"Talk to me," Holcroft spoke quietly into the cell phone.

"The pictures in his file show that Moore only had a little blood on his nose and right cheek. That happened while he was performing CPR. His physical exam showed no indication that he hit her. The damage to her throat was caused by a hard blow. He doesn't have that kind of power. The coroner shows Debra's head wound on the upper back portion of her skull. He says that wouldn't have killed her but probably knocked her out or at least left her barely conscious. His report asserts that this kind of head injury is caused by a blow from behind or falling hard backwards. Here's something else that may interest you. Debra Moore's neck was broken from the right side and wrenched toward the left. She could not have received both that type of head wound and a broken neck in the same fall. The coroner is writing this up as murder. His statement reads, 'Victim received a hard blow to her larynx. She then appears to have been thrown with great force down the stairs causing an injury to the back of the head that incapacitated her, allowing her assailant to then roll the victim on her side and fracture her neck with a harsh, twisting motion.'"

"Someone was hired to kill Debra Moore." Holcroft's suspicions were proving true.

"No kidding, and he is good at it. No one in the neighborhood saw or heard anything. There are no fingerprints, no shoe prints on the lawn—not even a hair that wasn't hers or her husband's. We're not going to catch this guy from the information we collect at the crime scene. He's a pro."

"The murder of Debra Moore, the mad cow situation at Biggs Ranches, and the explosion at Biggs' new house that killed his children—the circle is getting wider, not narrower. We need to find a way to narrow this down." Holcroft snapped his phone shut in midsentence.

"Rachel, this is Dr. Delcoma."

"It's good to hear from you, Doctor. Thank you for working so hard to help us." Rachel was appreciative.

"Rachel, I've done some more research on this virus. It should have pretty much run its course by now, and Jonathon should have about ninety percent of his strength back. He'll be at one hundred percent in less than a week."

"That is good news. Thank you for calling to tell us."

"That's not the only reason that I called." Dr. Delcoma caught Rachel's attention.

"Oh?"

"I know there have been some bad things happening to you and Jonathon. I know about the business, the cattle problems, and of course, the loss of your children. I saw on the news that Eli Moore's wife was murdered."

"Your point ..."

"I woke up last night thinking that someone may be out to get you."

"We already know that, Doctor." Rachel was turning cold quickly.

"I have a theory that may help," the doctor said carefully.

"Doctor Delcoma, we have theories coming out of our ears.

What we need is evidence. Thank you for calling." Rachel was out of patience.

"Please, do not hang up the phone! I can help! I can help you!"

Dr. Delcoma's urgent tone of voice caused Rachel to stop before the phone reached its cradle. She was upset but decided to listen. Dr. Delcoma was a good man who had always gone out of his way to help them. She owed him the courtesy of listening to his theory.

"I don't mean to be rude...." Rachel's voice was short and clipped.

"And I don't mean to upset you, but I care about you and Jonathon. I delivered your babies. I've treated your family for years, and you are good people. Please listen, and see if what I have to say helps. If it doesn't, then I will apologize for wasting your time and upsetting you needlessly," the doctor pleaded.

"You've helped us through stitches and broken bones. I'm listening. Maybe you can help us now."

"The virus that Jonathon has takes eight weeks to run its course followed by another three to four weeks of gradual recovery—a time span of nearly three months. Three months ago, your children were killed, and your ranches were infected with mad cow disease. Could it be possible that this virus was introduced into Jonathon's system as part of a sinister plot to destroy you?" Dr. Delcoma spoke quickly and confidently. He had rehearsed this conversation in his mind all night.

"I suppose that it's possible." Rachel began to review the timeline in her mind.

"More than possible, Rachel. More like probable. This is a rare virus. It originally came out of the southern part of the African continent. The last time someone on record had this virus was eleven years ago in Madagascar. An island off the east coast of the continent of all places! When was the last time Jonathon went to Madagascar?"

"Never."

"I thought so. What if someone brought the virus over here and infected Jonathon on purpose?"

"How would someone go about infecting him?"

"This virus can be contracted by ingesting it in a concentrated form. Jonathon could have drunk it. Most people don't come down with this, because the body kills it off when it shows up in small doses. Jonathon would have had to ingest concentrated doses of the virus for about a week in order to become as ill as he was."

"Wouldn't he know?" Rachel's mind was racing. "Not if it was in his coffee or orange juice. You know those little creamer cups you get at a fast food place when you buy coffee?"

"Yes."

"Three concentrated doses of the virus would fit easily into one of those."

"You have really done your homework!" Rachel was impressed and fearful at the same time.

"Here's my idea. What if you could find out who had the virus eleven years ago and see if anyone has taken his blood lately? There are many ways that your enemies could get a hold of the virus, but the easiest is to simply take a blood sample from someone who has had it. They take the blood sample and separate out the virus. Then they let it multiply in a lab somewhere, until they have enough to use. The virus would multiply quickly, if unencumbered by things like antibodies."

"How would I get the name of the last man who had the virus?"

"His name is Jonathon Buto, and he's seventy-three years old. I couldn't find out where he is now, but I'm sure that you can." The doctor sighed with relief knowing that Rachel believed him.

"I'm sure that we can. Doctor Delcoma, may I ask you a favor?" Rachel said kindly.

"Of course."

"Please keep this confidential. I don't want our enemies to know that we may have a lead. I also want you to stay safe."

Rachel wondered if their doctor would be the next to die at the hands of their enemies.

"I thought that through before I called you. If I think of anything else, I'll call again." Dr. Delcoma knew the risk he was taking.

"Thank you very much, Doctor." Rachel spoke from her heart.

Chapter Twenty

"Holcroft here. Talk to me."

"Bob, Miles Masterson."

"Miles, what's up?"

"My man has been keeping and eye on Doug Lister's activities. He has spent time with a few parishioners and a close friend of Biggs, Ron Milliken."

"The millionaire motivator?"

"Yes, I don't know why, but I think that Lister is a messenger and probably doesn't know anything his superiors don't want him to know."

"You may be right about that."

"I put another man on Ron Milliken, and I'm thinking of putting someone on Miguel Sameros."

"Has Sameros been spending time with Lister?" Holcroft asked.

"No, but he calls Milliken occasionally and had lunch with him today. I'm just looking for any thread we can pull."

"Me, too." Bob Holcroft appreciated Miles' ability to evaluate the possibilities.

"Do you have anything new?" Miles was hoping that he had gained the FBI agent's confidence.

"I'm not supposed to tell you FBI business, but I will because we're working together and I respect your integrity." Holcroft wanted Miles Masterson as an ally.

"Thank you. Same here."

"The coroner checked in on the Debra Moore murder." Holcroft filled Miles in on his conversation with Eli Moore and the coroner's preliminary report.

"Thanks, Bob. I'll be talking to you soon."

"Okay." Holcroft couldn't believe that he let Miles address him on a first-name basis. It was unprofessional, but Holcroft didn't care.

———⟶●⟵———

"The fire inspector just checked in with bad news," Rachel said as she and Jonathon were eating lunch by the pool. He had been swimming while she was talking on the phone and making sandwiches at the same time.

"What did he say?" Jonathon asked as he closed his eyes and took the first bite out of the pastrami on rye. "There isn't a deli in the world that makes a sandwich like you do!" He winked at Rachel.

"Thank you, dear, but I'm trying to be serious here." Rachel was glad to see her husband in good spirits. "They've looked into everything that we thought had any possibility of turning into a lead. Nothing panned out. The inspector said that this is either the best crime he's ever seen or the most tragic coincidence. He has to write it up as an accident."

"I'm not surprised." Jonathon shrugged between bites.

"Me neither, but I'm disappointed. I thought that at least we would learn something we could use."

"Whoever is out to get us has the connections to do it right. The local police would have closed the case on Debra Moore if Bob Holcroft's FBI team hadn't stepped in. We're fortunate to have his team helping us. Holcroft said that Debra's killer was a real pro—he set the stage for Eli to take the fall. It's a good thing the FBI knew what to look for."

"What do we do next?" Rachel was still hoping for clues from the African virus situation.

"I'm thinking that we need to talk to Pastor Doug. He's the only connection we have to whoever is after us." Jonathon still hurt from the thought that their pastor was somehow involved.

"You should check with Bob Holcroft and Miles before you do anything," Rachel warned. "We don't want to do anything that will mess up their plans."

"I will, but I think we need to lean on him. In my mind, he is a prime suspect in Debra's murder."

"We could use that as leverage to get him to talk. Maybe we should ask Bob and Miles to handle this." As she spoke, Rachel reached across the table and took Jonathon's hand. He was weeping softly.

⸻⸻⸻

"I'll find Miles, and we'll talk about it," Bob Holcroft promised Jonathon.

"Why don't you and Miles stop over tonight for coffee, and we'll run through what we know and make sure that we're all on the same page." Jonathon wanted to stay in the loop.

"We'll be there at eight, unless you here from us."

"How much longer will they hold Eli?" Jonathon knew that Eli's problem-solving skills would be invaluable.

"Probably two more days at the most. We can have him released at any time. They're only holding him because I asked them to." Holcroft had no trouble convincing the police chief of Eli's innocence. It took a much greater effort to persuade him to keep Eli locked up and away from the media.

"Let's make that part of our discussion this evening." Jonathon was concerned about Eli's emotional condition.

"See you at eight. I'll bring Miles." Holcroft hung and speed dialed Miles Masterson.

Chapter Twenty-one

"I have our next move," Doug Lister said with authority.

"Where shall we meet?" the man on the other end of the call inquired.

"There's a Holiday Inn about an hour and a half south of the city on I-35. Take the exit 131 toward Emporia; it's on the right. I'll get a room on the first floor. Be there at nine tomorrow night."

"I'll bring her with me," the man said.

"No, I've already made arrangements with her. You will come in different cars. You will arrive at nine, and she will arrive at nine fifteen. Come in the door at the south end of the parking lot. I'll meet you there." Doug Lister's tone of voice made it clear that there was to be no discussion about the plan.

"Got it."

Jonathon, Rachel, Bob Holcroft, and Miles Masterson sat at the kitchen table eating dessert and drinking coffee. Rachel explained her call from Dr. Delcoma about Jonathon's rare virus.

"I have a connection in the CIA that works in Africa; maybe he can uncover something on this Jonathon Buto." It seemed that Miles had connections everywhere.

"We need to work on the theory that the mad cow disease was

caused by injections. How would your adversary get his hands on serum containing mad cow disease?" Bob Holcroft thought that they should treat every theory as if it were a solid lead.

"There can't be too many places where it's available," Rachel interjected.

"I'll have my agent who worked with the coroner check it out. He's good at running down theories," Holcroft offered.

"What about the fire inspector?" asked Rachel.

"We need to drop him for now, Rachel. If something else points back to the explosion, then we'll get him involved again." Miles didn't like to drop any possibility, but he also didn't want to waste their limited resources on a dead end.

"When do we confront Doug Lister?" Jonathon was anxious to deal with his would-be pastor. Rachel crossed her arms and looked at the floor. When Jonathon had told her about Doug's involvement with Debra, Rachel was livid and was sick to her stomach, throwing up in the bathroom all night. Jonathon grimaced inside, knowing that this would be like pouring gasoline on an already dangerous forest fire. Explaining the situation was difficult, and Jonathon had tried to handle it delicately. Rachel saw through him immediately and demanded that he give her the information without sugarcoating it. Jonathon respected her request. She hadn't mentioned Doug Lister's name since.

"I suggest we wait a few days at least. Let's have Eli released tomorrow and see if that causes Mr. Lister to make another move. We should also leak the coroner's preliminary report to the media. That will make whoever is calling the shots nervous about what we know. Bob Holcroft was convinced that they needed to go on the offensive to get the enemy to make another move.

"I like that approach, Bob," Miles said matter-of-factly. "They may feel compelled to make a move that isn't in their plan. If they ad lib, they risk making a mistake. I have Ron Milliken and Miguel Sameros both under surveillance. If either one of them is involved, we'll see some activity with Doug Lister."

"You're watching Ron and Miguel?" Rachel asked in disbelief. "Miles, don't you think that's a little over the top?"

"Yes, and we may not learn anything except that your other friends are loyal to you. But the only solid lead we have is Doug Lister. Like it or not, both Ron and Miguel spend time with Doug. At this point, I don't trust anyone," Miles explained as Rachel leaned back in her chair and sighed.

"I'm with Miles on this," Jonathon weighed in. "We have to cover everything."

Bob Holcroft agreed.

"Okay, but I don't like it." Rachel put her face in her hands, trying to control her emotions.

"Too many disappointments in too short a period of time?" Jonathon asked as he put his arms around her.

Rachel nodded slowly.

<hr />

"Our preliminary investigation indicates that Debra Moore was not murdered by her husband. The coroner's initial examination of the victim's body concurs with our conclusion that someone other than Eli Moore murdered Debra Moore."

"Chief, when will the coroner's report be available to the press?" the local television reporter asked.

"The complete report will be available within five days."

"Do you have any other suspects?"

"I cannot reveal that at this point." The chief enjoyed the attention he received at press conferences.

"Will you be making another arrest immediately?"

"We'll let you know if that happens. Thank you." He was looking forward to being on television every night for the next few days.

The statement made by the chief of police drew reporters to the front steps of the city jail, allowing Jonathon Biggs to pick up Eli Moore unnoticed at the back door.

Eli was angry. "I know we had issues, but why was she telling people that I was a threat to her safety? I never did anything that even remotely resembled a threat."

Jonathon noticed Eli's anger. "I know, Eli," he said softly.

"Why would anyone want to kill Debra? She was a harmless socialite. She shopped, ate at the best restaurants, and pretended to be important with her upper-crust friends. Her life was harmless." Eli wanted answers, but there were none.

"She was being manipulated," Jonathon said sympathetically.

"I know, by every sincere-sounding organization that needed money."

"It goes deeper than that." Jonathon was preparing Eli to hear what the investigating team had learned while Eli was in jail.

"Deep enough to cause someone to murder her?" Eli said with disbelief.

"Yes, the people manipulating her are the same people who are out to destroy me." Jonathon still couldn't believe it himself.

"What? Why would they use her? The only thing that interested Debra about Biggs International was my annual bonus." Eli was incredulous.

"You are very angry toward her."

"You bet I am! She tells her friends that I'm an abuser and arranges to leave without talking to me about it. I knew we had problems. I'm the one who tried to discuss them with her. She just shut me off and did her own thing. Which, by the way, I paid for." Eli was yelling in the direction of the roof.

"Do you think you two could have worked it out eventually?"

"I doubt it. She wasn't interested in getting help."

"Her manipulators must have used her dissatisfaction with your marriage to pull her in and control her," Jonathon offered.

"But why would they kill her?" This all seemed unreal to Eli.

"My best guess?"

"Sure, why not?" Eli's frustration bled through into sarcasm.

"They wanted you out of the picture. You're the only one who could rescue Biggs International. They also want me to be personally devastated. I think that they were hoping that your arrest and conviction would turn me into a useless blob sitting in despair out by the pool."

"I'm glad you're doing better." Eli calmed himself down and looked out the window for a full minute. When he turned back toward Jonathon, he realized that there was something more on his mind.

"I have something to tell you and something to ask you. Which do you want first?" Jonathon inquired.

"Tell me." Eli was an information junkie.

"The FBI knew that you were innocent within hours of your arrest. Bob Holcroft wanted you to stay in jail to make our foes think they'd won. We were hoping they would get careless."

"Did they?" Eli was beginning to get angry again. The thought that he had been used without his knowledge irritated him.

"No, but keeping you confined allowed the police and FBI time to formulate the next part of their plan."

"Which is?" Eli crossed his arms and looked straight ahead.

"We're hoping that they panic when they hear of your release. We want them to make another move; hopefully, they will make a mistake in their haste and give us something to follow."

"I didn't like jail, but it was better than being at home thinking about Debra's body lying on the back steps." Eli wiped the welling tears from his eyes.

"Rachel's parents are traveling in Europe for another two months. Why don't you stay at their place? We're right in the back at the guest house, so we could be there for each other." Jonathon suggested.

"Good idea, I need some long talks with Rachel. Just like the old days. She rescued me from myself." Eli was pinching the bridge of his nose, hoping to stop the flow of tears from his eyes.

"Good, I'll send someone to your house to get your things," Jonathon said with enthusiasm.

"Now the question." Eli was back under control and ready for the conversation to move on.

"Would you please consider becoming the president of Biggs International?" Jonathon asked with care and respect.

"What? You're the president; it's always been that way." This was a day of surprises for Eli.

"I know, but you should be running things. I'll be the CEO and give you the reins."

"Why are you offering this to me now?" Eli couldn't believe what he was hearing.

"Because we will all be different to some degree when this is over. We've all lost something, and I want you to have something back. Plus, I want to keep the company in the family."

"When would this happen?"

"I've already talked to the board. Despite the fact that you're an ex-con, we want you to step up Monday." Jonathon Oliver Biggs and Eli Moore laughed together for the first time in a long time.

"Okay, if that's what you want." Eli surrendered with uncertainty.

"What do you want?"

"That's what I want too!" Eli smiled and laughed again.

"Done!" Jonathon Biggs pulled into the driveway.

<hr />

"Eli Moore is out," Doug Lister reported.

"What did you say?" The man pressed his palms firmly on the top of the pastor's desk and stood slowly to his feet. He couldn't believe what he had just heard.

"Eli Moore was released from jail this morning. The police chief made a statement declaring his innocence," Doug informed him.

"They must know that the Cleric used a pro." The man's voice broke with fear.

"Well, he did his job too well. Now we have a problem. I'll get a hold of the Cleric. He'll know what to do." Doug and the man both knew that the Cleric didn't tolerate failure.

"Are we still meeting tonight?"

"Yes, unless you hear from me, be there as planned." Doug Lister stood up and waved the man toward the door.

"This is not good!" The man shook his head as he left the room.

Chapter Twenty-two

"Ron Milliken just got on a plane to New York."

"What airline and flight number?" Miles Masterson wasn't surprised. Ron Milliken traveled to speaking engagements regularly. He was surprised that Ron had stayed around Kansas City for as long as he had.

"American 1226 arrives at nine tonight at La Guardia Gate A26."

"Thanks, I'll call ahead and we'll pick him up when he gets off the plane." Masterson dialed his phone and gave brief instructions. He made a second call. "Is Doug Lister on the move?"

"No, he's at home right now."

"Let me know if he becomes active."

Ron Milliken checked his bags at the curb and wound his way into the airport and through the tedious security check. He stopped at the first bathroom on the way to his gate and changed clothes. He had been wearing khaki slacks, a light blue shirt, and a medium blue jacket. He changed into blue jeans, a gray sweatshirt, and a Jeff Gordon NASCAR jacket with matching hat. He neatly placed the clothes he had taken off into his rolling carry on bag. He left the bathroom.

Milliken didn't turn toward the gate area as he left the bathroom. He weaved through the pedestrian traffic and became part of the crowd moving toward baggage claim. He stopped at a carousel and waited five minutes before he picked up a suitcase that wasn't his. He walked out between two families headed for the parking lot. At section C7, he pushed the unlock button on the keys he had in his jacket pocket and went to the navy blue Chevrolet Impala that lit up inside. He paid the parking attendant and headed onto the expressway, south out of town. He was sure that no one was following him before he went to the airport, but was in the habit of not taking chances. The game he played required complete anonymity. One moment of carelessness could be costly.

Commuter traffic was usually thick at this time of day because of rush hour. He took his time, knowing that he would arrive early. He had allotted two and a half hours for the one-hour drive. He had spent forty-five minutes at the airport and would need time at a truck stop to change his clothes back. He also wanted to eat. The timing would work out just right.

———⟫●⟪———

"Jonathon Buto died four months ago."

"How?" Miles Masterson asked.

"Heart attack. He had been ill for a long time. We checked out his medical records to see where he had his blood tested and found nothing unusual. We also asked the people working at the clinic in the hospital he frequented. They hardly remembered him. His doctor said that he was a quiet person who didn't complain and did what he was told. He also said that Buto didn't want to be on the transplant list for a new heart. The doctor said that at his age he wouldn't have qualified anyway." Miles' CIA connection had done his job well.

"Were there any life insurance policies?" Miles knew that his caller would have this information.

"Just one for one hundred thousand American dollars. It was fifty thousand, until the month before he died. He took advantage of one of those opportunities to increase his policy without a physical examination. The insurance company paid, no questions asked."

"Wife or children?"

"Wife died five years ago. Kids are grown and live in Paris. The older one went to college there and now works as an engineer. The younger one moved there after the mother died and attends the university. Nothing unusual about either one."

"Did you ask—"

"Friends and neighbors? Yes, they hadn't seen anything or anyone new come into his life recently. He kept to himself and had a day nurse stop in to check on him regularly. We're looking for her now. She left the company and moved out of her apartment two months later. She left no forwarding address. We're looking for relatives now who could tell us where she is."

"Be discreet. If she's connected in any way to this, we don't want to set off any alarms in the enemy's camp," Miles warned as he hung up.

"Frustrated, Miles?" Jonathon Biggs was curious about the phone conversation. The Biggses' living room had become the common meeting place for the team. Today, Miles showed up to talk while Rachel was making breakfast for Jonathon and Eli.

"Not really. I was hoping for more out of the Jonathon Buto lead. But we didn't get anything yet. It doesn't look like we will." Miles shared the content of the phone conversation. "Is there anything we're missing? Any little thing that happened that we haven't discussed? Any tiny detail we're missing?"

Eli spoke up, "I have one that seemed insignificant, until Debra was killed. I'm not sure it means much of anything now, but someone used my computer one night last week."

"Do you know who it was?" Miles asked.

"No, I checked the log book at the security station and saw nothing unusual. Ed, the day-shift guard, sent me a list of offices that were opened with keycards that night, and mine wasn't on the list. The FBI has been in my office since and checked my computer out thoroughly; they didn't find anything suspicious."

"Someone was in your office for a reason," Jonathon stated.

"It was Maggie," Rachel said from the kitchen. She heard the conversation and decided to come clean. "I asked her to look around."

"Maggie did that for you?" Eli was amazed. "She was supposed to be working for me and stalling you!"

"She works for you, but she's my good friend. I'm sorry, Eli. I was wrong not to trust you." Rachel still felt bad about her attitude toward Eli.

"We already took care of that. I'm sorry too. By the way, what was Maggie looking for?" Eli asked.

"Anything she could find. She discovered the beef proposal for the Argentina Ranch. She also found out that you were buying large amounts of Biggs stock in your name and Debra's. There isn't anything that you don't know about already," Rachel confessed.

<hr />

"Where is Doug? He was supposed to meet me," Ron asked expectantly. He didn't like changes within the plan, especially when they caught him off guard. He knew his present contact had a reputation for eliminating people who were no longer necessary.

"He called and sent me. He chose me because I'm familiar to you. You're in room 117. It's the first on the right." He handed Ron Milliken a keycard. As Ron walked down the hall, he wondered about his fate. He entered room 117.

Fifteen minutes later, as Ron Milliken waited impatiently in his room, the woman arrived in the lobby dressed in a plain business suit. Her hair hung loosely around her shoulders, and her black-rimmed glasses made her difficult to identify. She scanned the room for her contact and spotted him on the couch in the corner of the lobby. She knew him by sight, as they were very familiar with each other. She wondered why Doug Lister wasn't meeting her as planned. She slipped onto the couch next to him and whispered in his left ear.

"Where's Doug? He said that he would be here." Secret meetings always made her nervous.

"Doug had other obligations tonight. You get me." He smiled.

"I'm comfortable with that. Is the other party here yet?" Even though they had worked together often before, she knew his capabilities.

"Yes, but you won't be seeing him."

"Why not?" She was worried.

"You are in room 121. It's down the hall on the right. The phone will ring in five minutes." She received the keycard for room 121. She proceeded cautiously down the hall. Her hand was on the gun in her pocket. She walked softly, expecting the man in the lobby to come up behind her. She looked both ways and pressed the keycard into the slot on the door. When the light on the mechanism turned green, she took her gun from her pocket, turned the handle with her left hand, and pushed the door open slightly with her foot. Before she entered the room, she looked both ways down the hall again. The man in the lobby was gone. She entered the room slowly with her pistol poised. She wasn't going to be surprised. She moved the phone away from the window and stood in the far corner, weapon at the ready. She was glad that she had decided to carry her Glock 9mm tonight. It was light and fired easily without much recoil. She waited. Finally, after what seemed like an hour later, the phone rang. It had only been five minutes. It was Doug Lister.

"Why aren't you here?" She was anxious and angry.

"I received alternate instructions. You'll get another call in about a minute." The phone clicked as Doug hung up.

She waited.

One minute later, the phone rang again.

"This is being handled at a higher level. You will no longer be hearing from me."

"What's going on? I don't like this," she demanded.

"Neither do I, but it's necessary. We haven't succeeded in derailing Jonathon Biggs, so the Cleric is going to turn up the heat on him. He wants us to continue our daily activities until further notice."

"I've put a lot of effort into this. I want to be there when Biggs caves in."

"That's not up to me." Ron Milliken hung up and slipped quietly out of the hotel.

The phone in room 121 rang again. She crouched in the corner in case the call was being used to verify that she hadn't left the hotel. She didn't answer. The ringing stopped, and she crept quietly toward the door, being careful not to stand up and make herself an easy target. The phone rang again as her hand reached for the door handle. *They knew I wouldn't answer the last call. They know that I'm still in the room.* She crawled to the phone and picked it up.

"I have a significant assignment for you. Your next task is the most important one you have ever been asked to perform. It will be the final blow to Jonathon Biggs." She recognized the voice of the Cleric. He had trained her personally years ago. He was honoring her request to be there when Biggs caved in. She sighed with relief.

"I'm ready to serve you," she said firmly.

"I'll call you. Be patient. There are other pieces that have to be put in place first."

<hr />

"Mr. Masterson, Ron Milliken didn't get off the plane at La Guardia. The bag he checked is full of paper supplies. Notebooks, pens, stationary, and stuff like that. We have confirmed that his seat was empty at takeoff."

"That means he's still here." Miles Masterson now knew that Milliken was involved.

"What's next?"

"Keep an eye on his hotel, and see if he returns there. Where is Miguel Sameros?" Miles knew that the next move was being orchestrated as they spoke.

"He is at the Biggs International condo watching television. He ordered dinner in and hasn't left all evening."

Ron Milliken drove south to the Wichita airport and boarded a plane for JFK airport in New York. He was flying as Joseph Saltzer, a business man he had created for situations like this. He would be speaking in Manhattan tomorrow evening as planned. He loved a good adventure.

J.O.B.

PART
TWO

Chapter One

"Mad cow disease?"

Eli delivered the bad news on his first day as president of Biggs International.

"The Argentina farm. They discovered it this morning. One head infected."

"I'll get my team on it right away." Miles Masterson was stunned.

Eli called Maggie into Jonathon's old office, now his. He had told Jonathon that his present office was fine, but Jonathon wouldn't hear of it. Eli was moved in, and Jonathon took a vacant office across the hall.

"Maggie, would you notify the pilot that we will need the Biggs jet for a trip to Argentina. We'd like to leave in an hour," Eli ordered.

"How many will be traveling?"

"Miles and his team of four," Eli replied.

"And Jonathon Biggs," Jonathon Oliver Biggs said as he walked into Eli's new office.

"Could we make a short stop in Phoenix to pick up another member of my team?" Miles asked.

"Who?" Jonathon thought he knew everyone on the team.

"Breslin Kline," stated Miles Masterson.

Jonathon was sure of himself. "Breslin Kline is in Washington, DC, strapped to a desk."

"He was until yesterday. He's now a junior partner at Bills and Masterson." Miles smiled.

Jonathon was dumbfounded. "How did you pull that off?"

"I promised him more action. He gets to pick his assignments. I also told him that he would get to solve the Biggs case." Miles laughed. "He likes you guys."

"Did he actually say that he liked us?" Eli chimed in.

"He said, 'I liked working on the Biggs case,'" Miles clarified.

"He used the words 'like' and 'Biggs' in the same sentence?" Eli mocked with a short laugh.

"Good enough for me." Jonathon was obviously pleased. "He's in!"

"The Argentina ranch was supposed to be the last straw for Jonathon Biggs," the Administrator spoke cautiously. He was the Cleric's right-hand man, an expert in weaponry, martial arts, and the psychology of war. He was, in his younger years, the most dangerous assassin in the world. The Cleric had been his contact agent for many years and was one of only three people in the world who knew what he looked like. He was a powerfully built Samoan from the Hawaiian Islands whose forefathers had been renowned warriors and assassins.

"I know, but I had more planned for him in case he didn't fall apart on our time schedule." The Cleric smiled softly. He enjoyed the process of destruction. He loved the intrigue with all of the twists and turns in people's lives.

"He's turned out to be stronger than we thought. Jonathon Biggs is pretty tough for a spoiled, rich guy."

"Pretty tough won't save him." The Cleric snarled with delight.

Miles Masterson and his team boarded the Biggs jet with Jonathon and headed for Phoenix to connect with Breslin Kline.

While they were in the air, the flight attendant told Jonathon that Mrs. Biggs was on the phone for him.

"Jonathon, you have to come home right away!" Rachel was frantic.

"Pastor Doug was in a serious car accident about a half an hour ago. They're taking him to the hospital now. He's not conscious."

"What happened?"

"He lost control of his car on a back road and rolled it down the embankment and into a tree," Rachel blurted out.

"Was he alone?"

"No, Millie was with him. She was killed when the car hit the tree on her side."

"Who's giving you information?"

"Bob Holcroft. He's at the hospital hoping to talk to Doug, if he regains consciousness. I know that Doug betrayed us, but I still feel really bad about this. I wish we could help somehow." Rachel was crying softly.

"I'll grab a flight in Phoenix and be there as soon as I can." Jonathon wished that he could be there to comfort his wife.

"I already called Maggie. She fell apart, so I talked to Eli; and he said he'd make the arrangements to get you home. Call him when you get on the ground for your flight info."

"Okay, thanks. Is there anyone waiting with you?" Jonathon was concerned about Rachel. She had already been through enough, but it seemed that the problems kept on coming.

"Eli is sending Maggie over in the limo. We'll console each other. Maggie and Frank were really close to Pastor Doug. He helped save their marriage."

"I'm sure that Frank will come over too. Rachel, we know that Doug was involved in something bad the past few months, but we don't know why. I'm sure that he had his own reasons. These people trying to destroy us are truly evil; I wonder what they did to force him to get caught up in this mess." Jonathon was feeling Rachel's anguish.

"Now we may never know. Jonathon, do you think they did this to Doug and Millie?" Rachel asked fearfully.

"Bob Holcroft will have to figure that out. I love you, Rachel, and I'll be home soon."

"I love you, Bigg Time!" Jonathon hated to hang up the phone with Rachel sobbing at the other end. She needed him close right now, and he couldn't be there.

"Miles, Doug and Millie Lister were just involved in a car accident. Millie is dead, and Doug is unconscious. They're taking him to the hospital right now. Bob Holcroft is there, hoping to talk to him if he regains consciousness," Jonathon reported.

"What are you going to do?" Miles asked.

"Head for home when we land in Phoenix. Eli has arranged a flight for me."

Breslin Kline was waiting on the tarmac in Phoenix when the Biggs jet rolled up. Jonathon stopped to say hello on his way into the terminal.

"Breslin, it's good to have you back." Jonathon Oliver Biggs smiled as he shook hands with Breslin Kline.

"We will solve this case, Mr. Biggs. I've been studying on it since I left. I'm ready with fresh eyes to take another look." Breslin Kline spoke with his usual confidence that was often mistaken for arrogance.

"Go get 'em, Breslin!"

Breslin Kline smiled ever so slightly. "I like working on this case."

Jonathon smiled and walked toward the terminal. "I knew he liked us," he said under his breath.

Jonathon was met inside the terminal by an attendant and driven by golf cart to a private plane. "It's ready to go when you are," he was told as he boarded.

Jonathon walked up the short stairway and sat down. "I'm ready right now. Let's go."

"You told them not to touch anything until I arrived?" Breslin Kline asked as he stepped onto the Biggs jet.

"Yes, Breslin, they are not going to destroy the cow until you give the order. They've quarantined her for now, awaiting your arrival. The rest of us are here to help as we can. By the way, hello and welcome to a great future with Bills and Masterson." Miles extended his hand, and Kline shook it firmly.

"Thank you. I'm sure it will be a mutually beneficial relationship."

Miles Masterson winced and reminded himself that he hadn't hired Breslin Kline for his people skills. "Sit here and I'll tell you what has gone on since you left."

George Cousins, the assistant pastor, had opened the church for those who wanted to come and pray. He had assigned each deacon a group of families to call. The people needed to hear from their leaders at a time like this. Doug didn't have any living relatives, and Millie's mother was in a nursing home. George had no one to call, so he kept himself busy making funeral arrangements for Millie while he waited in the hospital's clergy room for news about Pastor Doug.

Miguel Sameros showed up to comfort the Biggs. Eli, Maggie, and Frank were there when he arrived. "I just heard about Doug. I am sorry for your grief. Do you mind if I stay in case you need someone to help?"

"I don't mind at all. You are such a good friend!" Rachel hugged Miguel and wept on his shoulder. "Jonathon was on his way to Argentina when the accident happened. He's on his way back here now."

"I'll pick him up at the airport when his plane lands," Miguel volunteered.

"That would be good. May I ride along?" Rachel asked, still hugging him.

"Let me rephrase that: 'I would like to take you to the airport to meet Jonathon when his plane lands." Miguel laughed.

"That would be nice. Thank you." Rachel turned and took a tissue from the box that Maggie was holding.

"Ron called me on my way over here and said he would be

in early tomorrow morning. He was devastated. He and Doug were good friends. He answered my voicemail during a break in his pre-seminar briefing. He's on in an hour, so there's no way to cancel and come tonight." Miguel informed everyone in the room.

"Why is this happening? I don't understand. Why Doug and Millie? Why them? Why now?" Maggie was breaking down again.

Rachel sat close to her on the couch. "I don't have any answers, but I'm glad that we're here to comfort each other."

"It just doesn't make sense," Maggie wailed.

"I know." All that Rachel could do was to hold her.

Chapter Two

"I want to know what happened, and I want to know right now!" Ron Milliken had a difficult time getting through his seminar. He was angry and called his contact person to get the real story about Doug Lister's car accident.

"What are you talking about?"

"Doug Lister had a car accident late this afternoon. His wife was killed, and he is unconscious. I want to know who ordered it done."

"Hold, please." The voice of his contact was unemotional.

"Mr. Milliken, what is this about Doug Lister?"

Ron repeated the short version to the Cleric.

"This is bad news, especially now when we are so close to the end." The Cleric sounded surprised.

"Are you telling me that you had nothing to do with this?" Ron asked suspiciously.

"I just heard about it from you. If I had ordered it done, I would have put out an order on you as well. We can't afford loose ends right now."

Ron was close to panic. "What should I do?"

"I don't know yet. This is a surprise to me. I will have to take some time to consider our next move." The Cleric sounded sympathetic. "You are good friends with Doug, aren't you?"

"Yes, he's the one that talked me into destroying Jonathon Biggs."

"Are you able to help the others that are grieving?"

"Yes, and I'll be with the Biggs tomorrow morning."

"I'm sorry, Ron. I didn't have anything to do with this. There was no good reason for me to want to hurt Doug."

"I believe you." But Ron Milliken wasn't entirely convinced.

"I'll call you in a few days to see how you're doing." The Cleric feigned a comforting voice.

"Thank you." Ron sounded relieved.

The phone went dead.

"I was hoping that Doug would be alone." The Cleric put his hands behind his head and leaned back in his chair.

"Millie was expendable," his administrator said matter-of-factly.

"I know, but I thought she had great potential."

"She happened to be in the car when the assassin's plan unfolded. It's amazing, but people trying to avoid a head-on collision will always turn to the shoulder of the road. In this case, the shoulder fell off into the woods. Do you think that Ron believed you?"

"Completely." The Cleric's laugh was filled with scorn. "We don't need his help with our next move anyway. By the time he realizes that destroying Jonathon Biggs requires eliminating his three best friends, it will be his turn."

"Just to make it more interesting, we should save Ron Milliken for last," the Administrator suggested.

Jonathon Oliver Biggs stood by Pastor Doug's bedside. Jonathon had experienced feelings all over his emotional spectrum these past few months. This present sensation was unfamiliar to him. Everything in his mind was pushing him to forgive. And yet, standing there staring his betrayer in the face drew anger and denial from his heart. Part of him said, "You deserve whatever you get." The other part felt sorry for this man who was a skillful deceiver.

Jonathon wept out loud and shook his finger in disgust at the broken man on his deathbed. "I forgive you," finally came from his heart to his lips. He left the room.

Doug Lister didn't make it through the night.

Pastor George Cousins was overwhelmed. He sat in the clergy room engulfed in a sense of numbness. He didn't have to call anyone right away, as it was three thirty in the morning. He and those in the waiting room were told at midnight that Doug was resting and would probably make it through the night. The doctor said that he was still very critical and not expected to live. If nothing happened in the next three days, a decision would have to be made about removing the life support. George prayed that God would intervene and either bring Doug out of the coma or take him. George looked up. "The Lord gives and the Lord takes away. Blessed be the name of the Lord."

The chairman of the deacon board was called at four in the morning. He wasn't sleeping and had three other deacons and their wives in his living room praying. He told Pastor George to go home and get some rest; the deacons would make sure that everyone was informed. A Deacon placed a call to the Biggs at six o'clock while they were making breakfast. They hadn't slept all night. Maggie and Frank went home emotionally exhausted at eleven. Miguel drove them after he and Rachel returned from the airport with Jonathon. Eli walked across the patio to Rachel's parents' house and went to bed at around two after Miguel fell asleep on the couch.

Rachel was trying to be quiet in the kitchen to give Miguel a few more minutes of sleep before breakfast was ready. She was exhausted, but Jonathon suggested that they get busy early and spend the day comforting the deacons and their wives.

"They will be drained with their responsibility to comfort every family in the church. They will need us to serve them so that they can serve others. Let's do whatever is necessary to help the helpful."

Miguel promised to help in any way he could. He was going to call the pastor of a sister church at nine and arrange for people to sit with the deacons' children all day to free them up. The church had six deacons, and three had small children. So Miguel was hoping to get two helpers for each home.

Jonathon was sure that he would be asked to share at the funeral service. He didn't want to. "Doug betrayed his best friends. I'm convinced that he had something to do with Debra's murder. I can't tell the congregation what I know, and yet they are mourning a hypocrite of the worst sort."

Rachel hugged Jonathon's neck. "Then I'm going to pray that Pastor George and the deacons don't ask you to share."

"Let God handle it? Good approach. I'm with you!" In spite of all that had happened, the Biggses' marriage was clicking again, stronger and more resolute that ever.

"Breslin Kline here."

"I was trying to call Miles Masterson."

"He left his cell with me and is enroute back to Kansas City as we speak."

"Breslin, this is Eli Moore. I'm assuming that Miles left you in charge down there."

"Your assumption is correct, Mr. Moore."

"You can call me Eli. It is good to have you back, Breslin."

"You can call me Mr. Kline. How can I help you, Mr. Moore?" Breslin Kline laughed under his breath.

As much as Eli enjoyed verbally sparring with Breslin Kline, he had to move on to the important issue at hand. "I would like an update on the situation."

"We put the animal down late last night. We called in an expert butcher to cut it up as per my instructions. We want to preserve the head, spinal cord, and hide intact. We are looking for the location where a needle carrying the disease may have been inserted."

"Can't you do that without butchering the cow?" asked Eli.

"I sent the ranch manager with two thousand American dollars to the largest hospital in the area. He paid the hospital administrator that sum of money to use their MRI machine. The whole cow will not fit in the machine, so we hired the butcher to trim it down so that it would fit. We're going to take the cow and two thousand more dollars to the hospital tonight after hours, and their technicians will run the test."

"It costs four thousand dollars to run an MRI on a cow?"

"Judging from what you've lost already, it's a small sum," Breslin Kline reminded him.

"True," Eli conceded.

"I'll let you know what we find. We'll bill you for the four thousand." Breslin hung up, uncomfortable with the feelings he had toward his new-found friends. Caring and being cared for by others was a new experience for him.

<hr />

The next morning Jonathon received a call from Pastor George about the funeral. Pastor George hoped that Jonathon would understand if he wasn't asked to share. The deacons felt that he had been through a great deal of grief lately and didn't feel right about adding to it. The deacons were each going to share, and Pastor George would speak as well.

Jonathon assured Pastor George that he understood and thought that it was a good decision. He explained to Pastor George that he was relieved, as he and Rachel were both tentative about him speaking at this time.

Rachel was on Jonathon's cell phone with Bob Holcroft while Jonathon was speaking to the assistant pastor. The call was short, as the FBI investigator explained to Rachel that so far nothing unusual had turned up in relation to the Doug Lister crash. He was putting one of his men undercover at the police vehicle inspection center to keep an eye on Doug's car while it was checked over by local authorities.

"Is it necessary to check up on the cops?" Rachel asked with surprise.

"I didn't like the way they handled the crash site. I got there later after I was told that Doug would probably never regain consciousness. They had neither a perimeter set up, nor did they make any effort to examine the car before the tow truck hooked it up and dragged it up the hill." The FBI agent expected the local law enforcement people to know how to handle an accident site.

"Did you ask them to do a preliminary exam of the car?" Rachel asked.

"It was too late when I got there. They don't know what I know, and I can't tell them yet."

"Thanks, Bob. Please keep us posted." Rachel turned to Jonathon. "Nothing new from the FBI. Who were you talking to?"

"Pastor George. He hopes I understand that I'm not being asked to share at the funeral." Jonathon smiled with relief.

"That went well! Did you make sure he knew that you were good with that decision?"

"I told him that I thought that it was a good call and that I was relieved. And I thanked him for his concern for my well-being."

"He's a good man," Rachel said.

"I know, and he's trying really hard to serve others in a set of bad circumstances," Jonathon said with respect for Pastor George.

"We've been there." She put her arms around Jonathon's neck.

"What do you mean 'been there'? We're still there." Jonathon held his wife close as he breathed a sigh of relief.

⟶⇒◆⇐⟵

"Breslin Kline checking in."

"How did the MRI on the cow go?" Miles Masterson enjoyed Breslin Kline's sense of directness.

"We found something important."

"What? Breslin, your sense of suspense is going to drive me up the wall!"

"We found a puncture site and a substantial piece of broken needle."

"What do you think we can learn from the needle?" Miles was pleased with this development.

"It's not the needle that's going to give us our lead. It must have broken off on the way out. We found it lodged in the tissue between the hide and the spinal column. It created a small pocket of infection that I'm hoping still contains some of the virus serum," Breslin informed his new boss.

"If we exam the serum we can see what else they mixed with the virus." Miles was getting more curious as the conversation unfolded.

"Thereby giving us a potential lead. We paid the resident surgeon at the hospital three thousand dollars to excise the section of the animal containing the infection pocket and needle. He did very well and left them intact. I shipped them to you this morning Fed Ex in a refrigerated container. It will be delivered to Jonathon Biggs' residence within the next sixteen hours."

"Good, that gives me time to find a lab to examine the contents."

"You could call Bob Holcroft with the FBI. They probably have a local lab where they contract their work."

"Good idea. I'll do that. Thanks, Breslin. Good work."

Miles Masterson closed his cell phone, paused for a second, and then reopened it to call Bob Holcroft. He explained the situation.

"We don't have the ability or the equipment to do this." Holcroft informed him.

"We need to bring in someone from the National Veterinary Clinic in Ames, Iowa, to help conduct the test. They know how to handle mad cow disease," Miles interjected.

"Good idea. Who do you know there?" Holcroft had come to realize that Miles had contacts that no one else did.

"Tere Waters is their senior chemist. She's good. I'll see if I can fly her in tonight and have her ready to start as soon as the package shows up."

Miles Masterson closed his cell phone again and thought for a full thirty seconds about how he was going to explain this to Tere

Waters without giving away too much information. They'd met during a routine investigation ten years ago and became friends. Miles had helped her purchase the first bull for her small ranch in Ames. She had been very grateful, as Miles had arranged an exceptional price on a prize bull. He spoke to Tere about once a month just to keep the friendship going. He also made a point of spending time with her whenever he was in Ames. He had decided on his approach, reopened his cell, and punched in her speed-dial number.

"Miles! How are you?" Tere Waters liked Miles Masterson.

"I'm good, Tere. How's Toro?"

"Must you always ask about the bull first?" Tere's laughter was contagious.

"He's important to me!" Miles teased. He liked Tere Waters.

"And I'm not?" She feigned insult.

"I was going to ask about you next." Miles flirted.

"At least I'm on your list. What's up? Are you in town?" She sounded anxious to see him.

"I'm in Kansas City, and I have a huge favor to ask."

"Name it."

Miles hoped she wasn't busy. "Would you be able to fly to Kansas City tonight with your chemistry set and help me out for a few days?"

"Right now things are pretty routine around here, so I could probably shake loose for a few good dinners with you. What will I be working on?"

"You'll have to trust me on that. I can't tell you until you get here." Miles was hoping that she wouldn't ask for more information.

"That makes it hard for me to know what to bring."

"Bring your whole road kit, and that really nice blue dress you wore when we went to Malone's for dinner," Miles responded.

She was flattered. "You remembered?"

"Of course! A woman named Maggie will be calling you with travel information and to tell you how to get to the private jet terminal."

"Private jet? Wow! You're going big!" Tere Waters wondered what could be so important that Miles would send a private jet.

"You're going Biggs—as in Biggs International's corporate jet. Maggie will call you within the hour."

"See you soon, Miles." Tere had been following the mad cow situation at Biggs International on the news. When she first heard about his children, she had wondered if the two situations were linked.

Miles ended the call and dialed another number.

"Jonathon, I need a favor. I want to borrow your jet tonight."

Chapter Three

Miguel Sameros had heard back from his father about their proposal to purchase Biggs European Manufacturing Division. The Sameros Ranch attorneys were busy drawing up the papers. Eli had the Biggs team of lawyers working on their end. Both parties wanted to expedite the agreement. Biggs stock began to drop again, but Jonathon and Eli showed little concern. They were more interested in solving what they now called "The Mad Cow Mystery."

The package was delivered to Jonathon twelve hours after it was sent. Jonathon hand carried the refrigerated container holding the infected portion of the Argentinean cow to a small warehouse he owned on the west side of the city. He leased the warehouse to Biggs International for storing paper documents. The warehouse had a temperature control system to keep the documents from deteriorating. He had also equipped it with a state-of-the-art computer system used for scanning each document and filing them for easy access through the computer system. The warehouse was operated by two Biggs employees whom Jonathon trusted. Jonathon kept an office in the building that he used to get away from the busyness at Biggs International headquarters when he needed time to think and plan. It was the perfect place to set up a small lab without attracting any attention. Jonathon pressed the number seven on his speed dial

"Miles?"

"Good morning, Jonathon. Has our package arrived?"

"Yes, I'm heading to the warehouse right now," Jonathon said as he placed the cooler in the backseat of his car.

"Give me directions, and we'll meet you there." Miles was anxious to get started.

"I'll just pick you up on the way. Is Dr. Waters with you?"

"Her room is one floor below mine, but she just went to breakfast with Rachel. I think Rachel is screening her." Miles laughed.

"You already did that. She's safe," Jonathon responded.

"I think Rachel is screening her... romantically." Miles chuckled.

"Miles, that's great! I didn't realize that you were interested in someone." The surprise was evident in Jonathon's voice.

"I'm interested, but Rachel is going to find out if Tere's interested in me."

"I'll call Rachel and have her deliver you both to the warehouse."

"Would you mind picking me up and having Rachel bring Tere separately?" Miles was suddenly sheepish.

"I guess I could do that. Why?"

"I'd like to talk to you about marriage. You and Rachel have a great one, and I'd like to pick you brain without Tere around." Miles sounded nervous.

"Does she know that you're thinking about marriage?" Jonathon was the one laughing now.

"No, I'm pretty sure she likes me, but I'm not sure how much. I think she's the one for me, and I don't want to mess it up." The usually confident Miles Masterson sounded very unsure of himself.

"I'll pick you up out front in ten minutes. We'll take the long way to the warehouse. I'll call Rachel and have her bring Tere out in a couple of hours."

"Thanks, Jonathon."

"No sweat." Jonathon was amused at Miles' discomfort with the subject of marriage.

When Rachel showed up with Tere Waters two hours later,

she winked at Jonathon. He smiled. They were match making in the middle of the greatest crisis of their lives. It was a pleasant distraction. Dr. Waters had two rolling metal cases full of equipment. Jonathon and Rachel left her alone with Miles to set up and discuss the situation at hand. Back in Jonathon's private office, they hugged each other and laughed out loud.

Rachel exclaimed, "Jonathon, they are perfect for each other!"

"Miles is acting like a junior high boy with a lifelong crush!"

—————

"Two of our people have checked in so far. The Biggs jet picked up a Dr. Tere Waters from the Ames Clinic last night and took her to KC. Miles Masterson met her at the airport, and Rachel Biggs is having breakfast with her right now." Ron Milliken was reporting to the Cleric. "Breslin Kline quit the USDA to work for Bills and Masterson. He's in Argentina heading up the investigation there. He shipped a package out to Jonathon Biggs last night by Federal Express. I don't know what's in it yet."

"Good, they're moving along in the investigation. Soon they'll discover our serum supplier."

"That's not good," Ron worried out loud.

"Yes, it is. When they discover him, he will be dead."

"That will create suspicion of a conspiracy."

"Exactly." The Cleric loved the cat and mouse game when he was the cat.

—————

Eli Moore had just negotiated his first deal as president of Biggs International. He had rescued the Argentina cattle deal that was pending. The buyer had agreed to go ahead with the purchase under more stringent testing parameters. The final sale would not be consummated or made public until ninety days after the ranch was declared clear of mad cow disease. When the buyer was told that Breslin Kline was in charge of the investigation, the deal was rescued. Kline was respected all over the world for his skills and integrity. Eli was pleased with the deal, as was Jonathon.

Maggie was working with Eli's administrative assistant, Connie, to get her up to speed on the various projects that Jonathon had been working on. Maggie seemed amiable about moving into the smaller office area and staying on as Jonathon's assistant. She was given a substantial increase in pay, as she was now the administrative assistant to the chief executive officer. She had asked for a few days off, as she had been working non-stop and needed to spend some time with her husband, Frank.

"When this is all over, you ought to give Maggie a bonus," Rachel had told Jonathon.

"We could send her and Frank on a trip to Hawaii." Jonathon loved being generous to people who worked hard.

⟹➤◄⟸

"This virus serum did not come from Iowa," stated Tere Waters. "It is either from Britain or Canada or both. There is no way to tell. But it is definitely Bovine encephalitis."

"What about the needle fragment?"

"I don't know, Miles. It could have been purchased anywhere. It's very stiff and larger than they needed to get the job done. We sedate the rats when we inject the virus into them at the lab. We also use a local numbing agent first, so the animal doesn't feel it when the serum is injected."

"Is it possible that this cow was sedated?"

"I doubt it. They probably pinched a fold of the skin hoping that the animal wouldn't notice until the needle came out. The cow probably moved as they were injecting the virus and the technician, perpetrator, bad guy, or whatever you want to call him withdrew the needle too quickly and broke it off just under the hide. A lighter needle would have bent without breaking."

"I don't understand why they would use the wrong needle. They successfully injected six other cows."

"Maybe they used a different person to do this one. Or maybe there were two people involved in the first six and only one person on the last cow," Tere responded.

"Good thinking! Smart, beautiful, and a great personality—Tere, you have it all!" Miles said brightly, hoping for a positive response.

"Miles, that was a nice compliment." Tere was blushing and fumbling with her instruments.

"I meant every word of it." Miles had walked toward her and was speaking softly in spite of his anxiety.

Tere reached out, took his hand, squeezed it, and let it go. "Thank you."

"Okay, let's talk about dinner." Miles' words didn't come out right. "I mean, let's talk over dinner."

"That would be nice, Miles. For now it might be good to explain our findings to Jonathon." Tere was getting back on track.

"Right! Good idea! Of course!" Miles punched the intercom button and spoke as professionally as he could. "Jonathon, we've come to some conclusions. Would you join us, please?"

After hearing Tere Waters' theories, Jonathon asked Miles about the next step in the investigation.

"We need to check out each ranch hand that has left each ranch. We will have to use photo identification." Miles was out of his flirtation mode and into his analytical mode. "Let's assume that they used the same person for the first six injections. Let's also assume that he worked on each ranch under a different name. Let's add the idea that there may have been two people on the first six jobs and that the Argentina job was done by only one of them."

"We have photo-identification cards on all of our employees," Jonathon interjected.

"Do you have them on you central computer network?" Miles asked.

"Only for people who work at headquarters. The ranches make their own ID cards." Jonathon made a mental note to have all ranch employees in the main computer in the future.

"Would they have a record of each employee's picture?"

"Yes, they take a photo and use the computer to make the card. I'm sure the pictures are still available."

"The ranches wouldn't share photos?" Miles was surprised at the lack of security involved in the ranches' hiring procedures.

"No," Jonathon spoke softly. "Until now, we haven't had to worry about sabotage."

"Jonathon, I'll need the rest of the day to get the ball rolling on this. Would you mind if I used your office here to make some phone calls?" Miles requested.

"No problem, Miles. Our people have already been told to give you whatever you need."

"It looks like Miles will be busy for lunch. So why don't we take Tere out and then come back and help her pack the equipment?" Rachel offered.

"Lunch sounds great." Tere looked seriously at Jonathon. "But let's not pack up just yet. I think you're going to need me for a few more days."

Jonathon caught Tere's look and asked the obvious question, "There's more?"

"Yes, there are traces of human blood on the cow's hide. I think the 'shooter' may have stabbed himself accidentally when the needle broke off."

"Could he get mad cow disease from stabbing himself with the needle?" Miles was intensely curious.

"We'll find out when you find him." Tere Waters slipped into her jacket and waved to Miles as she followed the Biggs to their car.

Chapter Four

"I want you to bleed some of the propane out of this tank, take it back to the lab, and test it," the fire inspector ordered.

"I don't know what good that will do, Greg; we've examined the whole house three times and found nothing."

"We know that the explosion was caused by a propane leak into the house. Any clues seem to have been destroyed when the place blew up." Inspector Greg Albright was sure that the Biggs children were murdered. He was determined to prove it.

"All we can say is that it appears to be the contractor's or the inspector's error. The dangerous gas detectors were not installed before the Biggs received their occupancy permit," his assistant protested.

"There is no code that requires the contractor or owner to have gas detectors, only fire detectors. The inspector is not liable, and the only thing that the contractor is in trouble for is not completing some of the details before occupancy. They do that all the time." Inspector Albright was becoming impatient with the conversation. He had a hunch and wanted his assistant to cooperate while he played it out.

"Has Jonathon Biggs filed a negligence suit against the contractor?"

"No, Biggs was anxious to move in before his daughter's birthday. They were planning a big party in their new house. Besides, Biggs is convinced that someone did this intentionally and that it is part of the stuff going on at his ranches." The conviction in Inspector Albright's voice was obvious to his assistant.

"What do you think, Greg?"

"I agree with him. How many new home explosions involving propane have we had?"

"None that I know of."

"Right, almost always it's older homes with outdated heating systems. Often the home owner tries to fix a gas line himself."

"Or tries to save money by reusing an old flex line. But they almost always smell it and call the gas company to check it out." The assistant was going along with the inspector's theory.

"So why didn't the Biggses smell the propane?"

"There are a lot of different smells in a new house." The assistant shrugged.

"But propane really stinks!" Greg was emphatic. "They would have known if they had smelled it."

The technician opened the valve on the propane tank and watched the level gage on the test container he had connected to the tank. "So we're testing for the chemical that causes the odor?"

"Yes, propane is odorless, so they put the smell in at the treatment plant. I'm curious about whether or not this propane smells." Inspector Albright was certain that there would be no smell.

The technician shut the valve when the test container was full. He sniffed around the fittings as he disconnected the main tank from the test container. "I can tell you right now that there is no smell in this tank of propane. I didn't smell anything in this line when I disconnected it. There is always a small amount of residue in the line." He knew his superior was right.

"Let's take it to the lab to make sure." Inspector Greg Albright reached for his cell phone.

<hr>

"Bob Holcroft, FBI." Holcroft listened for a moment. "I'll meet you there in an hour."

Curiosity coursed through Bob Holcroft's mind. He was still investigating the Biggs case, but every lead washed out. Whoever was conspiring against Jonathon Biggs was very good at covering his tracks. Debra Moore's murder was still unsolved and probably never would be. The local police wanted to bring Eli back in, but Holcroft was holding them off. The death of Pastor Doug Lister was not an accident, even though it appeared to be. Holcroft was still waiting for the car to be examined. When he arrived at the Biggses' home site, Fire Inspector Greg Albright was waiting for him.

"I know how the house exploded," Albright said as Holcroft unfolded his large frame from the front seat of the car.

"I hope we get a solid lead out of this. This case is like trying to wrestle an octopus. I can't get all the tentacles under control at the same time," Holcroft said hopefully.

"It was the propane. When propane is refined, the manufacturer puts an odorous gas with it. You see, propane is odorless, so if it leaks, you can't smell the danger. The odor lets you know that there's a leak. There is no odor in this propane. I sent a container of it to the lab to confirm, but I know I'm right. This was right under our noses and we didn't see it." Greg Albright was excited about his discovery.

Holcroft's curiosity had peaked. "You didn't find any evidence of a leaking pipe."

"They could have left a fitting loose. The basement would have filled with gas, and when the water heater ignited, it would have blown up, destroying the evidence."

"How could they time it to destroy the whole family?" Holcroft was impressed with the fire inspector's theory.

"The family was there all afternoon, so the timing didn't have to be perfect."

"Greg, can you stop the container from getting to the lab?"

"Why would I do that?" Albright was surprised at Holcroft's request.

"I'd like to keep this as quiet as possible. I need time to trace the propane to the source and find the person who loaded the truck and the driver."

"There's no company name on the tank," Greg offered.

"Good, I'll start there." Holcroft looked directly at Greg Albright. "I need you to get that storage container and keep anyone who knows about this quiet. I want to talk to the people involved, before they turn up dead," he said somberly.

"I'll take care of it. All local propane is prepared and loaded at United Gas Company. They're located on the south side of the city." Albright got the point.

"Thanks, Greg, I'll be in touch." Holcroft began to hurry away.

"Hold it, Bob, don't you want the rest of the story?" Greg held up a small piece of cloth.

"There's more? This is going to be a good day!" Holcroft was getting excited about the possibility of a solid lead.

Greg showed Holcroft what once was a bath towel. It had been burned and was now the size of a small handkerchief. It was rolled up tightly. Greg offered an explanation. "I found this over there under some rubble. Nothing to be suspicious about on the surface, but it was lying on top of a metal-door threshold. I think that someone was in the house earlier in the day setting up the explosion. I suspect that he rolled this towel up and tucked it under the basement door to seal the gas in the basement. That's why the explosion was so intense. Very little gas had seeped out of the basement to the upper level. When the door blew off, the towel stuck to the threshold." Albright handed the remains of the towel to Holcroft with an air of satisfaction.

"If what you're saying is a possibility to be considered, then how did the perpetrator get out of the basement after placing the towel?" Holcroft was skeptical. "The basement was not a walk-out."

Greg pointed to a large opening in the foundation. "But there is a safety egress on the west side." There had been a window built in as an escape route in case of a fire.

"Okay, I'll give it some thought. Thanks for your help, Greg."

Holcroft grunted, not sure what to think but hoping for the best.

"See ya." They both walked to their vehicles and drove off, Greg to retrieve the container and Bob to United Gas Company.

⟶►●◄⟵

Miles Masterson decided to check in with Bob Holcroft. When he called, Bob was on his way to United Gas Company to find out who drove the propane truck that delivered to the Biggses' new home. He also wanted to talk to the technician responsible for putting the chemical percaptin into the propane. Percaptin was mixed with the propane to cause an unpleasant odor that the home owner could smell to know that there was a leak in the system. Percaptin had saved many lives, as propane is an odorless gas. There was no percaptin in the propane that had exploded in the Biggs house.

Holcroft explained the situation to Miles, who asked him not to go directly to United Gas Company.

"Do you have time to stop by the warehouse? I'd like to show you Dr. Waters' findings from the Argentina cow. I think we need to have a strategy session."

Holcroft turned right instead of left and arrived at the warehouse fifteen minutes later. Miles was alone in the lab, as the Biggses had taken Tere Waters out for lunch. Miles brought Holcroft up to date on the lab findings and told him that the perpetrator's blood was on the needle. "Somehow in the process he cut himself with the needle. He may have some of the serum in his body right now. We're not sure, but we have to find him immediately."

Holcroft listened intently. "We have leads in two directions. If we get something good out of the propane people, maybe we can tie it to the mad cow conspiracy. The Argentina cow could produce some information, and the propane company could give us more info. We have to move quickly and decisively."

"Whoever is at the top of this conspiracy is willing to kill his own people to impede our investigation," Miles said, shaking his head with disgust.

"Debra Moore was killed by a professional, and I suspect that Doug and Millie Lister were also. People are expendable to the conspirators. I think they'll kill anyone that they think we might get to." Holcroft was concerned for the lives of future witnesses.

"The FBI walking into United Gas looking for one of their drivers and a technician may cause the deaths of those individuals before we ever get to talk to them. I have an idea!" Miles' voice gained intensity.

"I'm listening." Holcroft leaned against the desk and folded his arms.

"Let's break in tonight and look through their records. When we find out who the driver and technician are, we'll go get them at the same time." Miles was formulating the plan as he was talking.

"You mean send two teams to pick them up simultaneously?"

"Right." Miles' mind was flooding with the pieces of a plan.

Holcroft was concerned about the need for secrecy. "Where do we take them?"

"I'm not sure that you should know." Miles smiled at the FBI Agent.

"Why not?"

"Bob, it's a break in!" Miles was surprised that Holcroft had missed the obvious.

Holcroft slapped himself on the forehead. "I'm FBI; I can't do that!"

"I can. And I can stash them in a safe place."

"I want to interrogate them myself." Holcroft was insistent.

"I'll call you and tell you where to find them."

"We didn't have this conversation," Holcroft whispered.

"What conversation?" Miles mocked with a chuckle.

"Can we start over?" Holcroft laughed.

"Sure. Hello, Bob."

"Hello, Miles. Have you taken any action toward finding the perpetrator from the Argentina ranch?"

Miles explained that they were compiling a list of people's photos who had hired onto the Biggs ranches in the past six months. He asked Bob Holcroft to handle this part of the investigation discreetly.

One hour later, Miles was driving around with Jonathon Biggs talking about his next move with Dr. Tere Waters. "Jonathon, want to have some fun?"

"Rachel and I are not going out with you and Tere tonight." Jonathon laughed. "You have to take her out by yourself."

"I know. How would you like to go on a break-in with me? I'm going to slip into the United Gas Company tonight and go through their employee files. I want to find out who handled the propane that went to your house."

"What if we get caught?" Jonathon was astounded at his friend's invitation.

"I haven't been caught yet, and I've been doing this for a long time," Miles responded
confidently.

"What if they have an alarm system?" Fear was catching the words in Jonathon's throat.

"I'm sure they do. Let's go see the setup, then you can decide."

Miles drove by United Gas Company from each direction. He also drove down the road behind their compound. The compound was surrounded by a twelve-foot-high cyclone fence with barbed wire at the top. There were two guard shacks; one at the front of the compound and the other at the back. As they pulled into the parking lot to get a closer look, Miles said, "This is perfect."

The office building was not in the compound. It was an old metal building standing about fifty yards away. The building was close to the road with the parking lot behind. As Miles turned the car around to leave the lot, he commented on the two doors. One was marked *Employees Only* and the other said *Office*. "The alarm control pad is probably just inside the employee entrance. It probably has a four-digit code to disarm it."

Jonathon's anxiety was obvious. "How do we know what the four numbers are?"

"By tonight, I'll have a seven-digit master code to disarm their system." Miles spoke softly, hoping to calm Jonathon's fears.

"How will you get that?" Jonathon was sure he didn't want to know immediately after he asked the question.

"There are only four alarm companies in this area. The largest is Systematic Protection. I will have each of their master codes by tonight. My guess is that they use Systematic. I'm sure they'll have a sticker on the window that names the company."

"So we'll look at the sticker before we open the door...."

"And we'll use the appropriate code," Miles assured him.

"How will we get the door opened?"

"Jonathon, relax." Miles was laughing at Jonathon's naiveté. "I'll get the door opened without being noticed. Are you in?"

"I've never done anything like this before. It goes completely against my grain."

"Jonathon, someone wants to destroy you. They have killed your family and Eli's wife. Your minister was tangled up in this somehow, and now he's dead. We need this information to keep others from being killed. I'll pick you up at ten thirty. Wear black."

"Okay." Jonathon was used to being the leader not a follower.

Chapter Five

The late June night was sticky with humidity. The clouds were low in the sky, masking the glow of the moon.

Jonathon Biggs was dressed completely in black.

"You look good," Miles commented.

"Miles, I still don't feel comfortable about this."

"Jonathon," explained Miles, "during a war, there are covert operations going on all the time. You are at war. Someone wants to destroy you and everything around you. We are going on a covert mission to gain information about your enemy."

"You're right. What do you want me to do?" Jonathon was suddenly feeling better about the break in.

Miles handed him a long, police-style flashlight. "Hold the flashlight and watch for trouble."

Miles parked the banged up black compact car they were driving in the parking lot of an auto body shop next to United Gas Company. He pulled in between two cars left out for the night. The men slipped out of the car and kept a low profile as they ran to the employee entrance at United Gas. Jonathon spotted the sticker on the window that said *Protected by Fast-Alert Alarm Systems.*

"That's a really old company. I don't even have that on my master list." Miles was undisturbed by the discovery.

"What do we do now?" asked Jonathon furtively.

"I doubt that they have this alarm company anymore. We'll

look at the key pad when we get inside and take care of it." Miles took out two tools and unlocked the door with ease. "You look to the left for the keypad; I'll take the right," he whispered.

"It's here," whispered Jonathon, "and it says *Fast Alert.*"

"Let me have a look." Miles closed the door and stepped in next to Jonathon. "This alarm isn't even armed. All the indicator lights are off. Someone probably disconnected it years ago. We're clear. Let's find their files."

They proceeded down the hall toward the offices when Miles noticed a large, white board on the wall. It said *Schedule* at the top and was divided into sections. One section contained the day of the week, another the date. Also included were the names of the technicians on duty and the companies to whom the product was to be delivered. Next to the deliveries was a column that said *Will P/U* and listed the propane companies that would pick up at the United Gas facility.

"This is great!" Miles whispered as he looked over the white board. "We'll look up the companies that pick up their propane here. Their files will probably give us the dates and maybe the name of the driver and technician too."

"There are a bunch of filing cabinets in this office," Jonathon whispered as loudly as he could without talking. "Give me some names."

Miles was writing down the other names. "Let's try Hostler Gas. They seem to do more pickups than the others."

Jonathon began with the top drawer of the first cabinet on his left. When he opened the bottom drawer of the third cabinet, he found the Hostler Gas file. "No pickups on the date of the explosion or the day before. The technician signs off after the propane is loaded."

Miles gave Jonathon another name. As Jonathon pulled the files, Miles looked through each one for the appropriate information. After an hour, they found nothing.

"Let's look in the client files and see if we can find something," Miles suggested.

Jonathon began opening the other cabinets one drawer at a time and reciting the labels on each file. "Direct deliveries."

"Stop there! Let's look at that one." Jonathon pulled the file and handed it to Miles.

"Bingo! What was the date your propane was delivered?"

"March 16."

Miles began fingering through the file, looking for the date. He set the open folder on the desk. "Here's the paperwork on all the direct deliveries for March 16. None of them are routed to your house."

"What if someone got rid of the paperwork? My delivery was in the morning, so I assume the propane was loaded early the same day. Are there times listed on the paperwork?"

"Here's a load at seven. The next one was at eight then eight thirty… then eight fifty and so on—all morning. It looks like they loaded steady all morning. Wait a minute." Miles looked for details on each worksheet. "All of these trucks were loaded by the same technician at Loading Area 2. Let's go talk to this Alvin Worley and see what else he did between seven and eight o'clock on March 16."

Miles made a few quick notations into his Blackberry, while Jonathon replaced the files and set the room back the way it was before their visit. The men slipped out the employee door and made their way back to the car.

<hr />

At six o'clock the next morning, Alvin Worley walked out of his house toward the detached garage in his back yard. He liked this time of day, because everything was peaceful. The rush of life hadn't started yet. He always arrived at United Gas Company thirty minutes before his shift began. He liked to take his time in the morning making sure that everything was ready, before the trucks started coming in. Dealing with propane was dangerous, and he was a careful man. Alvin entered the side door of his garage and was greeted by Miles Masterson. Miles greeted him and introduced himself as a private investigator that needed valuable information in a murder investigation. He displayed his credentials for Alvin to inspect while he told him about the Jonathon Biggs explosion. Miles wasn't in the habit of giving out information with names attached but knew that he would have to gain Alvin's trust to procure the information he needed. He also knew that he was putting the man's life in danger by talking to him. He explained this to Alvin.

Alvin Worley was surprisingly calm. "Have you talked to my boss yet?"

"No, we don't know who is involved at this point," Miles answered. "We decided to start with the technician, you, and go from there."

Alvin's response was curt but calm. "Okay, ask your questions."

"Can you tell me about the morning of March 16? Was your routine changed?"

"We schedule everyone ahead of time, so the mornings are very predictable. Later in the day—especially in the winter—we load trucks for delivery companies that have run out of propane."

Miles handed him two pieces of paper. "These are the scheduled pickups for March 16. Do you remember anything unusual about that day?"

Alvin examined the documents and handed them back. "Yes, I remember that day very well. We began loading at seven as usual. I stay at the loading bays all day to make sure that there are no problems. I even eat my lunch out there. My boss, Bill Elkhart, called me into the office a little after seven thirty, so I left the area and went to his office. It wasn't a problem, because we had no one scheduled at that time. One of our trucks pulled up with a new driver, and I told him to park outside the bay and wait for me. I went in and talked to Bill. He said that it was time to give me an evaluation. He asked me how I liked my job and stuff like that. I told him I was happy here, and he told me that they were happy with me. He gave me an *Excellent* rating on my evaluation and a dollar an hour raise. I was pretty excited; a dollar an hour is a really big increase for United Gas. He asked me if I wanted to call my wife and tell her. I used his office phone and called her. She was excited too. I thanked Bill and went back to work."

"How long did your meeting take?" Miles asked.

"Exactly twenty minutes."

"Did you notice anything different when you returned to your work area?"

"No, I was back in plenty of time to load the eight o'clock truck. The new driver hadn't waited. His truck was gone. He was probably a trainee. They don't let them deliver product for the first two weeks, until they go through safety training and learn their routes."

"Alvin, do you remember what the new driver looked like?"

"Yeah, he walked right up to me. He was dressed in the company coveralls and cap. He was taller than me, probably about your height. Looked to be in good shape—the coveralls were a little small. He had a deep voice like a radio announcer—dark hair, mustache, dark complexion—that's about it."

"If I brought in an artist, could you describe him?" Miles asked anxiously. This could be the break they were hoping for.

Alvin looked at his watch and moved around Miles toward the driver's door of his car. "I could try. Hey, I have to go to work now."

"Can you call in sick today? I'll pay you for your time." Miles didn't want to appear demanding. Alvin had been calm so far, and Miles didn't want that to change.

Alvin shrugged. "I guess so. I have plenty of sick days left this year."

"Alvin, do you have a cell phone?"

"Sure."

"Use it to call work. Then we'll go see the FBI. You are a great help, and I thank you."

Miles' request made Alvin nervous, but he made the call to work and followed Miles to his car out on the street.

⟶⟶◆⟵⟵

Bob Holcroft met Miles Masterson and Alvin Worley in the small FBI office downtown. Miles and Alvin parked in the alley and came in the back door. They spent two hours with the FBI artist coming up with a sketch.

"That's him!" exclaimed Alvin.

"Can we remove the hat?" asked Holcroft

"Let's drop the mustache first." The artist manipulated the computer, and the mustache disappeared.

"He looks familiar to me." Miles spoke in the hushed tones of someone who wasn't quite sure.

"He looks familiar to you?" Holcroft asked.

"Yes, can we take off the hat and look at different hair styles?"

"No problem." The artist began to set up the necessary changes in the program.

"Mr. Worley, does this man look at all familiar to you?"

"I saw him that day at work, and he hasn't been around on my shift since," Alvin answered Holcroft's question directly.

"We're going to change the top of his head and hair style now. I want you to think hard about whether you've seen this man around the office or the compound. Try and picture him not dressed in coveralls but in a business suit or casually dressed," Holcroft instructed the propane technician.

"Okay, but I'm pretty much stuck out at the loading bays all day." Alvin was sure that he'd told them all he knew about the man in the too short coveralls.

"Maybe you've seen him at the mall or on the street or somewhere other than work. Try to think if you've seen him anywhere," Holcroft pressed.

The artist showed them different head shapes and hairstyles for the next hour. He kept track of the ones they thought had possibilities.

"That's ..." Miles blurted out. "I know who he is now. Put back the mustache."

The artist did as requested

"Mr. Worley, have you ever seen this man?" Bob Holcroft gave Miles a hand gesture to silence him.

"He's the man I saw at the loading bay, only he had a hat on," Alvin insisted.

"Are you sure?" Holcroft asked.

"Yes, like I said, he walked right up to me."

"If I put you in a room with a hundred men in coveralls with hats on, could you find this guy?"

"For sure," Alvin Worley said calmly and with confidence.

Holcroft turned to his partner. "Would you please take Mr. Worley home? Mr. Worley, thank you for your help. You are to tell no one about what we did here today. Do you understand?"

"Yes, sir, I understand."

When Alvin Worley was gone, Bob Holcroft turned his attention to Miles Masterson. "What was that about? You could have influenced him to agree with you whether he saw that man or not." He was angry at Miles' unprofessional behavior.

"I know, Bob, and I'm sorry. But I know this guy, and he's very close to Jonathon Biggs." Miles pointed at the pictures of the suspect.

"Who is he?" Surprised etched Holcroft's features.

"I'll let Jonathon tell you. Let's go to his private office." Miles was moving as he spoke, anxious to see Jonathon's response to the sketches.

Holcroft had the artist print four versions of the sketch. They arrived at Jonathon's warehouse within the hour. Jonathon came in ten minutes later.

"Let me handle the questioning from here," Bob instructed Miles. "I'll have to write a report on this, and it would look bad for me if you were anything more than an observer."

"Got it." Miles knew the rules under which Holcroft operated and didn't want to do anything to jeopardize his credibility.

"Jonathon, I'm going to show you four sketches. Tell me if you recognize this man." Holcroft produced the first sketch with the man wearing the cap and mustache.

"Yes, I know this man." Jonathon tapped the sketch nervously with his index finger.

"How about this man?" Holcroft lay down the second sketch.

"Yes, same man without the mustache." Jonathon was now leaning on the table, his weight supported by his arms.

"How about this one?" Bob Holcroft put the third sketch next to the second.

"Same man, no cap." Jonathon's face was bright red. As he stood up, he clenched his right fist and slammed it into his opened left hand.

Holcroft quickly set the fourth sketch on the table.

Jonathon Biggs looked directly at Miles Masterson. "It's Ron Milliken," they said together.

<hr />

"Alvin Worley didn't go to work today," the Administrator reported.

"Where did he go?" retorted the Cleric.

"We don't know; we weren't watching him." The Administrator winced.

"Do you think that he can identify Milliken?" There was a hard edge to the question.

"I seriously doubt it. He was in Bill Elkhart's office when Milliken was there."

"They've discovered the propane?" The Cleric was putting the pieces together as they spoke.

"Yes, I'm sure that they have." The Administrator was calm.

"Let's make some arrangements, and then we'll call Ron Milliken."

The Cleric realized that Jonathon Biggs' team was stronger than he expected. He decided to take them all down after Jonathon was destroyed. One by one he would break them. The more people he could destroy, the better.

Chapter Six

Jonathon Oliver Biggs was pacing the floor back in his living room. Rachel sat on the couch crying softly.

"How could he be involved in this? We've known him for years." She began to sob.

"This is betrayal at its worst! We need to confront him and get as much information as possible. He's like.... He's like Judas!" Jonathon started for the sliding door that led to the pool. Rachel stepped in front of him as he began to open the door.

"Jonathon, you're not going back there. Your days sitting next to the pool depressed are over." Rachel was blunt and direct.

"Rachel, this keeps getting worse as we go along. The people involved in trying to destroy us are our friends. We've trusted them. Pastor Doug and Millie shared so much of our lives. Now Ron, one of our most trusted friends.... Is there anyone we can still trust?"

"Yes, Miles is here and will be even after this is over." She pointed to Miles sitting on the couch.

He rose and walked up next to Jonathon. "I'm here to stay."

"And don't forget your newest friend, a skeptic won over!" Breslin Kline left the stool at the kitchen counter and approached the group as he spoke.

"And most of all, Jonathon," Rachel spoke softly as she put her arms around her husband's neck, "you can trust God."

"Rachel..." Jonathon looked at her in astonishment.

"I know that I've been mad at Him. I haven't wanted anything to do with God, because of the pain we've been through. This past week, for some reason, I've been watching and praying. Not for God to solve anything or even to make sense of this for me; but for Him to give me some sense of peace and stability inside. I have a long way to go, but I'm experiencing some relief and extra strength."

Jonathon closed the door and turned to embrace his friends.

"Change of plans, Ron." The Cleric's Administrator explained the situation at United Gas Company.

"What do you want me to do?" Ron felt fear inside that he had never experienced before.

"We've arranged for you to speak at a few of the major corporations in Europe." The Administrator spoke with his usual calm.

"When?" Ron was trying to control his voice to keep the fear from spilling out.

"You'll fly to Heathrow today and Frankfurt tomorrow. I'll contact you at the hotel tomorrow evening with your itinerary."

"Do you think they suspect me?" Ron Milliken was thinking about Debra Moore and the Listers. He knew that he was being sent to meet his death.

"No, but we're being careful. We want to keep you out of harm's way." The Administrator said the words, but Ron didn't believe him.

"Thank you."

"You're a good friend, Ron. I'll talk with you tomorrow in Frankfurt."

The phone went dead.

"We can't find Ron Milliken." Bob Holcroft was at Jonathon's private office talking to Miles Masterson and Breslin Kline. "He was supposed to be on a flight to Seattle to speak at the Seattle's Best Coffee corporate convention. He never boarded the plane. We checked with the people at Seattle's Best, and they said that his agent called and cancelled this afternoon. His agent said that a secretary had made a mistake on Ron's calendar and booked him twice for the same dates. Ron's agent is unavailable right now." Bob Holcroft's cell phone rang, and he stepped out of the room to take the call. When he returned five minutes later, he was visibly upset.

"Ron Milliken is on a flight to Heathrow Airport in London. The best we can do now is to have one of our agents in England follow him and see what comes up."

"That may not be a bad thing," said Breslin Kline. "Maybe, he'll lead us to the person who is holding all the strings."

"I hope so. It's the only play we have right now," Miles said.

"I received your text message," she said anxiously.

"You are alone?" he clarified.

"Yes, completely."

"Is your phone secure?"

"You gave it to me! Of course it is." Every time she talked to the Cleric he asked her the same questions.

"Good. It is time to take out Rachel Biggs," he informed her.

"Are you sending someone?"

"No, you will take care of it," he commanded.

"Is it supposed to be another accident?" She wanted to do it right.

"No, I want it to look like murder. I want Jonathon Biggs to have a picture of his wife's bloody dead body in his mind forever."

"Do you have a place in mind?" she asked.

"Their living room. I want him to know that we can get close to him whenever we want to."

"It may take a few days to plan." She felt a sense of pressure and anticipation at the same time.

"Make sure that they know it was you." The Cleric would change her identity immediately after the assignment was completed.

"I'll call you when it's over." She wanted to affirm his trusting her with this mission.

"No, I'll call you after I hear about it on the news."

<hr />

Breslin Kline had copies of all the employee identification cards from each of Biggs' six ranches. He and Tere Waters were looking them over when Miles came into the room.

"Find anything yet?" he asked expectantly.

"No. We're sorting them out by the dates they were hired and the dates they quit," Breslin informed him.

"This doesn't look like it's going to produce any of our hoped-for results." Tere had decided to stay awhile to help out and to spend more time with Miles.

"I think we should start with the last ranch and check out the employees who left within two weeks of the time we estimate the injections occurred." Breslin was trying to sound convincing, even though he knew that this approach was a long shot.

"Okay, maybe we'll get lucky and find the guy who poked himself with the needle. Right now, we have to try anything we can think of." Miles was anxious to find anything that would move the investigation along.

Breslin Kline began to review where they were in the investigation. "We know that the Biggs home explosion was intentional and that his children were murdered in a well-planned manner. We should continue to pursue the propane company management to see if there are any more leads.

"We are certain that the mad cow disease serum was injected into one animal at each of the seven ranches. Tere has estimated the injection dates as closely as possible. She has also determined that the serum could not have come from Ames, Iowa, but could be from either Britain or Canada. Our best guess is Canada, as it would be easy to bring it across that border undetected," Breslin continued.

Breslin stood and began walking in a large circle around the room. "There is a connection between the home explosion and the mad cow incidents," he continued. "That connection is the destruction of Jonathon Biggs. The person planning Jonathon's demise obviously wants him to suffer immeasurable emotional pain, as well as financial loss on his way down."

"Debra Moore, Eli's wife, was somehow involved in this with Pastor Doug Lister and maybe his wife as well. Debra was murdered by a professional. Doug and Millie died of injuries in an auto accident, which I believe was professionally orchestrated. They were probably conduits of information to the head of this disaster crew. Debra was trying to help Biggs fail financially. All three of these people were murdered for their efforts."

Breslin stopped across the room from Miles and addressed him directly, "We now have a suspect in Ron Milliken, who is presently enroute to Britain then on to who knows where. We hope that by tailing him we can discover something useful. It might behoove us to kidnap him, before his superior has him killed as he did the others. Waiting and following him doesn't seem to be a good idea to me," Breslin concluded by crossing his arms and maintaining eye contact with Miles.

Miles stepped close to Breslin. "How would you kidnap Ron Milliken? The FBI is following him, so we would have to avoid them."

"I would take him in his hotel room early in the morning and send out a decoy for the FBI to follow to the airport. The decoy would change clothes and slip away unnoticed." Breslin made it sound easy.

"What would you do with Milliken?" Miles continued the inquiry.

"I would take him into another room in the same hotel and confront him with what we know. I would remind him that his boss is in the habit of killing people after their usefulness has been exhausted. I suspect that he's very high on the hit list. Maybe he'll give us something."

"What if he doesn't talk?" Miles was very interested in Breslin Kline's proposition.

"I would hold him—until he missed his next appointment—and turn him loose." Breslin cracked a mischievous smile.

"Why?" Miles became more intrigued with each question he asked.

"Because missing his appointment disrupts the plans of his leader. The leader will decide that Milliken is disposable and will act quickly to get rid of him. Whoever is at the top of this doesn't need any loose ends left alive."

"So then we would give up on Ron Milliken?"

"Oh no! We would watch to see who shows up to kill him, thus picking up another lead," Breslin said triumphantly.

"Very good." Miles was impressed. "If I leave immediately, I can be in his hotel room before he wakes up in the morning."

"Two quick questions for you, Miles. Can you find out where he is staying? And do you have resource people in London to help you?"

"The answer to both questions is *yes!*" Miles wrote three phone numbers on a sheet of paper and handed it to Breslin Kline. "The first number will get me a first-class ticket on the next British Airways flight to Heathrow. The second number will connect you with a friend who will watch for Ron Milliken at the airport and follow him to his destination. The third number is a man named Mr. James Bolton. He will make sure that Milliken stays alive, until I get there."

"Head for the airport right now. I'll take care of these details." Breslin spoke quickly but clearly as he ushered Miles out to his car.

"Make sure that someone follows up on the employees that left the sixth ranch. If we get information from Milliken and an employee, we could finally get a step up on the perpetrators," Miles instructed.

"I'll handle it myself," Breslin promised.

Tere Waters climbed into the driver's seat. "I'll deliver him to the airport Mr. Kline." She smiled and squealed the tires, leaving the warehouse parking lot.

Chapter Seven

Miles located Ron Milliken's room on the third floor of the Sheraton Park Tower on Knightsbridge in London. He left his contact—whom he knew as Mr. James Bolton—in the room that Bolton had reserved for him on the fourth floor. "Not ideal, but we can make it work."

Miles had no trouble acquiring a keycard for Milliken's room through Mr. Bolton's contact at the front desk. At three thirty-two in the morning, Miles silently slipped into the sleeping man's suite. Ron lay sprawled out and snoring on the king sized bed. Miles glided patiently and quietly to the far side of the bed. With flawless agility he pounced on his victim, sitting on Milliken's chest while planting his knees on his shoulders. He thrust the chloroformed kerchief over the nose and mouth of his quarry and held it there until the man was unconscious. He dialed upstairs on his cell phone and calmly told his accomplice to move out according to plan. Less than one minute later, Mr. James Bolton was holding the elevator door open on the third floor, as Miles Masterson entered carrying his prey over his shoulder. When they arrived on the fourth floor, Bolton slipped out when the elevator door opened and checked the hallway. Momentarily he whistled a soft "all clear," and Miles strolled down the hall and into their room. The duo secured Ron Milliken's hands and feet with duct tape and placed a kerchief in his mouth. They sat and watched CNN news for the next hour until their captive began to stir.

"Hello, Mr. Milliken. I advise you not to struggle, as you will become increasingly uncomfortable, if you do," Miles spoke through a ski mask with a gentle British accent. "I do not intend to harm you. We will leave that up to your principal. He seems to be eliminating each of you as your usefulness declines."

Milliken settled back onto the bed, breathing deeply as if he'd run a long distance.

"Mr. Milliken, I would like to talk to you about your involvement in the demise of Jonathon Biggs. We can place you at United Gas Company's loading bay the morning a delivery of propane was made to the Biggs residence. We can also prove that the load delivered contained no percaptin (the safety gas that gives odor to propane). We have also determined that Debra Moore was involved and murdered as a result. The Listers— Doug and Millie—were killed in an auto crash made to look like an accident. Since we know these things, I assume that the person directing these operations knows them as well. It is my assumption that you will be the next dead person on this trail of destruction."

Miles nodded toward Mr. James Bolton. Bolton brought a microphone toward the bed and at Miles' instruction taped it to the top of the headboard just above the prisoner's face.

"Allow me to explain our plan for you, Mr. Milliken," Miles continued in a monotone. "I want you to tell us everything you know about the organization that controls you. I want to know who is at the head and whoever else you know who is involved in any way. Tell me your story. If you choose not to, and you may, I will release you to go your way. Soon thereafter, you will be murdered by your employer.

"I must add that you will not be released until after you miss your next speaking engagement. This will cause your leader to wonder where you are and what has transpired in the meanwhile. You could contact him immediately upon your release and tell him what happened. I doubt that he'll be sympathetic. He's likely to kill you within hours." Miles maintained his demeanor and tone of voice. "Disappearing is another option for you to consider. But I think that if we can find you—he surely will. He's much better at this than we are. When he finds you, my best guess is that you will die after he bleeds you for any information you may possess. Nod, please, if you understand these options."

Milliken nodded frantically; his eyes gave away the magnitude of his fear.

"If you cooperate with us, we will protect you until you receive a just trial and your sentence has been determined. Nod, please, if you understand what I am saying to you."

Once again, the hostage nodded.

"I would like to remove the tape and kerchief from your mouth, allowing you to communicate with me. I will not do so unless you promise to be on your best behavior. I don't want to make this any more difficult than necessary."

Ron nodded slowly. He was sweating profusely and trembling slightly.

Miles removed the tape and kerchief.

"I need a drink of water." Ron gasped.

Bolton held the glass to Milliken's lips as he drank deeply, until he coughed. Bolton wiped the excess water from Ron's face as Miles nodded for him to speak.

"This may come to you as a great surprise; but I'm glad this is over for me. I was planning on being killed soon anyway. I realize that my usefulness is limited at this point, and I saw the writing on the wall for me. This will give me an opportunity to explain myself and clear my conscience before they get to me. There is no way that you can protect me. They are well organized, intentional, and patient. Every contingency is carefully calculated from every possible angle. They never fail."

"Who are 'they,' and who is the leader?"

"We call him *the Cleric*. He orchestrates personal disasters in the lives of successful people. The *EXclesia*—that's what his organization is called—carries out his plans. His right-hand man is known as *the Administrator*. I don't know what either of them look like. I've only talked to them a few times, as I generally receive my instructions through an EXclesia operative. Recently, I spoke to the Cleric himself, after Doug and Millie Lister died. He assured me that he didn't set them up. I believed him, maybe, because I didn't want to admit to myself that I was going to die at the end of this as well. The Administrator relayed the plans for this trip to me yesterday and told me that you were on to the United Gas situation. He tried to reassure me that I was safe, but I knew that they just wanted me out of the mainstream when they took me out."

"How long have you been involved with the EXclesia?" Miles wanted to keep him talking.

"Five years."

"So you have helped orchestrate the destruction of other successful people like Jonathon Biggs?"

"I guess so. They usually just use me to do reconnaissance and send back information about the victim's organization and family. Some of the companies that hire me for my consulting skills have CEOs or presidents that are targets of the Cleric. I get to know the leadership and some inside information that the Cleric uses as part of his planning. He is very patient, and it sometimes takes years to set up his targets. I haven't been involved this deeply until now. They have used my friendship with Jonathon and his family to get inside of his life and business."

"How can you say that you are his friend after what you've done to him?" Miles said harshly.

Ron Milliken's voice broke. "I've been an unwilling participant in the grip of an evil manipulator."

"Tell me about it." Miles didn't believe him.

"About seven years ago, I began to self-destruct—too much success in business and as an international playboy. I was doing designer drugs and gambling a lot. Over a two-year period of time, I lost more than I had. I owed over two million dollars between the U.S. and Europe. I leveraged all of my property and my business interests but still fell short. My life was caving in when I met Doug Lister. He was a master at managing debt and getting people back on their feet. He loaned me over two and a half million dollars to straighten out my financial mess. I was working with a company in Turkey, and one of the executives took me to an underground party. I got stoned pretty good, and the next thing I know, I'm in a prison cell all by myself. They wouldn't let me call anyone, including the U.S. Embassy. After about a week, Doug Lister showed up with another man and told me that I was probably going to get the death penalty or, at very least, life in prison. They left and came back two days later and told me that maybe they could get me out. They offered me an opportunity to work for the Cleric and be free of my debt. I was desperate, so I agreed. They got me a couple of consulting contracts, and I in turn gave them inside information that eventually helped bankrupt both companies. One of the CEOs killed himself out of despair. I told Doug that I wanted out because I felt that I was somewhat to blame and didn't want that on my conscience. I received a call from the Cleric, telling me that I was directly to blame. He threatened to ruin my life if I didn't cooperate with his plans. I have continued to serve him ever since."

"How did you get involved in the Jonathon Biggs situation?"

"I've been friends with Jonathon for years. Success has always come easily for him. He has a life of few problems and many benefits. He took over his dad's growing business and married a great girl from a prominent family. Good things just come to him. He doesn't seem to have the issues that the rest of us have to deal with every day."

"So you've been close to Biggs but jealous at the same time?" accused Miles.

"At first, I just envied him. Then, as my problems increased, I became angry, because he had no problems. I remember thinking about him while I was in the Turkish jail cell. Jonathon would never get himself into that kind of situation. He's too good—nobody can have that much success and happiness without messing it up. I have hoped for him to fail—so when I had an opportunity to bring him a little discomfort, I enjoyed it," Ron confessed with a sob.

Miles was astonished. "You enjoy destroying someone's life?"

"I did at first but didn't realize how far it would go. After Debra Moore was murdered, I had second thoughts. Then when Doug Lister was killed, I knew I couldn't get out without being next. I cooperated with the Cleric, hoping that he'd be happy enough with my work to keep me around. When Jonathon told me that his family was killed because of an odorless propane gas explosion, I realized that I was the one who murdered his kids. I can't live with this any longer! I can't fix it either! I know I'm a dead man, so use me to get to the Cleric. When it's over, I'll disappear for good."

"Tell me about the Cleric." Miles was looking for any information he could use to capture him.

"He contacts me by cell phone. He has a new one delivered by messenger service every week or so. He never acts quickly. He's smart, evaluating every possible outcome and planning for it. The lives of those he chooses to destroy collapse around them. The Cleric likes the process of bringing his victims to the edge. His goal is to push them to the point of suicide by ruining everything that's important to them. If time passes and the victim doesn't try to kill himself; the Cleric arranges an accident. He wants his victims to end their lives in a state of mental and emotional anguish." A tremor of fear coursed through Ron's body as he talked. Miles and James Bolton looked knowingly at each other. Ron Milliken was going to die at the hand of the Cleric, and he knew it. He also knew that he couldn't stop it. They were hearing the confessions of a dying man.

"You said that he has an administrator who works closely with him."

"Yes, I've only talked with him on the phone recently. They seem to be more personally connected to destroying Biggs than the others they've ruined." Ron began to settle down as the trembling subsided for the moment.

"What brings you to that conclusion?" Miles asked carefully.

"I have always dealt with an EXcelcia operative until the Biggs thing started getting serious. Both the Cleric and the

Administrator have called me directly—they didn't do that before."

"Why are you in England?"

"The Cleric told me that Jonathon had discovered the propane scheme. He didn't want to risk my being identified, so he personally arranged for me to be out of the USA." Ron began to tremble again. This time was less severe.

"What happened the day you went to United Gas?" Miles probed.

"I received a call from Doug Lister the night before, asking me if I knew how to drive a truck. I told him I did, and he instructed me to wait in the back of a McDonald's parking lot next to my hotel. When I arrived, my cell rang, and I was told to go to the truck parked next to the dumpster, put on the uniform in the front seat, and drive it to United Gas. An operative would meet me at the loading dock and tell me what to do from there."

"What did he look like and what was he wearing?"

"Doug told me to look for the guy with an orange cap with ear flaps and one of those orange and black plaid hunting coats. He was taller than me, probably six three or four, looked to be in good shape—muscular, athletic. He wasn't there when I drove up to the loading area."

"Someone else saw you," Miles stated.

"Yes." Ron was surprised that Miles knew about Alvin Worley. "One of the dock workers came over and told me that he had to meet with his boss. He said that I was to wait until he came back in a few minutes. He went across the parking lot and into the office. After about five minutes, I was getting edgy and thought about leaving. A man came up from behind and told me to stay where I was. He backed the truck into the bay and loaded it up. When he pulled out, he instructed me to drive it back to McDonald's and park it. He told me to leave the keys under the mat on the floor and the coveralls on the front seat. I did and went back to my room."

"Did you see anything or anyone after that?"

"The window in my room afforded me a view of the dumpster

at an angle. About ten minutes after I got back, a man in dark clothes and a baseball cap walked from McDonald's to the truck, put on the coveralls, and drove away."

"When you wore the coveralls, did you notice a company name or an employee name printed on them?"

"Yes, now that you mention it! The name was Franco. That's F-R-A-N and C-O, as in *company*. The employee name was Frank."

Miles dialed his cell phone. "Check out a Franco—that's F-R-A-N and CO as in 'company.' See if a delivery driver named Frank works there. Also, ask Mr. Worley if he knows anything about this company or the driver."

Ron Milliken began to sob uncontrollably. "What have I done? I deserve to die for hurting the best people I know! What can I do to help you catch the Cleric?"

"Ron, I think you are the next one of his people scheduled to die," Miles said without emotion.

"Somehow I'm not surprised. If he succeeds, I have it coming. Do you want to follow me and see who tries to take me out?" Ron was anxious to cooperate. It was as if he needed to make up in his dying what was lacking in his life.

"Something like that." Miles was unmoved by Ron's sorrow. In his book you didn't betray your friends—no matter what. He considered Ron to be untrustworthy and weak, until proven otherwise. "If you saw the guy who loaded the truck, would you recognize him?"

"Yes, I think so. Without the hat it might be confusing. I think I could."

"You may need to recognize him quickly, if you want to stay alive." Miles shook his finger in Ron's face.

"You think he's the one that the Cleric will use?" The fearful tremors returned.

"Maybe. Why didn't the Cleric send him to drive the truck, load it, and deliver the propane to Biggs' house? I think he uses this guy to do hits for him. The Cleric probably needed someone to help with this but didn't want him exposed to too many people. Professional killers don't like to be seen if they don't have to. You are expendable, so the Cleric didn't care if you were recognized, because he's planning on killing you anyway. In order to help, you'll have to put yourself in harm's way and see who comes after you."

"Okay," Ron said deliberately.

Chapter Eight

"You still struggle, don't you?"

"Yes, and I will for the rest of my life," Rachel Biggs answered her close friend.

"What is the hardest part for you?"

"The loss of my children. Our lives were family oriented. Did you know that we had dinner together every day? Jonathon insisted on it even when the kids were involved in high school events. Sometimes we would eat at three thirty in the afternoon just so that everyone could be together. Jonathon and I even picked the kids up at school for lunches together occasionally. I miss all of that." Rachel reached for the tissues on the coffee table.

"Are you still angry?"

"Oh, very... I want to see whoever did this brought to justice. Actually, at first I imagined how I would watch them die. It was fast and bloody sometimes, slow and painful others. I'm through that part of the grieving process, but I don't know how I will react when I face them in court someday. I know that Jonathon will catch them all. He's a relentless person—not vicious or hurtful—but he never quits. The people that are helping him make up an interesting team. But they are all very sharp people on a mission that they are determined to accomplish." Rachel spoke with conviction.

"Do you worry about Jonathon?" A gentle question.

"At first, when he was depressed and sitting out at the pool all day, every day. I wondered why he didn't kill himself. I was so hurt and angry that I told him to go ahead and die too. I can't believe what I said to him. For some reason, I thought that he would leap into action and solve this puzzle. That's what he has always done. Jonathon takes care of those he loves. I know now that he can be knocked down emotionally just like everyone else. He knows I'm sorry for the things I said and the way that I acted. When he decided to get involved, things began to come together. He is a leader and knows how to make things happen. Worry? Yes, I worry that they'll get him before he gets them. But I know this has to be done. The official types can't figure it out. When others give up, Jonathon gets going. He is able to accomplish things that everyone thinks are out of reach." Rachel leaned back into the comfortable chair and gently wiped her eyes and nose with the tissue.

"Rachel, I'm glad that you feel comfortable sharing your hurt with me."

"I appreciate being able to talk with a trusted friend. Until today, I have only talked about this with Jonathon. Some days I feel like I've been hit with a wave of grief, anger, and hopelessness. It all comes back quickly and sweeps over me so completely that I can't control my own feelings. It's like I get caught in the wave and can't get out. Reliving the pain may last up to a day or two, or it may be over in an hour. When I'm through the wave, I'm exhausted and usually go to bed for a while." Rachel laughed gently, thinking she sounded foolish.

"I knew that this was unbelievably painful for you. But I had no idea how much you were suffering. I wish I could have been more of a comfort to you. I guess that I've been afraid to ask deep personal questions—afraid that trying to help more would stir up your pain again." Now Maggie reached for the tissues as a small tear fell from her eye.

"You have been a great help to me and Jonathon. When I showed up at the office angry and started barking orders, you were calm and competent. Thanks for being careful and letting me vent when I needed to." Rachel was sincere in her appreciation.

"Thank you, this is the hardest thing I've ever done. I see your hurt, but for now, I need to help the team. Trying to give them any information I can to keep the investigation moving. My role is to provide support in any way I can."

"You do, and it's appreciated very much. Your glass is empty. Can I get you some more water?" Rachel took the glass and walked to the kitchen.

"Yes, thank you. With a slice of lime, please." Maggie slipped her hand into her purse as Rachel moved across the room to the kitchen. As she grasped the weapon, she shivered for a second. Regaining her composure, she thought about how pleased the Cleric would be when he heard about Rachel's death on the evening news. Her shiver turned into determination. She quietly rose to her feet and walked casually toward the kitchen. The Cleric's training took over as she moved toward her target.

As Rachel opened the refrigerator she heard a footstep too close behind here. Before she could turn around, Maggie grabbed her hair, pulled her head back, and slit her throat.

Maggie lowered Rachel to the floor. She was bleeding profusely and trying to talk. All that came out of her mouth was a rasping gurgle. Maggie noticed that the dishwasher was open. She placed the combat knife in the silverware tray. "Nice touch!" she whispered to herself. She took off her bloodied blouse, washed up in the kitchen sink, and put on a clean one from her briefcase. The Cleric had been right about the amount of blood and wise to tell her to bring a change of clothes.

Rachel was still now, her eyes closed. Maggie carefully stepped over the pool of blood and walked outside to her car. She got in and drove away.

"How did you feel about your first kill?" Guillermo was in the Cleric's "Circle of Three." The Circle was made up of the

Administrator, Guillermo, and Maggie. Each was completely trusted by the others and, most importantly, by the Cleric.

"It was weird, because I had known her for so long. She was always nice to me, and I had to work through that before I got to the house. I'm sure the Cleric will be very pleased. I feel good about that. I did something I had never done before. The power to take a life is intoxicating. I feel like I was born for this." Maggie was excited and pleased with herself at the same time. She was talking fast, because the adrenaline was still working in her body. This was an exhilaration she had never experienced before. She now understood why Guillermo enjoyed killing.

"We have been trained by the best. You look good." Guillermo smiled that soft smile that caused Maggie to melt inside. She had parked her car in a long-term lot two miles from the airport and took the shuttle to the International Terminal. She had two bags with her filled with books for weight and crumpled news-paper for bulk. The shuttle driver placed the bags on the side-walk, received his generous tip, and drove off. Maggie signaled a Sky Cap to take her luggage inside to be checked. She gave him the flight number and a twenty dollar bill. As he took her luggage inside, she headed for the airport parking garage Level 3 where Guillermo was waiting with a change of clothes and the other accessories she needed. After changing in the back of his Cadillac, she looked like a different person altogether. The lon-ger brunette wig with the dark brown contacts looked good on her. The burgundy blouse and dark lipstick made the adjustment complete. She was no longer the efficient, administrative-assis-tant type but now a very attractive, thirty-something woman. Guillermo found her especially alluring.

"You followed the directions exactly, right?" Guillermo asked.

Maggie was proud of herself. "Of course, I've worked on this for years. Getting into Biggs International, earning their trust, and connecting with Rachel took a lot of patience. Six years is a long time to spend setting someone up. I know this job is personal to the Cleric, so I did it to perfection. What's next?" She was sure the Cleric would be pleased.

"We drive straight through to Denver tonight. You'll pick up a car and head for Vegas, and I'll grab a flight to Paris. Its time to take care of our friend Ron Milliken."

"Will we have time for a little romance?" Maggie scooted over and nuzzled his ear with her lips. "I miss you so much," she whispered.

"Absolutely, we have a room at the Airport Marriot. We'll order in and enjoy our time together. You are the love of my life, you know?"

She whispered into his ear, "I know. And you are mine. I'm glad the Cleric approves of us being together."

"He likes the idea. Keeping loyalties close is important to our success." Guillermo turned his head, and his lips met hers.

Maggie was anxious for the Cleric to hear the news and call to congratulate her. "Do you think they have discovered Rachel's body yet?"

"I don't know. It's been a couple of hours already. Anyone walking into the room would notice her, right? If they have found her, they're already covering the airport trying to figure out what plane you're on. Tomorrow night, you'll be in Vegas then on to Mexico. You should be back home within two days with no complications." Guillermo was always confident.

"It will be nice to be home and relax a little. The destruction of Jonathon Biggs has taken a long time. And it's not over yet. He and his friends are very persistent. I thought he was going to end it all a few times, but his wife kept fighting to find out what really happened. I think she energized him."

"Those days are over!" Guillermo laughed.

"Maybe I should have taken her out sooner." Maggie snickered with delight.

"No, the Cleric has a reason for every step we take. Every move is calculated to bring the target down with maximum suffering. The destruction must be emotional, as well as physical."

Guillermo had learned well under the tutelage of the Cleric and the Administrator.

"He especially wants Jonathon Biggs to suffer! He's suffering now that I took care of his wife. I know him; this will definitely destroy him. He can't survive without her." Maggie had seen them together for six years. She was sure that Jonathon Oliver Biggs could not live without his Rachel.

The next morning Guillermo and the newly made-over Maggie split up at the Denver Airport Marriot. She was wearing an auburn wig and had disguised her nose to look wider and rounded. She kept the dark-brown contacts and felt satisfied that no one could recognize her even at close range. She took the VW Passat left for her at the airport and headed for Las Vegas. Guillermo took an international flight to Paris to plot the demise of Ron Milliken. They both anticipated that Jonathon Biggs' grief would end his hunt for the Cleric.

The Cleric had not contacted Maggie yet. There was nothing on the news either national or local about Rachel Biggs' death. Maggie presumed that Jonathon's friends would keep it quiet for a short time to let him deal with his grief.

Chapter Nine

"Rachel, I can't believe I almost lost you!" Jonathon Biggs was whispering as he sat next to his wife's head in the ambulance. He held a bloodied note in his hand. On it was scribbled almost illegible words:

Stop Maggie

―――⟶●⟵―――

Bob Holcroft was at the Biggs residence with Breslin Kline and two of his most trusted FBI agents. He had the rest of his team checking the airport, bus, and train terminals for Maggie. They had tried to contact her husband, Frank, without success. Holcroft assumed that he was gone for good, disappearing with Maggie. Holcroft himself was at the Biggs residence with the local police, looking for clues as to Maggie's whereabouts. He was hoping to learn something that would lead him to Maggie's contacts. She had been with Biggs International for six years. Jonathon found her through a professional search agency. She had worked as an administrative assistant for the chief financial officer of a large, privately owned pharmaceutical company in Europe that had folded after a series of family tragedies. She was personable and seemed, until now, to be a loyal employee and friend.

"How could she be involved in taking down the Biggs?"

Holcroft mused to himself. "Waiting six years to kill someone is a long time. She must be part of a larger organization that has perfected the art of ruining good people."

"Are you talking to me, Bob," Breslin Kline broke in, "or to yourself?"

"To myself. This is getting more complicated as we go along." Holcroft's large, muscular build made the thinner, shorter Breslin Kline look small and weak. The two men had developed a bond of respect.

"Yes, but this could be our big break. Maggie messed up. If we can find her, maybe we can follow her to whoever is leading this organization," Kline chimed in to Holcroft's thought process.

"I hope so." Holcroft's cell phone began to play "Born in the USA." He answered and put it on speaker for Breslin Kline to hear.

"We found a Sky Cap at the international terminal who we think handled Maggie's bags. He picked her luggage up at the curb, but she didn't follow him into the terminal. She never checked in and wasn't on the plane. One of the guys outside saw her cross into the parking garage. If it was her, she's traveling alone. That's all we have so far," the agent at the other end of the phone said. "Right now we're going to access the cameras on each level to see if we can spot her hooking up with somebody."

"Keep me informed, thanks." Holcroft snapped his phone shut.

"She left by car." Breslin Kline was stating the obvious. "Either picked up a car or someone picked her up. Can you fill me in on what happened here?"

"It looks like Maggie came up behind Rachel when she was at the refrigerator." Holcroft pointed as he spoke. "Maggie tried to cut her throat but didn't get the jugular. She caught her low by the collar bone and ripped upward from right to left. Rachel fell to the floor over here and eventually got to the phone. She called 911 but couldn't talk, so they dispatched a squad car to the address. Jonathon drove up about two minutes after they got here. My guess is that Maggie saw all the blood and assumed that Rachel was dead so she fled."

"I just came from the hospital. She had a note in her hand telling Jonathon that it was Maggie and to stop her. She's going to need surgery on her esophagus and vocal chords and about eighty stitches in her neck. She should be able to talk softly in a few days. If we want to talk to her before that, we'll have to bring a notepad," Breslin Kline said in his official voice, but it had come out softer than usual.

"How's Jonathon holding up?" Holcroft asked. He had convinced the police Chief to keep Rachel Biggs' attack quiet. Holcroft had to promise the Chief that he would get credit later for being an important part of the investigation.

"He was in shock at the house. But now I think her note has sent him to a new level of determination. Once she's settled and rested, I'm sure he'll want to meet with us back at the warehouse."

"Good, we will stop them, Breslin! We'll figure out this tangled web of evil and rip it out by the roots." Holcroft was trying to convince himself as much as he was trying to convince Breslin Kline.

<hr />

"Inspector Holcroft, come into the kitchen. I've found something!" one of the agents called out.

Holcroft and Breslin Kline walked carefully into the kitchen, trying not to disturb any evidence.

"Check this out, sir." The agent pointed to the bloody combat knife in the dishwasher. "There's the weapon."

"Let's take some pictures and get this knife to the lab!" Holcroft commanded.

"This is a disturbing development," Breslin Kline whispered to Bob Holcroft.

"I know. Let's get out of here so we can talk. Agent Miller, call me on my cell in an hour with an update."

"Yes, sir."

Holcroft knew Miller was a good man and would be thorough in his examination of the scene. He and Kline walked outside.

"Your car," said Holcroft.

When they were seated in Breslin's Buick LeSabre, Holcroft began to say what they both knew to be true.

"They wanted Jonathon to know that Maggie killed Rachel. Did you see that knife? Maggie didn't even wipe it off. Her prints will be all over it. This is psychological warfare. They're trying to destroy Jonathon Biggs' life one piece at a time. This was designed to be his last straw." Holcroft was surprised by the audacity of Rachel's would-be killer.

"But they have failed, and we have a lead." Breslin Kline sensed that the hunt was on.

"I wonder who else around Jonathon has been planted in his life by the enemy."

"So far we have his pastor, his vice president's wife, his buddy Ron Milliken, and his administrative assistant. Why go to all this trouble to destroy him? They could have simply had him shot." Breslin Kline wondered for Holcroft to overhear.

"Or they could have waited thirty minutes and blown him up with his kids," Holcroft added.

"Someone wants him to suffer," Breslin Kline stated, as only he could.

"Yeah, and they're good at getting what they want." Holcroft shook his head.

"Are you certain that you killed Rachel Biggs?" The Administrator reminded Maggie that the news had been strangely silent about the brutal murder.

"I cut her throat from one side to the other. She bled all over me and the floor. She was definitely dead before I left the house. I put the knife in the open dishwasher for Jonathon to find." Maggie wasn't concerned.

"Nice touch!" The Administrator was impressed at her presence of mind on her first kill.

"I was taught by the best!" Maggie responded. "The Biggs are family people. They are probably keeping this quiet until Jonathon is able to be seen by the media without falling apart. They'll announce soon enough."

"You know them better than anyone. I'm sure you're right. We've booked a flight for you on Mexicana airlines. Leave the car in the ESPN Zone parking lot on the strip and take a cab to the airport. You'll be flying to Mexico City, where our limo will meet you and take you to the Cuernavaca mansion. Just hang out there until we call you in." The Administrator was specific and direct.

"Got it. I can tan and swim for a few days." Maggie tapped *End,* and her conversation with the Administrator was over. She lit up a fresh cigarette and laughed out loud as she blew out the smoke. "So goes your life, Mr. Jonathon Oliver Biggs. Up in smoke!"

"Maggie did what?" Miles Masterson was in shock as Jonathon Biggs told him about Rachel. "Rachel survived? What is her condition?"

"Miles, just listen, and I'll answer all of your questions!" Jonathon was emotionally exhausted and lacking in patience.

"I'm sorry, Jonathon. It's just that this is such an evil plot. I've seen a lot of wicked scheming in my life, but this is a whole new level of evil!"

When Jonathon had finished telling him about Rachel and Maggie, Miles reviewed his plan to use Ron Milliken to draw out the Cleric.

"Jonathon, Ron's sorrow over what he has done seems genuine. He came up with this plan, even though it may cost him his life. He calls the leader the *Cleric.* He let himself get trapped by and used beyond anything he could have imagined. He will probably be dead within a few days—I'm sure the Cleric will take him out."

"Let me talk to him," Jonathon ordered.

"Are you sure? This guy has been part of destroying your family. Maybe you should just let him be … He'll get what he has coming when they kill him. And maybe we'll get the Cleric." Miles didn't think it was a good idea for a highly emotional Jonathon Biggs to have to deal with Ron Milliken.

"I'm sure. I need to talk to Ron. Put him on."

"Okay." Miles Masterson handed his cell to Ron Milliken. "Jonathon Biggs wants a word with you."

"Jonathon, I'm so sorry!" Ron wept. "I can't believe how I've betrayed our friendship and hurt you and your family. I wish I could fix it or go back in time and change what I've done."

"Ron, you need to help us get the Cleric and break up his organization," Jonathon said calmly.

"I will. I'm sure that they'll try to kill me soon. The Cleric doesn't like loose ends, and I've become one. He disposes of people when he's finished with them. I'm okay with dying—God knows I deserve it and more—but I want you to know that I am sorry." Ron was sobbing uncontrollably.

"Ron, you have to live through the next few days, until we can meet and talk about this face-to-face. You need to hear my pain before you can ask for true forgiveness. I want you to know everything I've gone through so that when you ask for forgiveness, you know what you're asking for. Stay alive until then!" Jonathon commanded his betrayer.

"I'll try!" Ron handed the phone back to Miles. He and Jonathon spoke quietly for a few minutes before they hung up.

Ron Milliken was terrified but determined.

Miles Masterson and Mr. James Bolton, formerly of British Intelligence and Scotland Yard, moved into the room attached to Milliken's. Ron had an evening flight scheduled to Germany and was to speak the next morning to the leadership at Daimler Motors. Masterson and Bolton had decided that Ron would lay low until he went to the airport. They expected something to happen before he boarded his flight. They were also certain that Milliken was being watched. Miles Masterson was thankful for the help of Mr. James Bolton. Bolton was in his mid-forties, retired from Scotland Yard after a stellar career with MI6. In his early thirties Bolton was considered the most dangerous man in the world. Short at five-foot six and unassuming, he could move around freely without being noticed. His fighting skills were unparalleled. In retirement, he was contracted to train agents from Israel's Mossad and America's CIA and Black Ops units. He was calm and efficient.

Guillermo was also determined. He had flown into Paris and connected to London last night.

Guillermo checked in with his contact in London who was watching Ron Milliken.

"Nothing unusual so far. He came down to breakfast at seven. He had oatmeal and coffee. The only person he talked to was the waitress. At breakfast he read the paper and returned to his room. An hour ago he sent his suit out to be pressed. He's in his room right now."

"A man of simple habits—predictable to a fault. Did you get the things I asked for?" Guillermo asked his cohort.

"Yes."

"I'll meet you in the alley by the service entrance in twenty minutes. I won't approach until someone else is going in to make a delivery."

"Got it."

Guillermo waited until the water delivery people propped the service door open and began to load their dolly and roll it into the storage room. He walked in behind them. His agent in London walked by the door as he entered and handed Guillermo a fanny pack containing everything he had requested. Inside the hotel, Guillermo made his way up the stairwell to the third floor of the Sheraton Park Tower on Knightsbridge. He stopped at the landing on the third floor to prepare. He took a flask of whiskey, a bottle of water half empty, and two small bags of powder from the fanny pack. He poured the powders and the whiskey into the water bottle and shook it until it was mixed thoroughly. He then proceeded to Ron Milliken's room.

Guillermo knocked on the door of room 312.

"Yes," Ron's voice sounded through the door.

"Your suit, sir," Guillermo responded, knowing from his contact that Milliken had sent his suit out to be pressed.

Milliken opened the door. Guillermo grabbed his throat and punched him in the stomach at the same time. Ron Milliken let out a gasp that turned into a soft squeak as Guillermo forced him backwards onto the bed.

"The Cleric wants to see you," Guillermo lied. "You are to drink the contents of this bottle—it will put you to sleep. When you are out, I will transport you, and you will wake up in the Cleric's mansion. If you resist or refuse, I have been instructed to shoot you in the stomach and watch you bleed to death slowly. Will you cooperate?"

"Yes," the word was hard to get out.

"Too bad, I wanted to watch you die. Sit up and drink this." Guillermo handed the bottle to Milliken and held him at gunpoint as he drank down the contents. "Drink it all—every drop."

"How long does it take to work?" Ron Milliken couldn't stop himself from trembling.

"About ten minutes. You should lay down, so I don't have to pick you up off the floor." Guillermo was enjoying himself waiting for Ron to go unconscious.

Within ten minutes, Ron Milliken began to spasm. As the intensity of the spasms increased, Guillermo found a pair of socks in Ron's suitcase and stuffed them into his mouth to keep him quiet. Milliken's eyes rolled back in their sockets, and he lay quietly. Guillermo removed the socks and put them in his fanny pack.

"You will be found dead when you miss your flight." Guillermo laughed for his own benefit as he left the room and headed down the stairwell to the service entrance.

"I'm on him," stated Mr. James Bolton

"I'll take care of Milliken," said Miles Masterson as he punched the buttons on his cell phone.

Within five minutes, a man and two women arrived at room 312. They confirmed that he was still alive, but that his breathing was shallow. They immediately started a saline IV and pumped his stomach. He threw up but was otherwise unresponsive.

"Will he make it?" asked Miles Masterson.

"I think so. I don't know whether he'll have brain damage or not. We won't know until he comes around."

"What was in the bottle?" Miles wanted to know the details.

"My best guess is heroin and some kind of slow-working poison. He also smells like alcohol. The poison would have moved into his system first and killed him. This was designed to appear as if he overdosed while doing drugs and drinking. We have to get him to drink fluids as soon as we can revive him."

"I'm downloading their conversation and sending it to the Yard for analysis." The man was working quickly but calmly. "This will probably take an hour or so. We may not even get a voice match at all from our records."

The third member of the team had dusted the bottle and the door for fingerprints. "There are no prints anywhere. I can see where he grasped the door knob but left no prints. He wasn't wearing gloves, so he must have covered his finger tips with something."

"Or had his fingerprints surgically removed. He is a professional." Offered the man at the computer.

Miles' cell beeped. "Mr. Bolton, where are you?"

"I'm outside of the sandwich shop two doors down from the hotel. He left the building through the service entrance in the alley. When he came to the street, he stopped in for lunch. He's eating a sandwich and reading a book as we speak."

"Do you recognize him?"

"No, I've never seen him before. I did get a good photo of him though. I'll send it into MI6 at the first opportunity."

"Good."

"Would you like me to capture him or just continue to follow?"

"Let's follow him and see where he leads us. Thanks, Mr. Bolton."

"Out."

Chapter Ten

"Sir, we have her on film in the parking garage. The Sky Cap identified her as the woman who left her luggage with him."

"Good job!" Bob Holcroft was pleased as the agent at the airport told him that they had camera footage of Maggie in the parking garage.

"Thanks, she got into a 2005 Cadillac Escalade on Level Three. A man was waiting in the car for her. The attendant at the pay booth remembered them. She said that a man and a woman gave her a fifty dollar bill and were impatient about waiting for change. She said they went west on the Interstate," the agent reported.

"They are probably driving to another airport to confuse us. She'll have to change her looks, so there's a good possibility that they'll get a room somewhere. Check the gas stations, rest stops, and hotels along the highway and see if anyone can identify the car. A Cadillac SUV is pretty noticeable. Also check the rental agencies to see what you can come up with. I've sent her picture out across the country. Let's see if she turns up."

"I'm driving to Vegas right now. I'll follow the instructions unless I hear differently," Maggie reported to the Administrator.

"I would feel better if Rachel Biggs' death was confirmed by the media," the Administrator said.

"Not to worry, she's dead. Jonathon Biggs and his team are so messed up right now that they can't even think straight. The news will pick it up soon." Maggie sounded confident, even though she was beginning to have some doubts. She had reviewed the scene over and over in her mind and found no flaw in her actions. The amount of blood and Rachel gurgling before she died convinced Maggie that the kill was a good one. "Why are they waiting to announce it to the world?" she mused to herself as she drove toward Las Vegas.

———❊———

Breslin Kline and Tere Waters were back at the office with Jonathon Biggs discussing their next move. Breslin Kline's phone beeped.

"Good!" Breslin sounded optimistic. "See if you can get a DNA sample to the lab right away. I'll have Dr. Waters coordinate with the Pima County Sheriff."

"Another piece of the puzzle?" Tere Waters was very intrigued after hearing her name in connection with the investigation.

"They found a body in a cave by Sabino Canyon in Tucson. It was partially decomposed and some small animals got to it. The Sheriff reported that the body was placed in the back of a shallow cave and covered with rocks. I doubt if this is our mad cow delivery man, but I'd like you to look at his DNA and compare it with the information you have on the broken needle. The Pima County Sheriff will be calling you with the information," Breslin said with a glimmer of hope.

"We have been unsuccessful in identifying any of the people who worked at the ranch around the time of the injections. I hope this turns up something, because we've exhausted most of our leads in that direction." Jonathon sighed.

"Shouldn't you be with Rachel?" Tere Waters interrupted.

"She was sleeping when I left two hours ago. I feel like she's expecting me to solve this right away." Jonathon threw his arms up into the air with frustration. He appeared exhausted and overwhelmed but determined.

"Listen Jonathon, you have a great team of people working on this from both sides of the Atlantic Ocean. We're starting to get some breaks. Go to Rachel and let us do what we do best. We will get the Cleric and we will get him soon. Tell Rachel that Miles has a lead in Europe that is hot and that Holcroft has a nationwide search going for Maggie. We're close. Tell her that." Breslin Kline was surprised at himself. He had prided himself for never getting emotionally close to a situation. When he left the FDA to help Jonathon, he did it out of respect and intrigue. But now he was experiencing deep feelings for Jonathon and Rachel and the investigation team. "I also think it is time for you to call a press conference naming Eli Moore as President of Biggs International and have him speak to the mad cow issue. We want the public to know that you are moving ahead and back in business. I'll make some calls and get the quarantines lifted and acquire a statement from the FDA spokesperson that we can use at the press conference."

"Good, Breslin, set it up. I'll call Eli on my way back to the hospital."

"Rachel, Breslin got the quarantine lifted on all six ranches. We're calling a press conference at four thirty, just before the evening newscasts, to announce the reopening and Eli's promotion." Jonathon was enthusiastic for Rachel's sake. She needed good news to help her through the healing process.

GOOD, Rachel wrote in large, shaky letters on the ever-present notepad at her bedside. Jonathon brought her up to date on the investigation.

"I want you to think about what you want our lives to be like after this is over. I think we're close to finishing this, and I want to be looking ahead with you." Jonathon was trying to see ahead to a positive future for them.

"Okay," Rachel wrote. She had tears in her eyes. She was beginning to see Jonathon return to himself. When he was at his best, she never worried. She knew that she was a changed person.

Trauma does that to a person. She would always have a sense of loss over her children and the scars of betrayal from Maggie, Ron, and the Listers. She wondered if she could ever build a friendship again without worrying about being set up. Trust had always been a natural part of their lives, and now she wasn't sure if she could trust anyone but Jonathon again.

"We have a great group of people helping us, Rachel." Jonathon spoke softly. "Can you believe that Miles took on this investigation, not caring whether he ever gets paid? I asked him the other day to keep track of his expenses and hours so that someday I could pay him. He laughed and said that helping me was his hobby, and he didn't charge for hobbies."

Rachel smiled softly. "Ha, ha!"

"Breslin Kline, the stuffed shirt perfectionist, quit his job to help us out. At first I thought he just wanted the challenge of solving an extremely difficult case, but now I think he actually likes us. He seems concerned about us as people."

"That's not like him!" Rachel was laughing and writing at the same time.

"I think that Tere and Miles have something going romantically. They call each other three or four times a day. I wouldn't be surprised if they end up together. I'll bet that you'll be the Maid of Honor at their wedding."

She wrote, "I know, but it seems so obvious. I wonder if Miles is ready to settle down and stay in one place for a while. He might be someone who could help Biggs International."

"By the way, Eli told me to tell you that we didn't lose all of our children. He's still around and considers himself to be our son." Jonathon held her hands in his. Every few minutes he would lift one of her hands to his lips and kiss it gently. She liked that and smiled with each expression of his undying love for her.

He's right; Rachel was crying freely and appreciating the moment. Jonathon must have read her mind about not trusting people. He had just named people who had given of themselves to help the Biggses. That was the kind of loyalty that lifelong friendships were made of.

Rachel closed her eyes and put her head back on the pillow. She felt Jonathon dabbing her face with a tissue. Then he kissed her. It was one of those, "I'll love you forever" kisses. She smiled and went to sleep peacefully. *How long has it been since I have slept peacefully?*

⟶◆⟵

"His name was Joseph Miller. He was a vagrant cowboy. Working wherever he could for food, lodging, and a little money. Served time twice for breaking and entering. First time was in county lockup for a year and the second was in a medium security facility for two years—hard working and well liked but unsettled. The sheriff has traced him back to three or four ranches; one was the Biggs Ranch in Tucson. There is no record of him being at the others, but he could have hit those places between jobs. It's a long shot. I'll have more when the DNA on the needle is compared to his." Tere Waters was on a conference call with Miles, Eli, Bob Holcroft, and Jonathon. Breslin Kline was in the room with her.

"How long will that take?" Jonathon asked.

"Probably tomorrow, but it could be later tonight," Breslin replied. He and Holcroft had called in favors to get this done quickly. They were both confident that the comparison would be completed soon.

"I was hoping for four thirty this afternoon. This would be a great thing to put in the press conference. I suppose we could tell them that we have a lead." Eli wanted the press conference to have maximum favorable impact for Biggs International.

"What about finding Maggie?" Jonathon probed.

"We came across a hotel clerk who kind of recognized the picture. Apparently, she came in two days ago as a good-looking brunette and checked out the next morning with brownish red hair. He said she looked completely different. We had an artist come in and draw up both looks. It's definitely Maggie. She changed her nose, hair, and clothing to make herself look plain. She obviously wants to blend in."

"What about the driver of the car from the airport? Did anyone see him?" Miles asked.

"Yes, they came and left the hotel together. That's what surprised the desk clerk—same guy but a different-looking woman. Her transformation was enough to get his full attention. Our artist also did a work up on him. I'll email the pics to you as soon as we're off the phone," Holcroft explained.

"They're making small mistakes. Giving us opportunities." Breslin's mind was going a mile a minute. "Miles, what about your man who is following the assassin?"

"He's still on him. He went to a small, local bed and breakfast about an hour ago. He just slipped out the back door of the place and is presently strolling through the market. Mr. Bolton thinks he's waiting for the news to announce that Ron Milliken's body has been found. After that, he'll probably leave the country."

"Did you get a photo of him by chance?" Breslin asked, already knowing the answer.

"Yes, and as soon as Mr. Bolton delivers it to me, I'll email it to each of you."

Breslin had already pieced the possibilities together. "I wonder if it will match the sketch from the hotel clerk."

"Breslin, what is going on in that mind of yours?" Holcroft asked lightly.

"If Maggie and this assassin were together in Denver, and he left to kill Ron Milliken, then my best guess is that they will get back together again at some point." Breslin Kline was amazing everyone once again.

"What are the odds?" Eli asked.

"Not very high unless the Cleric's circle of trust is small," Holcroft inserted. "What if he considers Maggie dispensable? He will probably send this killer back to her to take her out of the picture."

"So she could be in grave danger?" Tere Waters was surprised that the Cleric so willingly killed his own people.

"Yes, or he could want to keep her alive. At any rate, if we watch them both and they reconnect, they may very well lead us to the Cleric's lair," Breslin Kline said with finality.

Chapter Eleven

Jonathon Biggs opened the press conference with the announcement that Eli Moore was the new president of Biggs International. He explained that he would still be the CEO but not have day-to-day duties. He introduced Eli and stepped back from the podium.

"Thank you, Jonathon. I have worked at Biggs International since my high school years. I began in the mail room, because Jonathon believes that all good leaders ought to understand the people that work for them. At Biggs International, we have the best workforce in the industry. We value people and productivity. One of the core values we hold to is honesty; we will continue that great legacy.

"We have been through a great crisis," Eli continued with confidence. "The FDA and the FBI have both come to the conclusion that someone sabotaged all six of the Biggs ranches by injecting the mad cow virus into one animal from each ranch. We have not apprehended the culprit yet, but we continue to pursue every possible means to bring them to justice. As a result, our ranches were quarantined by the FDA. This action on their part was the right thing to do. Biggs International suffered significant losses as a result. We have survived with help from friends and the loyalty of our workers and stockholders. The FDA has lifted the quarantine on all six Biggs ranches. We recently entered into a purchase agreement with the Rancho Vasquez in Argentina; I am pleased to announce today that we are moving ahead with that purchase. I would like to thank the Rancho Vasquez in Argentina. Their leadership team has been trusting and patient since we added them to our group of ranches. They are good people and will continue to work with us to expand the industry."

"I also announce to you today the pending sale of Biggs International's European Manufacturing division to Sameros Ranches Incorporated. The sale of our manufacturing division will provide more than enough cash flow to cover our debts and move us back into the forefront of the cattle industry." Eli paused for effect.

"I am pleased to be the new president of Biggs International. I am proud of my relationship with the Biggses, not only in the business sense, but as a part of their family."

Eli answered questions for a few minutes and closed the press conference.

The Cleric watched the news conference live on CNN from his mansion. He was furious.

"They said nothing about Rachel Biggs." The Administrator was surprised.

"They are going to great lengths to cover it up. Although Jonathon Biggs certainly doesn't look like a man whose wife has just been murdered," the Cleric responded with sarcasm.

"Is it possible that she lived? Maybe she is barely clinging to life at this moment." The Administrator knew that something had gone wrong.

"It is possible. It's more than possible. Something is very wrong with this picture." The Cleric was becoming more agitated. "Where is Maggie right now?"

"Driving to Vegas. She should be there in a few hours. Her plane leaves this evening at five for Mexico City. From there, she'll take the limo to Cuernavaca."

"Get her on the phone!" hissed the Cleric.

"That's the same guy!" Holcroft declared.

"Absolutely!" Breslin Kline chimed in.

"Can MI6 or Scotland Yard identify him?" Jonathon leaned over and spoke into the microphone on the conference room phone.

"No positive identification from British Intelligence, Scotland Yard, CIA, FBI, or anyone else. No one knows who he is." Miles was in London relaying the information.

"What is he up to now?" Jonathon asked.

"He spent the night at the bed and breakfast. He got up early and went for a run. We haven't seen him since he returned. He's hanging around for a reason. I don't think he'll leave until he's sure that Ron is dead," Miles reported.

"What is Ron's condition at present?" Breslin Kline asked carefully.

"He's in guarded condition. The heroin and the poison didn't have much time to work before we got to him, so he may survive. There is going to be some residual damage, but the doctor isn't sure how much yet. They are still concerned that his heart can't handle the next few hours."

Bob Holcroft had an idea. "Let the news media know that Ron Milliken had a drug overdose last evening and is in critical condition. Make sure that they clearly state that he is not expected to live through today."

Miles liked Holcroft's idea. "Good, let's see what our assassin does when he hears the news."

Holcroft continued. "We're showing his picture to all airline employees in the international terminal in Denver. He was seen at a hotel with Maggie two nights ago. I'm interested to know what name he used on the flight manifest. Can we find out what name he gave to the bed and breakfast?"

"Too risky, it's a small place. It would be impossible to stay inconspicuous. Let's leak the news about Ron to the media and see what he does next."

"Okay, Miles, keep us informed. We'll watch CNN and Fox

News to hear the announcement." Jonathon pressed the end button on the phone.

<hr />

"Ron Milliken is dead!" proclaimed Guillermo the assassin. "I'm coming home."

"Good, I'd like you to stop in Kansas City. I'm concerned about the Rachel Biggs situation." The Administrator's request surprised Guillermo.

"Why? Maggie took care of her already." Guillermo had been listening to the news and heard nothing about Rachel Biggs. He wondered what the Cleric would do next. Now he knew.

"We want to be sure that she's dead," the Administrator said flatly.

"Maggie said she was… What's the problem?" Guillermo was getting irritated.

"As I'm sure you know, there has been no announcement made about her death. The news hasn't reported the attack at all. Jonathon Biggs had a news conference today and didn't appear as a man who was mourning the loss of his wife. Something is wrong in Kansas City."

"It's obvious that Biggs is keeping it quiet for business reasons. I don't want to show up in the aftermath of the situation. I have never gone back to the scene. That's why no one knows who I am. In and out and gone for good. I don't go back, and I won't this time," Guillermo insisted.

"Guillermo!" It was the Cleric speaking. "We need you to go to Kansas City."

"Let's say that Rachel Biggs is still alive. So what? You have made your point. We got into Biggs' living room and cut up his wife. He knows that we can get to him anytime we want to." Guillermo had never questioned the Cleric before.

"I want you in Kansas City to find out who is helping Jonathon Biggs. The USDA faded out on this thing weeks ago. I know the FBI is still working on it, but they have to be ready to call it quits. Biggs has someone else helping him from the inside. Find out who and then we'll decide how to deal with the situation." The Cleric sighed with impatience. He was developing Guillermo to take on more responsibility and, eventually, to take over EXcelsia. Wanting to be part of the decision-making process was good. The Cleric was glad for the exchange.

"I'll be there tomorrow," Guillermo conceded.

<hr />

"We have Maggie!" the FBI agent said as he rushed through the airport. "She's at the Vegas airport waiting to board a plane to Mexico City. Do you want her detained?"

"No, I want her followed. Get on the same plane. Fly first class so that you don't lose her when she gets off." Bob Holcroft didn't want to lose Maggie now. "She's going to lead us to the Cleric."

"Can do!"

"I'll send John Doe as soon as I can get him a flight out." Holcroft wanted his man backed up, but didn't want to go through the Mexican Federales. He had worked with them before, and they had wasted valuable time with interviews and paperwork. "John Doe" was a private operative who did special jobs for Holcroft. "Has Maggie made contact with anyone?"

"I don't know. She appears to be alone. We spotted her inside the airport, so I don't know how she got here or if she has called anyone. I have to go get my ticket. I'll talk to you later."

<hr />

The assassin spent the next two days locating and following the various members of the Biggs team. The area around the Biggs International condos seemed to give him the best opportunity to strike. Guillermo spent time each day moving up and down the street disguised as a homeless man.

J.O.B.

PART
THREE

Chapter One

"Breslin Kline is dead! He's dead!" Miles' voice exploded into his cell phone.

"What?" Bob Holcroft didn't believe what he had just heard.

"I just drove up to the condos, and the police were everywhere. I recognized Breslin's car, so I stopped and ran up to the first cop I saw. He told me that a man was shot a few minutes ago. He pointed to Breslin's car. He was sitting in the front seat with a bullet through his forehead. That's all I know right now. I'll call you back when I get more." Miles was in a state of panic.

Bob Holcroft walked into Rachel's hospital room late that evening. Jonathon was asleep in the chair next to Rachel's bed. She was sleeping soundly. Holcroft tapped Jonathon on the shoulder and motioned to meet him in the hall.

"The local police found Breslin Kline dead in his car in front of the Biggs condos," Bob Holcroft explained as he attempted to maintain a professional demeanor.

"Not Breslin! Why? How? This is unbelievable," Jonathon Biggs blurted.

"The Chief of police knows that we were working with Breslin on your case. He called me as soon as Miles identified the body." Holcroft was struggling to maintain his composure. He enjoyed working with Breslin more than anyone he had served with in his career.

"Are they sure it was murder?" Jonathon wanted to be told that it wasn't true.

"A single shot came through the windshield and hit him in the forehead. He died instantly. We're dealing with the same killer who went after Ron Milliken," Holcroft said, feeling sadness and anger both at the same time.

"I thought we had him covered. What happened?" Jonathon's tone was harsh.

"We did. We lost him in the lunch crowd downtown by the courthouse. He turned up two hours later in the bar across the street from the courthouse. He had a drink, made a phone call, and left. He's at the airport Marriot right now."

"How could you 'lose him' for two hours? Aren't you pros at this stuff?" Jonathon said accusingly.

"Surely you didn't think that we were all safe?" countered Holcroft. "The Cleric has had people killed before and will try again. His man is an expert. He's the best I've ever seen. I hate it when a guy like this gets the better of us. Back off, Jonathon. We're all at risk here and have no pretenses about the danger involved. His next target could be any one of us."

"We have to stop him. Let's get everyone together for a strategy session." Jonathon forced himself to be calm.

"I didn't share information with the police. I still think the killer will lead us to the Cleric. We will bring these people down!" Holcroft didn't know if his tears were tears of determination or sorrow. He decided that it was probably both.

⟶⟩●⟨⟵

"I got Breslin Kline," explained Guillermo, standing alone at the end of the bar. "It was too easy."

"Are you sure no one saw you?" the Administrator asked.

"No one has ever seen me!" exclaimed Guillermo. "I picked up the silenced Glock 40mm from the locker at the airport. I took a cab downtown and wandered through the lunch crowd for a while then slipped into this bar. I had a drink and left out the back alley door, put on my homeless beard, cap, and jacket, and moved into position in the small walkway between the Biggs International condo building and the apartment building next door. I got lucky when Kline drove up five minutes later. As soon as he stopped in front of the building, I walked in front of the car and shot him in the head through the windshield. I walked across the street, into the alley, and back to the bar. I changed, and now I'm having a drink, talking to you."

Upon hearing the news of Ron Milliken's condition, Guillermo had taken the next flight to New York. From New York he went to Dallas and from there to Kansas City. Miles Masterson and James Bolton followed him. Bolton took the same flights and Miles followed, as he was concerned about being recognized by Guillermo. When he arrived in Kansas City, the FBI picked up the surveillance duties. Guillermo took various cabs to different places in the city most of the day and into the evening. There didn't seem to be any pattern to his movements. He settled for the evening at the airport Marriot. The next day at mid-morning he took a cab downtown and proceeded from there. He was certain that he wasn't being followed but always assumed that he was. His movements were designed to confuse anyone who may have been tailing him and to keep him from being the object of anyone's attention.

"What about Rachel Biggs? Is she alive or dead?" The Administrator wanted more good news for the Cleric, who was listening in on the conversation.

"I don't know. She isn't showing up at any of the hospitals or morgues."

"Come on home. Let's let things cool off while we decide how to finish this. Jonathon Biggs is tougher than I thought," declared the Cleric.

"But he will go down," Guillermo said confidently.

"Yes, Guillermo, go down he will, and he will suffer." The Cleric was concerned but enjoying the challenge.

Chapter Two

"She's been in there for three days. I don't think she's coming out any time soon," FBI agent Miller commented to John Doe.

They were sitting in the maid's quarters above the garage of the mansion across the street from the one in which Maggie was staying. The walls around the house were twelve feet tall with sharp glass imbedded on top to discourage climbing burglars. Just inside the wall, out of sight from the street, was a two-foot wide band of razor wire in case someone made the wall. Maggie was inside the large compound enjoying a much-needed rest, lounging by the pool and being pampered by two servants who took care of everything from cooking and cleaning to protecting her. The Cleric had placed this loyal couple at the mansion ten years ago. He wanted his vacation getaway to be very safe. The couple, Sergio and Alma Garcia, was also used from time-to-time for various assignments as needed by the Cleric. They were fiercely loyal to him.

"Holcroft wants us to wait around to see if the guy that shot Kline shows up," John Doe said plainly.

"Have you completed your surveillance evaluation yet?" the FBI agent asked.

"Yes, and the system is tight. Cameras and motion sensors as well as lasers. Getting in at night is impossible. The daytime would be easier, because most of the lasers will be off, but the motion sensors by the walls will still be active." John Doe was an expert in virtually every area of covert operations.

"The only person to leave the compound is that Mexican lady. She gets groceries and supplies and comes back in. I wonder if the Cleric is in there with her. If we go in, we'll need more people. We would have to strike hard and fast and hope we get the Cleric." Agent Miller was not anxious to try an assault.

"If he's not in there, then we'll have lost our person who can lead us to him." As John Doe was speaking, his cell phone vibrated. It was Bob Holcroft with an update.

"The assassin is now in Mexico. He crossed the border on foot at McAllen, Texas. He grabbed a cab in Reynosa and headed for the airport. Bolton and Miles Masterson are on him," Holcroft reported.

"I hope his moving gets Maggie out of the compound," John Doe said. "If we have to go in we'll need more men and equipment. This place is really secure. If we go through the gate or over the wall they'll know immediately."

"I'm coming down as soon as we know where the killer is headed. I'm flying to Tucson in Biggs' jet. We'll fly in when we're ready to take them on." Holcroft wanted to be in on the capture.

"Just exactly who is *we?*" John Doe was hoping for a special ops team.

"Me and Jonathon Biggs. He insists on following this through to the end himself. We're having a short briefing in five minutes and will be off after that. I'll call you when we're in the air."

"Or I'll call you if there is any movement here."

"Good, thanks. Would you make a few calls to acquire the equipment you think we might need? Tell him that money is no object." Holcroft knew that John Doe could get whatever they needed quickly and quietly.

"Jonathon Biggs has deep pockets," John Doe responded.

"He wants to finish this," Holcroft stated explicitly.

John Doe didn't want an untrained person in the way. "Biggs knows that he's not going in with us, right, Bob?"

"He's insistent on confronting the Cleric himself. We're working on the details now."

John Doe was adamant. "Having an amateur around could cause this mission to fail—not to mention that he could get us killed or be killed himself."

Holcroft didn't like being told the obvious, as if he hadn't thought of it. "I will inform him of the risks and your concerns. Is there anything else?"

"No, sir. Thank you."

"How do you want to do this?" Guillermo asked the Administrator.

"Stay at the house in Monterey tonight. Use the car in the garage when you leave tomorrow night. Stop for a drink at the Staybridge Hotel. Leave at nine o'clock; go out the service door on the side of the building. There will be a red pickup with the keys in the visor. When you start the engine, Maggie will come out and meet you. Take the usual precautions and drive here."

"I'll call when I get into town. We'll do the usual double check to make sure I'm not followed." Guillermo had been trained well by the Administrator.

"Good, see you tomorrow."

"Yes, tomorrow."

Holcroft, Jonathon, and Eli were in the conference room of the downtown offices at Biggs International.

Bob Holcroft was laying out the plan for moving in on the Cleric. "Jonathon, you know we can't bring you in on the fight. You could be killed or put one of us at risk."

"I thought you might feel that way. This may sound absurd to you, Bob, but I think I am qualified. I am on the SWAT practice team. I'm part of the group of volunteers they use as criminals to simulate various situations. I've been doing that for fifteen years and have been in nearly every possible scenario used in their training exercises." Jonathon tried to be as convincing as possible.

Holcroft wasn't impressed with Jonathon Biggs combat resume. "That's good, Jonathon, but it is not live combat with weapons that shoot real bullets that could get you or one of us killed."

"I'm also the captain of the state champion paintball team. Last year we defeated the FBI team in a field drill and a warehouse battle. By the way, the Marines came in third," Jonathon added.

Eli interjected, "Bob, Jonathon is a nationally ranked sharpshooter with a pistol in both still and moving targets. He helps train cadets at our police academy in perpetrator recognition drills. We have been working on this stuff since I was fourteen. We are very good."

"Two things," Holcroft stated firmly, pointing his index finger at Eli and then at Jonathon. "One, this is not a drill, and two, does *we* mean that you want to come as well, Eli?"

Eli Moore nodded in affirmation.

"Bob." Jonathon tried not to sound as if he were pleading. "They could have killed me at any time. They don't want me dead; they want me ruined and suffering. This is about destroying me and everyone close to me. I have to be involved at every level. Breslin Kline has been a friend for less than a year, and he's dead. I'm not going through life wondering which friend or loved one will be next. Mexico is not your jurisdiction, so you can take anyone you want. We've been in this together since the early stages; let's finish together!"

Jonathon could tell that Holcroft had changed his mind.

"Okay, but you wear vests and headgear." Holcroft waved his finger emphatically in each of their faces.

"Done!" Jonathon offered his hand to Holcroft. They shook.

"By the way, Bob, how are you arranging to go into Mexico as an FBI agent?" Eli asked.

"I'm on vacation. I haven't had one in years, so I'm due.

Mexico sounded nice, so I thought I'd visit for a few weeks with my friends Jonathon and Eli." They all laughed.

"I thought that stuff only works in the movies!" commented Eli.

"I'm not sure if it will work, but I'm going anyway!" Holcroft smiled.

Jonathon answered his cell phone. "The jet is ready. Let's go!"

Chapter Three

"The Chrysler New Yorker that brought Maggie into the compound is leaving. There are two people in the front seat. One is the Mexican woman we have seen before; the other is a man close to her age. I'll bet anything that Maggie is in that car!" Agent Miller was ready for some action.

"We sit still," replied John Doe. "I'll let my man up the street pick up the New Yorker. This is a defensive move to get anyone who may be following her to go after the first car. There will be another car in a few minutes. We'll take that one."

"I didn't know that you had a man down the street! You need to tell me these things." Agent Miller didn't like to be left in the dark.

"I only give out information if and when it becomes necessary. That's why Holcroft called me. He knows I'll get the job done without a lot of attention or collateral damage."

"I'll call Holcroft and tell him she's moving." Agent Miller picked up his phone.

"Good, then you can pack up the gear and head home. Your help has been invaluable, but it's time for you to step out. You will never get jurisdictional approval to follow this to its conclusion," John Doe ordered.

"What! We'll see about that." Agent Miller punched a button on his cell to speed dial Holcroft. When he hung up, he began packing up the equipment, grumbling under his breathe, but loud enough for John Doe to hear.

"There she goes. Beat-up, blue pickup. Hispanic man driving. That's her for sure!" John Doe headed for the door.

"She's not in that car! The driver is a Hispanic male, and there is no passenger," Agent Miller said.

"She's the driver. It's easy for a woman to disguise herself as a young man. I don't have time to explain this to you." John Doe walked out of the building and got into the driver's seat of an old Chevrolet Impala.

Agent Miller grabbed his super high-powered binoculars and took another look as the blue pickup drove by. The driver was a very young-looking Hispanic male with a thin mustache. "He's wearing work gloves to hide his feminine hands while he drives. He's Maggie! Who is this John Doe?" He packed his gear and headed out of Mexico.

———◆———

"Maggie's moving in Cuernavaca," Holcroft informed Jonathon and Eli. "I'll let Miles know."

"The assassin is headed toward Monterrey. He walked right through the terminal in Reynosa and got into a black Ford LTD. We're on him. If he goes all the way into Monterrey, it'll take between two and three hours depending on the road conditions. I'll bet that Maggie will come to him. Maybe the Cleric is staying in Monterrey." Miles Masterson and James Bolton were enjoying the pursuit.

"Stay on him, Miles. We'll be there in less than three hours."

Holcroft hung up and asked Jonathon, "Can we change our flight plan and go into Monterrey, Mexico?"

"No problem. I'll call a friend in the Federals, and he'll take care of it quietly."

"Great." Holcroft eased back into his seat. They would need at least some rest before they arrived in Mexico.

———◆———

"She has switched vehicles. She is now on a small yellow motor bike." John Doe's contact man called to him on the radio.

John Doe was two blocks behind.

Maggie had pulled up to the pump in a gas station. A young man had pulled in behind her on a motor bike. She reached into the bed of the pickup truck took out the helmet that was there, put it on, and switched places with the driver of the motor bike. He pulled out behind her and blocked traffic while she scooted down an alley.

"She's going down an alley. Turn right and pick her up on the next block."

"I'm on it!" John Doe responded. "Do you think she made us?"

"I doubt it," came the reply. "She doesn't seem to be in a hurry. She's probably following their protocol just in case."

"I see her now. Go south in case she dodges down another alley. I'll stay with her from here."

Ten minutes later, John Doe was talking to Bob Holcroft on the Biggs jet telephone. "She has pulled into the airport and is getting off the motorbike right now. She's going to fly somewhere. She's walking toward a twin-engine Cessna that appears to have been waiting for her? Do you want me take her now?"

"No," Holcroft said firmly. "She's coming to meet someone in Monterrey. We'll be waiting for her. Get a flight up here as soon as you can in case I need you for backup. Also, can you arrange for some tactical gear in Monterrey right away?"

"No sweat. I'll have it delivered to a room at the Staybridge Hotel. Check in as Enrique Diaz. What are you going to do next?" John Doe didn't want to miss the fight.

"I don't know yet. I want to see who she meets and where they go. I'm hoping they lead us to the primary," Holcroft said.

"Just like the days when we chased drug runners in Louisiana." John Doe laughed.

"Only fewer bugs and no swamps—I'll talk at you later." Holcroft turned and began to explain the situation to Jonathon and Eli. He then called Miles Masterson. "We'll be there in twenty minutes. Stay on the assassin. We'll connect when they rendezvous."

Chapter Four

Miles Masterson and Mr. James Bolton followed Guillermo to a small, simple house on the busy outskirts of Monterrey. Miles left Mr. Bolton to keep an eye on Guillermo and flagged a cab to the Staybridge Hotel. He knew that he couldn't leave Mr. Bolton alone all night, as they were both exhausted and prone to making a small but crucial mistake. Together they could take turns watching and sleeping.

Miles introduced himself to the desk clerk as Enrique Diaz and received a key to room 120. He called Bob Holcroft as soon as he opened the packages from John Doe.

"Your friend John Doe is really connected down here!" exclaimed Miles Masterson. "He sent two wooden crates with vests, AK47s, some flash bang grenades, and ten pistols."

"Are there two Desert Eagle Forty-fours in there?" Holcroft asked.

"Yes, with right and left shoulder holsters. I take it that they're for you?" Miles Masterson wasn't surprised that the big man liked big weapons.

"I like the forty-four. Big noise, big hole. Backs the bad guys down real quick," quipped Holcroft.

"Good. I hope we don't need all that fire power." Miles shook his head.

"We will. This Cleric person is a strategic thinker. He'll be well protected." Bob Holcroft was sure of himself.

Jonathon Biggs, Eli Moore, and Bob Holcroft arrived at the Staybridge Hotel within an hour of the conversation with Miles Masterson. They decided to form teams to watch Guillermo for the night. Eli and Jonathon went out to give Mr. Bolton a break. Miles and Bolton would take over in four hours.

Bob Holcroft went to the airport to watch for Maggie. He returned two hours later. "She's staying here."

"What room is she in?" Bolton was already thinking about surveillance issues.

"Room 123. Across the hall and one door down."

"I better tell Jonathon and Eli to stay away." Holcroft didn't want Maggie to see either of the men from Biggs International.

"I'll walk down the hall and put a listening device next to her door. I'll also check the perimeter for other possible means of exit," Bolton volunteered.

Bolton left the room to perform his tasks. Ten minutes later there was a knock on the door.

"*Servicio de quarto.*"

Gun in hand, Miles Masterson approached the door. With Holcroft standing to his left, he slowly opened the door.

"John Doe," whispered Holcroft. "What a relief!"

"I brought you some tacos, chilaquiles, and Coca-Cola," he said as he walked into the room. "It's a little crowded in here— looks like an FBI project. Six agents in one room. Not to worry." He placed a key in the door between rooms and opened it. "I got you another room. Biggs has more money than the FBI." He laughed and pointed at Holcroft.

"Maggie is across the hall," Holcroft rasped.

"I know, I checked the register at the front desk. She is the only other person besides Enrique Diaz to check in tonight. She registered under the name Feliz Santigo. She also ordered room service. I delivered her's first. She appears to be settled in for the night."

"How rested are you?" asked Miles Masterson.

"I'm fine. I've been sitting around in Cuernavaca for the last three days. I'm good to go. What do you want me to do?"

"We need a four-wheel drive pickup truck."

"It will be in the parking lot behind your room with the keys under the floor mat within an hour. Anything else?"

"Maybe you could spell Jonathon and Eli while they watch the assassin," Miles suggested.

"Not a problem. Where are they?"

Holcroft gave him the location, and John Doe left the room. At the door he said, "*Gracias, Senor. Buenas noches!*"

As soon as John Doe left, Bolton tapped on the window. Miles opened it and he climbed in. "I'm glad we're on the first floor!" Bolton said. "She has an outside window just like this one, only it opens to an alley not a parking lot. There's a reason she has that room. She can escape easily enough through the window or be picked up by someone out in the alley. I set up a camera at each end of the alley and a listening device beneath her window. She won't be going anywhere without us."

Bolton picked up a plate and placed a scoop of chilaquiles and a taco on it. "I love Mexican food," he said in his British accent. He booted up his notebook computer and connected to his various devices. The men took turns sleeping and watching the computer for movement.

———

"I'm here to help," whispered John Doe as he slipped into the backseat of the surveillance car. Both Jonathon and Eli were awake.

"I know." replied Jonathon. "Holcroft said that you would be coming."

"You need to take turns sleeping or you won't be alert when this comes down," John Doe warned. "I'll take the next two hours."

"It's hard to sleep with all this coming to a head," Eli admitted. "But I'll try."

"I brought you guys some weapons for later. Glock nine millimeters and AK47 fully automatic rifles. Do you know how to use the AK?"

"Wow, that's some serious firepower!" Jonathon proclaimed.

"If you didn't want to fight; you shouldn't have come along," John Doe stated bluntly.

"Oh, we're in all the way. I'm just surprised at your ability to procure such exceptional equipment on short notice. And yes, we have used the AK47 before at our gun club. We both own Glocks as well," Jonathon pronounced with a serious tone in his voice. He wanted John Doe to know that he could handle himself in a conflict.

"Good, get some sleep. I'll wake you in two hours."

Jonathon didn't realize how tired he was. He put his head back in the seat and closed his eyes. When John Doe woke him, four hours had passed. Guillermo the assassin hadn't left the house.

John Doe had Jonathon drive around the block and find a different parking place that was less conspicuous in daylight. He sent Eli into a small restaurant to get breakfast and coffee. While he was gone, John Doe had a heart to heart with Jonathon Oliver Biggs.

"I don't know what to do with you all day. I can't send you back to the hotel because your former assistant is there. I'm also sure that the assassin knows your face. Because you are a public figure who has been in the news recently, someone might recognize you."

"In other words," said Jonathon, "I'm easy to spot."

"Yes, and you guys are not experienced at surveillance. I snuck up on the car last night, and you didn't even see me coming. If I were the assassin, you'd be dead right now."

"I know we lack experience, but we're here for the duration. So give me the picture, and I'll do whatever I need to do to help." Jonathon was not going to be sent packing at this point.

"I have to keep you with me, but I have to keep my eye on the house at the same time. I'm going to send Eli out after we eat to buy hats for you both. I hope that no one looks closely. We'll need to move the car every once in a while. I may even get out and walk around on the street, while I send you around the block a few times."

"I'll do whatever you ask. But I'm here to stay." Jonathon was clear.

"Okay."

Thirty minutes later, Eli was wearing a new baseball cap that looked well-worn, because John Doe had rubbed dirt on it and poured coffee around the bill. Jonathon had a straw hat that he crumpled up, so it looked well used. He pulled it down low on his forehead hoping to shade his blue eyes. At intervals all day, John Doe had them driving up the street, parking on the opposite side and generally maneuvering to avoid being noticed by the assassin. He got out occasionally and walked around, blending in with the business of the street. Fortunately, the traffic was moderately heavy all day and pedestrians were traveling up and down the sidewalks shopping and hanging around. Jonathon thought that the cars, the crowd, and the noise affectively kept them anonymous.

The day passed at the hotel in the same way. Maggie stayed in her room.

Chapter Five

"We don't have anyone left in Kansas City to keep an eye on Jonathon Biggs," the Administrator said.

"I know. Can we get more of the mad cow serum?" The Cleric had a new plan for the Biggses.

"Yes, but then we'll have to send Guillermo to take care of our guy inside. How much are you thinking we need?" The Administrator was taking mental notes. He never forgot anything he was told. He had the equivalent of a photographic memory for things he heard.

"Two doses." The Cleric smiled. "One for Jonathon Biggs and another for his wife, if she is still alive. I want you and Guillermo to go. I'll keep Maggie here with me. She would be easy to recognize, because they know her so well."

"Excellent, sir! I sometimes miss the days when I was active in the field." The Administrator was ripe with enthusiasm.

"You were the best—and you still are. You trained Guillermo well, but you are the true master of demise. Your skills are still sharp, and your mind is even sharper. You have been a great help to me here, but now I need you out there finishing Biggs in the most agonizing way possible." The Cleric smiled with affirmation.

"Thank you, sir. I've been keeping up practicing on some of the locals." The Administrator rubbed his palms together in delight.

"How about the farmer from Saltillo? That was good work." The Cleric liked to hear every detail when someone was killed.

"He couldn't even scream out in pain as I tortured him." The Administrator had selected the farmer at random from the outskirts of Saltillo, a city about 350 kilometers from the mansion in Ciudad Victoria. When the Administrator had tortured and killed him, he incinerated the body completely in the furnace of a local factory.

"His family will suffer for years wondering where he went. The note was a great touch." The Cleric reviewed how the Administrator had left a simple note written by the farmer during the early hours of torture. "I need a better life, good-bye." He placed the note on the steering wheel of the farmer's truck near the United States border at Juarez.

"It was good practice!" The Administrator erupted with glee.

"We'll lay out the plan with Guillermo tonight. You are personally in charge of this one."

"I will not fail you, Cleric."

"I know. You are the master of demise! You don't know how to fail."

"He's moving!" Jonathon Biggs saw Guillermo the assassin drive a black Honda Civic out of the garage attached to the house. He turned right and blended into traffic. Jonathon was driving and slowly pulled out four car lengths behind him. Suddenly, Guillermo made a quick right down a small side street. Jonathon turned right on the same street, but the Civic wasn't in sight. They drove down the street looking both ways at every intersection but didn't find the Civic.

"We lost him!" Eli said in frustration.

"No we haven't!" said John Doe. "He's changing cars. That's him on the sidewalk to the right. See the Civic parked there. Pull over for a second, and let's see what he gets into."

"He's hailing a cab. We're on him!" Jonathon was excited by the chase.

"Move quickly up behind the cab. He won't be watching for someone following him," John Doe instructed, and Jonathon obeyed.

They followed the cab for ten blocks, until it pulled over and Guillermo got out. He went into a men's clothing shop. The cab waited outside.

"Pull into that parking space," John Doe ordered. It was a space two cars ahead of the cab. He got out and went into the narrow alleyway next to the shop. Suddenly the cab drove off without the assassin. Moments later John Doe came out of the narrow alleyway between the buildings and got into the back seat of the car.

"He's gone."

"Do you think he spotted us?" Eli asked.

"I doubt it. These were well rehearsed defensive maneuvers. By the time I walked to the back alley, he was gone."

"How do you know that he isn't still in the shop?" Eli asked as if it were obvious.

"He left the cab like a man in a hurry. He was using the shop as his entrance to the alley behind." John Doe was already calling Holcroft. "He's on the move. He's a top level pro. He lost us in less than five minutes."

"I'll bet that she moves soon too. Someone just delivered a red truck to the alley outside of her window," Holcroft said. "Come back to the hotel and keep an eye on the lobby. I'll set someone up in the alley. I'm betting that Maggie and the assassin go to the Cleric together."

"Got it. What about the big guy and his pal?" John Doe wasn't being sarcastic. He still wasn't sure that Jonathon and Eli would be anything but a liability when the action picked up. John Doe knew the value of instincts learned from years of training and experience. His trained eye told him that Jonathon Oliver Biggs had just enough instinct to get himself killed. In his opinion, Eli Moore didn't have any hope of surviving a fight.

"Take me about two blocks from the hotel. Park and stay in the car. Put the vests on under your jackets and keep your weapons discreetly handy. If the assassin meets Maggie here, this thing will unfold in a hurry. When I call, get to the front of the hotel fast. Start moving on the first ring. Answer while you're moving. Got it?" John Doe hoped that they would follow his instruction when the action started.

"We're ready!" Jonathon and Eli chimed in together.

"Don't say that!" rebuked John Doe. "I've been doing this for years, and I'm never really ready. Just pay attention and do what you are told. Men will die tonight. We want all of ours to walk away!" That said, John Doe left the car and walked toward the lobby of the hotel.

Chapter Six

"Mr. Bolton, will you cover the alley in the direction the truck is facing?" Bob Holcroft was strapping on his Desert Eagle forty-fours over his vest. "Miles and I will be in the truck. Beep me twice on your two-way when that truck moves. We'll drive by the alley entrance, and you can hop into the back of the pickup. When they get where they're going and the assassin moves to get out of that truck, I want you to shoot him dead. We want him out of the picture, before he can put his skills into action against us. Dead, Mr. Bolton, one shot dead!"

"With certainty, Inspector." Mr. James Bolton was completely calm inside and out.

"Miles, you drive and do exactly as I tell you. We must be quicker than they are, or we will lose our advantage."

"Ready." Miles Masterson climbed out the window and into the truck provided by John Doe. He started the engine and broke out the back window with the butt of his rifle.

Holcroft joined him, saw the broken window, and remarked, "Good idea. Mr. Bolton will be able to hear us clearly this way."

Mr. Bolton left through the door carrying his small notebook computer, which he was using to view the surveillance cameras he had set up. He had a Glock 40mm in his belt under his jacket and one stuck down the small of his back. He arrived in the alley via the rear exit and set up his computer behind a dumpster that provided him protection from view. He quickly programmed the destruct mechanism to destroy the computer when he pressed the ESC key or Function F12. He waited.

—>•<—

John Doe stopped in the lobby and picked up a newspaper. He then went into the Hotel lounge and ordered a Coke with lime. He sat at a table in plain view and read the paper while he drank his Coke. He told the waiter that he was waiting for a lady named Elena. He knew that he would look awkward while waiting, so he made up a woman friend to make the awkwardness appear normal.

Guillermo the assassin was sitting at the far end of the bar slowly drinking tequila. Fifteen minutes later, at nine o'clock, he slid from the stool and strolled casually toward the restrooms. When he was out of sight, John Doe punched his phone and notified Bob Holcroft. Holcroft nodded to Miles Masterson, and they positioned their vehicle near the entrance to the alley. They could see the dumpster, but not Mr. Bolton, who was completely concealed next to it.

John Doe got up and shrugged his shoulders in disgust, as if he had been stood up by the pretend Elena. He tossed down a generous tip and walked dejectedly out to the street with his phone handy.

Guillermo slipped into the driver's seat of the truck and quickly found the keys under the visor. Ten seconds after he turned the ignition, Maggie came through the window in her room and slid gracefully onto the seat next to him. She gave him a kiss on the cheek. "It is so good to see you again. Let's go home!" Unseen by either of them, Mr. James Bolton was signaling Holcroft and Masterson.

Guillermo put the truck in gear and pulled out of the alley. Mr. Bolton pressed the ESC key on his computer and heard the gentle hiss as it began the self-destruct process. Guillermo turned right out of the alley and drove at a reasonable rate of speed out of town. Miles and Holcroft quickly picked up Mr. Bolton and followed. Seconds later, Jonathon Biggs pulled up in front of the hotel, and John Doe casually got in the backseat.

"Give them room, but keep them in sight," instructed John Doe. "We want to be able to catch up to Miles quickly when we have to, so keep that in mind as you position yourself in traffic."

"We're close to the end, aren't we?" Jonathon Biggs breathed.

"I hope so, Mr. Biggs. Let's get this cleaned up tonight, so you can all go on with your lives," John Doe answered.

"And spend some time healing from our wounds." Eli thought of Debra and the Listers. He was glad for Jonathon's sake and his own that Rachel had survived.

They drove for four hours through the desert and into the hills around Ciudad Victoria.

<hr />

Maggie snuggled up to Guillermo. "When this is over, let's go to Cuernavaca and spend some serious time together. I'm sure the Cleric will give us a few months of rest after all this time."

"He's going to want to savor the victory for a while, before he moves on to the next family. I'm sure that he'll give us plenty of time off. But why don't we go to the Swiss Alps or someplace that normal people go for romantic interludes."

"Oh, good idea! I'll go anywhere with you." She leaned over and kissed him firmly on his lips.

He put his arm around her and asked, "Do you think the Cleric will let us get married soon? Or at least give him grandchildren?"

"He hasn't talked about it yet. I'll try to discreetly ask him." She kissed him again with more passion this time.

"Let's finish off Jonathon Oliver Biggs and get on with our trip to the Swiss Alps!" Guillermo held Maggie close and whispered, "Because I love you," in her ear.

They were entering Ciudad Victoria, a beautiful city in the hills of northern Mexico.

"The Administrator just drove by. We'll pull over here and let him run his surveillance check so we know we're not being followed." Guillermo pulled over to the side of the road.

Holcroft spotted him and told Miles to turn left at the first opportunity. They turned a block before they would have driven by the couple. Holcroft was on his cell with John Doe and told him to have Jonathon turn right on the same street.

"This guy is slippery. I hope we don't lose him now," Holcroft said.

"We won't," stated Mr. James Bolton.

Miles smiled broadly. "Please tell us how you know that, Bolton."

"While I was waiting so patiently behind the dumpster, I decided to give us some security. I slipped along the alley wall and placed a tracer under the front bumper. Would you like me to activate it now?"

"Please, sir, activate the tracer now." Holcroft was shaking his head. "That was risky."

"Not if you are Mr. James Bolton." Miles laughed. Bolton had been the premier stealth agent in Britain for years. He was rumored to have been in Prince Charles' quarters while the prince was in the room taking tea.

Holcroft instructed John Doe to drive three blocks down and move parallel to the street where Guillermo was parked. Holcroft decided to keep visual surveillance in case Guillermo and Maggie decided to change vehicles. He had Miles drive around the block. As they came around, the truck began to move again. Miles settled in two cars behind and casually followed. Holcroft kept the other car informed and within two blocks.

"All clear," said the Administrator over his cell to Maggie. "Give me five minutes lead and come in to the mansion."

"He's been doing this for years, and we've never been followed." Maggie giggled.

"He says it only takes one time," Guillermo, always cautious, commented.

"I'd like to see someone take on you and the Administrator. You two are the most lethal people in the world. Even if someone did find us, they wouldn't live to talk about it!" She leaned over and kissed him again. This time with admiration.

"True," Guillermo responded by returning the kiss with a longing pause at the end.

"Well, shall we go to the mansion? I think the Administrator has had enough lead time," Maggie spoke breathlessly.

"Let's go." Guillermo went around the last curve and pulled up to the security box at the gate. He put in the combination, waited for the cameras to confirm their identities, and began to edge forward as the gates slowly opened into the compound.

"Miles, as soon as that gate opens enough, I want you to ram him and push both of us through it. Start moving now!" Holcroft ordered.

Miles Masterson accelerated the four-wheel-drive truck toward the gate. As Guillermo moved forward, he looked in the mirror and saw the truck right behind him. The collision knocked the couple back into their seats as Miles powered both vehicles through the gate. Guillermo stomped on the brakes too late, as both trucks were careened into the compound.

"Come now!" yelled Holcroft into his two-way.

"We're ten seconds behind you!" John Doe's voice came back.

Guillermo pulled his pistol and kicked the door open. As he began to roll out of the truck, Bolton's bullet caught him directly below his nose and severed his spinal column on the way through his head.

"Great shot, Mr. Bolton," Holcroft shouted as he and Miles bailed out of the truck.

"I was aiming for his forehead but he moved." Mr. Bolton shrugged.

Jonathon Biggs, Eli, and John Doe came screeching up in the car, nearly sliding into the wreckage. All three jumped out and joined the others as they moved up the driveway.

"Bolton, take the right flank and move quickly to the back of the house. John Doe, take the left. We'll spread out and go through the front door. Everybody run, now!" Bob Holcroft relished a good fight.

The mansion was a large two-story building that was narrow and long. There was a pool and a small pool house in the back. The front of the mansion had a wide, stone porch with a roof that wrapped halfway down each side. The porch in the back was similar. Each bedroom upstairs had a small balcony accessed by a single door. Mr. Bolton and John Doe made their way to the back of the house quickly.

Miles blew the door open with his AK47 and ran in low. He covered the door while the others followed. Jonathon and Eli did well at this exercise. "Where are your helmets?" Holcroft yelled at the two executives.

"We forgot them in the car," Jonathon yelled without apology.

"If your head gets caved in don't come crying to me!" scolded Miles.

"The right rear is secure," reported Mr. Bolton.

"The left is secure," John Doe chimed in.

"They're going to make us find them," said Holcroft. "Let's split up. Miles and Biggs, you take that side of the house. I'll take Eli and cover this side. Bolton and Doe, make your way in from the back. Maybe we can squeeze them."

As he was speaking, a burst of shots were fired in the backyard followed by two quick single shots. "Two of them came from the pool house, a man and a woman. One fired an automatic weapon. Both are down. Both are down." The voice of John Doe came over Holcroft's two-way.

Five minutes later, the groups came back together in the foyer of the mansion. "There is no one in the house," Miles Masterson reported. Everyone nodded in agreement.

"We found no access to a basement," Eli spoke up.

"The floors are concrete with marble tile, so maybe there isn't a basement," Miles surmised.

Jonathon Biggs knew about mansions. He'd been around them all his life. "No, there is always some kind of small cellar or pantry in these types of mansions. A place used in the old days to store food. Let's look around the kitchen and see if they covered up an entrance."

Jonathon and Miles headed for the kitchen while Holcroft and Eli went out to the pool house to see about the shots.

"This is the couple from Cuernavaca," John Doe informed Holcroft. "They must have flown here yesterday while we were watching Maggie and the assassin."

"We'll check out the pool house. Bolton, take Eli and look around the perimeter of the wall. See if you can find an escape route. Eli, this is the part where people get shot. Are you sure you want to continue?"

"Yes!" Eli was emphatic.

"Then get going," ordered Holcroft.

John Doe whispered to Holcroft as they entered the pool house, "Remember those drug houses along the border, the ones with the trap doors and tunnels in the closets? I'll bet there's a trap door in here somewhere and in the main house too."

"Good point." Holcroft informed Jonathon and Miles about John Doe's observation and asked them to check the closet floors and walls for access doors to a tunnel or basement room.

John Doe went directly to the master bedroom closet when he noticed the door was open. "Bob, I found something. See the seam in the carpet? It's too wide. I'll bet that's the door to a tunnel."

"The man and woman John Doe shot out back by the pool house probably came out here to watch the Cleric's back so he could get away." Holcroft punched the button on his two-way and brought everyone up to speed.

"We don't see any escape access along the wall on the perimeter," Eli checked in. "So we're tapping at sections with our weapons to see if there is a hollow spot."

Chapter Seven

"Cleric, we need to leave now!" The Administrator had heard the shots outside and knew intuitively that the two, quick single shots meant that Jonathon Biggs and his crew were close at hand.

"They have discovered the tunnel in the pool house." The Cleric was matter-of-fact as he looked at the surveillance monitors in front of him. The two of them were in a large, cavernous room below the house. It had a black marble table in the middle and a fireplace at one end large enough for a man to stand in straight up. The ceiling was at least fifteen feet high and covered with sound-dampening material. There were two, smaller rooms located at the opposite end of the fireplace at the back of the large room. There were three openings entering the large room, one on each of the side walls. A tunnel from the kitchen led to one, and another tunnel from the pool house led to the other. The third was in the center of the back wall. This served as the escape tunnel through the perimeter wall to the outside.

"They have the pool house covered," the Cleric said from the smaller of the two ante rooms. The room was the hub for the surveillance system on the property.

"I'm arming myself right now. What weapons do you want to carry?" The Administrator was in the other room selecting the weapons he would use against Jonathon Biggs and company. Every wall in the room held weapons of various types from different eras of warfare. "I'm taking the small crossbow and two forty-caliber pistols with laser sights; if I have to I'll take a few of them out quietly and blow the others away with the forties."

"Just give me the Uzi. If there's going to be an open confrontation, I can spray the room and distract them while you finish them off." The Cleric's strategic mind was clicking.

"I'll give you a thirty-eight with the Kevlar piercing rounds in case you get in a close situation. Do you want your robe now?" The Administrator was already putting on his dark brown hooded robe.

"Yes, please," the Cleric responded with respect. "They've discovered the kitchen entrance, and two of them have found the secret door through the wall. They are trying to open it now. It looks like Jonathon Biggs is here! He's in the kitchen. Someone else is with him. We'll have to destroy them in here." The Cleric had a sense of anticipation in his voice, much like an athlete looking forward to the contest.

The Administrator came into the surveillance room and helped the Cleric into his purple hooded robe. They returned to the main room and stood by the marble table.

"To The Dark One, for The Dark One: deceive, discourage, and destroy," chanted the Cleric.

"To The Dark One, for the Dark One: deceive, discourage, and destroy," chanted the Administrator.

"Oh, Dark One, empower us to do your will: to the destruction of Jonathon Biggs and all that he is!" the Cleric prayed, placing both hands open palms down on the marble table.

"Oh, Dark One, we are you servants. Use us to destroy your enemies and to give you praise!" the Administrator responded, standing behind the Cleric with his hands on the Cleric's shoulders.

When the prayer ended, both men simultaneously pulled up the hoods on their robes. Their faces were barely visible.

The Administrator moved quickly and quietly into the shadows in the back corner of the room. The Cleric stepped forward and took his place in front of the marble table, as if to greet his enemies.

"Let Biggs and Eli Moore live for a few moments. I want to address them, before they die."

The Administrator stood silently in the corner and waited. He liked the contest, but he loved the killing best of all.

<hr />

"We've found the exit in the wall but can't get it opened. We may have to use one of the grenades," Mr. Bolton said, checking in with Holcroft.

"We're above a tunnel from the pool house. We'll get out of the way. Give us thirty seconds and blow the wall." Holcroft and John Doe closed the trap door, waiting for the explosion. "Did you copy that, Biggs?"

"Copy that, Bob. Miles found a button behind the refrigerator. When he pushed it, a set of cabinets moved from the wall to reveal a steel door that must lead to an escape tunnel. I wonder if your tunnel and ours both end up at the same exit or if there is more than one way out of here."

"Can you get the steel door opened?"

"Affirmative, Miles picked the lock with his forty-five." The rest of Jonathon's sentence was cut off by the explosion at the wall.

"Everybody go. Use your flash bangs as needed. These tunnels could be booby trapped," Holcroft commanded.

"Let's move!" Miles commanded in a hoarse whisper. Jonathon moved through the door quickly.

"We're going in!" shouted Eli as he and Mr. Bolton entered the tunnel at the wall. Mr. Bolton went first with Eli a few steps behind.

John Doe dropped the six feet into the pool house tunnel with Holcroft nearly on top of him. As they landed, four spikes came out of the wall. Two of them pierced Bob Holcroft's right leg.

"Booby trap! I'm hurt—got it in the leg. Doe, keep moving, I'll tie these up and be right behind you. Be careful!" Holcroft grimaced in pain and frustration. "We can't let Biggs get there before we do. He could make a fatal mistake."

John Doe helped Holcroft up the tunnel a few feet and left him.

"Biggs will be here first—from the kitchen. Remember don't kill right away," said the Cleric in a soft, affirming tone.

"Tunnel on the right. Crossbow to the arm and leg." The Administrator knew that the Cleric liked the details of the contest. He enjoyed the anticipation as much as the Administrator enjoyed the killing.

"Good." the Cleric continued to wait quietly for his guests.

Chapter Eight

A flash bang grenade rolled a few feet out of the kitchen tunnel and exploded. The Cleric and the Administrator did not move. Jonathon Biggs *had* made a fatal mistake. In his adrenaline-rushed excitement, he ran into the room, moving his rifle from side-to-side, looking for a target. The grenade appeared to confuse him more than his enemies. A short arrow whooshed through his arm. As he was realizing what had happened, another arrow penetrated his thigh, stopping when it hit bone. Miles Masterson dove on him from behind, knocking Biggs to the floor. A third arrow hit Masterson on the top of his right shoulder as he fell. He groaned and rolled off Biggs as a fourth arrow hit him within inches of the last one.

The Administrator walked out of the shadows and stood three feet to the left of the Cleric. He had a forty caliber pistol in each hand.

John Doe rolled out of the pool house tunnel into the main chamber. At the same time, Mr. Bolton and Eli crawled into the room from the wall tunnel. All three aimed their weapons in the direction of the Cleric.

The Cleric lifted his robed arms, hands visible and unarmed. "Welcome to our worship chambers. Mr. Biggs, I know you're not dead, because my Administrator and I decided ahead of time not to kill you right away."

Jonathon Oliver Biggs struggled to his knees.

"It is fitting to have you kneel before me." The Cleric laughed. "This has worked out better than I had planned."

"The Dark One has been good to you," said the Administrator with reverence.

"What is this all about?" shouted Jonathon Biggs. "Why did you kill my family? Who are you to take the lives of innocent people?"

As he was speaking, Maggie appeared through the kitchen tunnel. She was armed with a pistol. She walked up directly behind Jonathon and placed the muzzle of her weapon against the back of his head.

"You forgot about me in the truck. Big mistake, Mr. Biggs!"

"I want an explanation!" demanded Jonathon, ignoring Maggie. "Are you such a coward that you hide in Mexico while other people do your evil work for you? I did nothing to deserve this! I don't know you or why you would want to destroy me, nor have I, to my knowledge, ever done anything to harm you."

"Yes, you have. Do you remember a boat accident twenty years ago?" the Cleric began.

"I do. A woman was killed because her drunken husband caused a collision. My wife, Rachel, rescued their twelve-year-old son from the lake. What does that have to do with you murdering my family?"

"You have a good mind for details, Mr. Jonathon Oliver Biggs. If you recall, the man was taken into custody for driving a boat while intoxicated and involuntary manslaughter for the death of his wife. The accident occurred on a weekend, so the arraignment wasn't until Monday morning. The man was released on twenty-thousand dollars bail and disappeared without his son. He disappeared, never to be heard from again. You raised his son as your own and gave him every possible luxury and advantage. A life his father never could have provided for him."

"That boy has grown to become a good and respected man," Jonathon yelled at the Cleric. He had no concern for the gun held to his head by Maggie. "His success is not a result of what he was given but the result of his character and hard work. Are you trying to tell me that you..." Jonathon's voice trailed off as Eli stepped forward. "Are my father?"

"Yes, but don't get sentimental," the Cleric mocked. "You don't think that I actually love you or care about you in any way, do you? I left that life behind and found a new one. I do, however, hate you, Jonathon Oliver Biggs. You stole my son and deluded him with your riches. I watched you from a distance for years, and when I was ready to come for my son, it was too late. Your lifestyle was ingrained into him. You are the typical, wealthy heir who was given everything and passes it on to his children. Now you have no children! Your wealth is about to fail you altogether. Even your wife was killed by her close friend Maggie—in your own kitchen, no less!" The Cleric released a scornful laugh.

"You are not my father; Jonathon Biggs is my father. The Biggses raised me after you killed my mother and deserted me." The anger and hurt were evident in Eli's voice. He forced himself to speak evenly as he lifted his pistol and aimed it at Maggie's head. "I will kill Maggie if you don't drop your weapons."

"You don't understand, Eli. Your wife, Debra, worked for us. When we were finished with her, I had her killed. So as you see, we're all about death. We worship the Dark One, the one your Bible calls a 'murderer by nature and the father of lies.' There are cells like ours all over the world, plotting to bring ruin to 'good' men like your 'father' here. We've had many successful endeavors." The Cleric enjoyed explaining his conquests. "A powerful man in Europe commits suicide after his wife is found dead of a drug overdose. A wealthy Japanese businessman drives his car over a bridge because he is accused of murdering his wife and children as they slept. We did the wife and kids, he did himself. Our goal is for you to die in despair by your own hand. But for you, Mr. Biggs, we'll make an exception." The Cleric didn't appear to be concerned about the situation at all. "Go ahead and shoot Maggie. She has served her purpose and can be released at any time."

"But father!" Maggie blurted in shock and surprise. Jonathon felt the barrel of her pistol tremble against the back of his neck.

The Cleric turned his back on his daughter. "Kill them now," he whispered to the Administrator as he turned.

As he spoke, Bob Holcroft lumbered into the room, dual Desert Eagle, forty-four pistols in his fists. He fired both in quick succession. The first bullet hit the Administrator square in the chest, driving him off his feet and to the floor. He was dead before he landed. The second bullet drove through Maggie's left shoulder. Her gun went off as she was hit.

"Biggs is down!" yelled Miles Masterson, lying wounded on the floor. "She shot him in the head!"

The Cleric spun around, sliding the Uzi from beneath his robes. As he turned, Bolton and John Doe fired simultaneously from different directions. John Doe's bullet penetrated the Cleric's right eye, as Mr. Bolton's bullet entered his left eye. The Cleric's head snapped back, as if he were experiencing whiplash. He seemed to gather his balance for a split second and stared with empty sockets at his shooters. He crumpled to the floor, dead—forever.

Epilogue—Three Weeks Later

The team gathered in the Biggses' living room after the memorial service for Breslin Kline.

"Breslin would have been pleased with that service," said Miles Masterson, the new executive vice president of Biggs International. Miles proposed to Tere Waters on the airport tarmac the moment he returned from Mexico. She said *yes* immediately. They would be wed the following month, and Jonathon and Rachel Biggs would be their best man and matron of honor.

"I knew he liked us all along!" declared Jonathon Oliver Biggs. His head was wrapped in a bandage covering his right ear. Maggie's bullet creased the right side of Jonathon's head and took off the top half of his ear. He had already decided not to have plastic surgery to repair the ear. He figured his hearing was fine, so why bother?

"I thought it was fitting that we buried his ashes along the west ridge of the ranch," whispered the recovering Rachel Biggs. Her voice was affected for life. She would never be able to shout again. She told the doctor, "If I need to make a big noise, I'll buy an air horn!"

"I hope he knew that we all cared for him. He had a tough time building relationships with people. But he built a good one with us." Bob Holcroft was showing his compassionate side. He insisted that Breslin Kline was the best partner he had ever had. Holcroft, Mr. James Bolton, and William Louise (John Doe's real name) decided to start a covert investigation group to thwart the progress of "Dark Cell" groups like the one operated by the Cleric. Jonathon and Eli agreed to provide financial support.

"I hoped that Breslin would have continued working for Bills and Masterson. I'm sad and disappointed. I appreciated his candor and really enjoyed our verbal sparring sessions." Eli Moore laughed at the short but quality friendship he had enjoyed with Breslin Kline. Eli would continue as president of Biggs International. He was in the process of completing the sale of the European Division to Miguel Sameros and his father. The cash flow from the deal would give Biggs International a profitable year and a much-needed stock boost. Rachel Biggs insisted that Eli receive counseling to recover from the discovery that his father was a murderer and to deal with the issues raised when he discovered that Maggie was his half sister. She would be spending the rest of her life in a Mexican prison for her crimes. She was the only person in the Cleric's circle who had survived. Her husband Frank's body was found in a dumpster behind a strip mall outside of Kansas City.

Ron Milliken remains in a coma in England. Jonathon Biggs is hoping that he regains consciousness so they can talk about forgiveness. The doctors are not hopeful.

Breslin Kline will be missed.

Please read on!

God created each of us on purpose; with a purpose.
The most profound question we can ask in life has two parts:

1. Do you know your Creator?
2. Are you pursuing His purpose for your life?

This book is about the unrelenting efforts of the devil to keep you from answering the first question and living the second.

The devil is rarely given credit for his best work! We tend to blame God when things go wrong and life is painful and difficult. Often, however, the blame lies with the evil one.

Paul, the Apostle, tells us that he masquerades as an angel of light—looking good but scheming with evil strategies to keep us from realizing our purpose for being created. We also learn from this great apostle that Satan is well organized and has his own demonic legions to influence people and nations away from God's best (2 Corinthians 11:14; Ephesians 6:12).

Jesus pointed out that Satan is a murderer and the father of lies. His capacity to deceive and destroy is beyond our comprehension. The Apostle Peter says that he is like a roaring lion seeking someone to devour. If you are trying to live for God; the devil is having you stalked (John 8:44; 1 Peter 5:8).

Jesus is more powerful than the devil. On the cross and through His resurrection, He defeated sin, death, and Satan. He will come again one day—hopefully soon!—to set things right. Remember this: Jesus wins! If you belong to Him, you will share in His ultimate victory. You will also have His power to live the life for which you were created (1 John 4:4).

Job said it well,

> I know that my redeemer lives, and that in the end he will stand upon the earth.
> And after my skin has been destroyed, yet in my flesh I will see God;
> I myself will see him with my own eyes—I, and not another. How my heart yearns within me!"

Job 19:25–16 (NIV)

e|LIVE

listen|imagine|view|experience

AUDIO BOOK DOWNLOAD INCLUDED WITH THIS BOOK!

In your hands you hold a complete digital entertainment package. In addition to the paper version, you receive a free download of the audio version of this book. Simply use the code listed below when visiting our website. Once downloaded to your computer, you can listen to the book through your computer's speakers, burn it to an audio CD or save the file to your portable music device (such as Apple's popular iPod) and listen on the go!

How to get your free audio book digital download:

1. Visit www.tatepublishing.com and click on the e|LIVE logo on the home page.
2. Enter the following coupon code:
    826e-5fb0-5306-88e6-c408-78db-8206-008f
3. Download the audio book from your e|LIVE digital locker and begin enjoying your new digital entertainment package today!